CW01663981

HONG KONG BOY

To Kath Crompton

Happy Reading

Clive Hunsworth

Hong Kong Boy

by

Clive and Dorothy Himsworth

The Pentland Press Limited
Edinburgh · Cambridge · Durham · USA

© Clive and Dorothy Himsworth 1999

First published in 1999 by
The Pentland Press Ltd.
1 Hutton Close
South Church
Bishop Auckland
Durham

All rights reserved.
Unauthorised duplication
contravenes existing laws.

British Library Cataloguing in Publication Data.
A catalogue record for this book is available
from the British Library.

ISBN 1 85821 659 1

Typeset by George Wishart & Associates, Whitley Bay.
Printed and bound by Antony Rowe Ltd, Chippenham, Wiltshire

To the memory of my father Eric Himsworth CMG,
my mother 'Billie' Himsworth (Defence Medal) and to
the help received from my brother Dr Brooke Himsworth,
all of whom were interned in Stanley Camp.

Contents

Acknowledgements

We would like to acknowledge the help received from P. Pollock, archivist at King's School Canterbury. To Neville and Sylvia Long of the Overseas Missionary Fellowship. To David Fletcher for showing us around the First World War section of the Tank Museum, Bovington and for the use of the library. To the librarian at the School of Oriental and African Studies, London University and University of Hong Kong.

We would like to express our thanks to the Adult Education writing group, Sevenoaks, for their comments on our work and particularly its convenor, Camilla Bourcier.

CHAPTER I

Chihli Province, North China, 1900

'Our Gracious heavenly father, who created all the earth and everything in it, the land, the clouds, the water. We ask you to look down mercifully on your needy people. Lord of the harvest, Lord of sowing, we pray for rain, that your people may live and eat the produce of their labour.'

John, who was just eight at that time, started to fidget on his bench. His legs barely touched the ground. He was willing his father to stop talking. Today was his birthday, and he was longing to start reading his lovely new book Grandfather Watts had sent him. It was *Jungle Book* by Rudyard Kipling; how exciting it looked. He loved the story of Rikki Tikki Tavi. The words rolled off his tongue as he said them over and over again in his mind. Mother said he was like the little mongoose in the story, inquisitive or something like that; it was a big word and John was not sure what it meant.

John's mind began to wander again; his mother touched his leg and whispered to him to sit still. He looked up and caught his father's stern gaze and he tried to concentrate on what he was saying.

John had been born in Hong Kong, but had lived for the past seven years in the Chihli province of China. He still found the language difficult to understand. He knew his father was praying for rain, they had not had any for almost a year. His amah Chang had told him only yesterday.

'Everyone will starve if we don't have rain, as the crops will not grow. They're all withering in the fields under the hot sun.'

John had never known what it was to be hungry, but as he liked food he felt it wouldn't be very pleasant.

The service at last came to an end, and John ran off to play. His mother told him he could not go outside the mission station, but today he did not mind this restriction, because he knew they would be having a special cake for tea. John wanted to find a quiet place where he could read his book without interruption, but close enough to the house to see all that was going on and to smell the cakes being baked.

That night John woke with a start. 'Bother,' he said to himself, he was having such a lovely dream, all about trains, great big ones with funny faces on the front. Mother often told him and his sister, Amy, stories about where she had lived in England in a town called Tunbridge Wells. Her father was a train driver. John thought he would like to go to England, and be a train driver too, when he grew up.

There were strange noises outside. John listened intently for a moment, then unable to identify the sounds, he leapt out of bed and flung back the shutters, startling his sister into wakefulness.

'Amy, Amy, hurrah,' he cried, 'Look, it's raining. Come and see, Chang is singing, and dancing like mad in the pouring rain.'

Side by side, thrusting their hands out to catch the drops, the children saw their father rush out into the courtyard to quieten the commotion.

'All our troubles are over,' shouted Chang, 'God has heard your prayers.'

Rumours were rife in the Chihli province of China at this period. Reports had reached the mission station where John's father, the Rev. Eric Aldcott worked. The Empress Dowager had put out edicts to kill all the Christians and foreigners.

John was vaguely aware of a feeling of unrest within the mission station. He was a bright child, and he missed little of what was going on around him. He noticed that his mother seemed preoccupied most of the time. There seemed to have been lots of deacons' meetings, and John had the feeling the grown-ups knew something he didn't.

The next morning, John was playing in the courtyard when he noticed a stranger walk in. Very quietly he drew himself into the shadow of the cypress tree, then crept through the shrubbery and across the courtyard until he was within earshot of the window where his father was talking to the stranger.

'I've received telegraph wires from various cities around you. All the mission stations have been destroyed by the Boxers, and many missionaries have been killed. You're in great danger if you remain here. There are Boxer soldiers all around you.'

Eric Aldcott's voice sounded strangled as he replied, 'So it's not just rumours, it's true.'

'You must leave the mission as quickly as you can,' continued the stranger, 'you've no time to lose, it's unsafe for you and your family to remain here, but you must go under cover of darkness.'

There was a slow, dead silence in the room. John had heard enough and knew he must not be seen. He trembled with apprehension as he turned from the window, and stealthily recrossed the courtyard. When he reached the safety of the shrubbery he threw himself flat on his tummy, his breath coming in small gasps.

John felt the panic rising, he didn't want to die, there were so many things he longed to do. He straightened himself, brushed himself down, and then sped off in search of Chang.

He found her in the washroom. Dashing in, he shouted 'Chang,' and tugged at her sleeve, 'Chang.' His small soft lips were trembling. Chang noticed his muddy clothes and ruffled hair.

'What are you doing, you naughty boy, rushing in like a gust of wind,' she chided him.

'I'm sorry,' John apologized. He swallowed hard, and with a troubled face enquired, 'Chang, who are the Boxers, and why do they want to kill us?'

Chang stared at him, a slight shadow of fear in her dark eyes. 'The Boxers are evil men who blame the Christians for the drought,' she told him. 'They think the gods are angry because hundreds of people who've become Christians stopped worshipping them, and they're the cause of all our calamities.'

'Are they going to kill us?' he asked, in a tiny voice which shook with fear.

'No, you're quite safe here,' Chang assured him, not knowing of the visit from the stranger that morning. 'Now that the rains have come, all our worries will be over.'

'But Chang, Father had a visitor today and he told him we would all be killed if we don't leave the mission station.'

Chang hesitated for several seconds, then turned back to her washing and said, over her shoulder, 'Nonsense, child, no one will hurt you, you must have made a mistake. Now don't bother me any more.'

John caught the note of evasion in her voice, and knew better than to ask more questions. He turned away slowly, although he still didn't understand.

At dinner, John ate little and said nothing, he was conscious that his parents were strained and quiet too. They seemed to be engrossed in their own thoughts. Only his sister Amy, sitting next to her mother at the table, kept up her usual chatter. Her big blue eyes danced merrily, and her fair hair curled prettily around her small angelic face as she tucked into her food, with the hearty appetite of a healthy three-year-old.

'I've something I want to tell you all,' John's father's voice echoed around the room. 'We're going away for a little while. John and Amy, you must go to bed early, as we have to leave when it's dark.'

'Oh goodie, where're we going Father?' asked Amy.

'Up in the mountains.' he replied.

John's mouth went dry. Unable to contain himself any longer he asked in strangled tones, 'Why, Father, is it unsafe to stay here?' He dreaded the answer, but he had to know.

'Our lives are in the Lord's hands, and we must trust Him,' was his father's reply.

That night, John was aware of Chang packing clothes in a bag. He was not sleeping as soundly as usual, and he was having awful dreams. He was just drifting off again, when he was gently shaken by his amah.

'You must get dressed very quickly and quietly,' she told him in urgent tones, then turned to wake Amy, and hurriedly dressed her.

'Where're we going,' John asked anxiously, as he yawned and rubbed his eyes.

'To Mr Wang's brother who has a farm up in the mountains. You must both be very quiet and do exactly what your father tells you, and we will be safe. Now no more questions,' she added hurriedly, anticipating a host of 'whys and wherefores'.

The clock in the courtyard was striking midnight as the little band set off. The streets were quiet, so different from the usual hustle and bustle of the daytime. The windowless shops were shuttered. By day they would be open, spilling their wares into the street. The coolies, balancing their poles on their shoulders, would be jostling with the rickshaws, and peasants pushing handcarts. There was always the noise of teaming people in the stifling, sweaty heat. In their Chinese clothes the occasional passer-by hardly gave the party a second glance.

Amy was being carried by her father, and John found his hand held very tightly by his mother. She was hurting him, but John sensed he must not make a fuss. They had reached the town wall by this time. John felt both panic and excitement mounting in him as he watched his father lift Amy into a large basket, and then climb in beside her.

They were lifted over the edge of the wall, and John heard the rope rasping as they were lowered. His heart was pounding as his turn came to go over. In the pitch black, he was led by the deacon to the basket, and helped to climb in. He hung on tightly to the sides as he was gently put over the wall and lowered down. The basket scraped against the side of the wall. John's hands shook, his mouth went dry, and for a few seconds he thought he might fall, or the basket break with all this rough treatment. Then he felt solid ground, and a great sense of relief, as his father helped him out of the basket. 'Hold Amy's hand,' he whispered.

John watched as his father gave two pulls on the rope, and the basket went up to fetch his mother, and then the deacon, who was to guide them to the farmhouse.

John held on tightly to his father's belt as they moved slowly forward in the dark. The night was warm and sticky as they trudged along. The paths between the fields were rough and slippery after the rains. Several times John stumbled and would have fallen, but was saved by his father. The journey had been strangely uneventful, and John's fears had been overtaken by a terrible feeling of weariness, but still he plodded on.

They reached the foot of the mountains just as dawn was breaking.

'Not much further now. It's only a short climb to the farmhouse,' Mr Wang told them, encouragingly, as he stopped for a moment and pointed to a little house cut into the side of a hill. They were welcomed warmly by the family who were to shelter them for the next three weeks. John's mother laid out their bedding, and he fell, fully clothed, into an exhausted sleep.

When John woke the next morning, the Wang family had already gone to the fields to tend the wheat and vegetables. To John, the mountains meant freedom, holidays, fun, and best of all, picnics, with lemonade and rice cakes. He found his mother preparing breakfast with Mrs Wang.

'Mother, can we have a picnic today?' John burst out, as soon as he caught his mother's eye.

She shook her head, and with a stricken look said, 'No John, I'm afraid we can only go out when it's dark, for fear of being seen.'

John's face fell, and a puzzled expression knotted his eyebrows, 'You mean we have to stay indoors all day? We can't go out to play, or even have a picnic? What can we do then?'

'You'll have your lessons, as usual. I know it's hard, but you must try to understand that we're all in great danger.' She leaned towards him and ruffled his hair affectionately.

The house was small; the days dragged slowly by. John longed to be outside playing or even to go to the fields with the Wang children. Whenever voices were heard passing, they had to crawl into the cave at the back of the house. John thought he would die of suffocation, it was so small and dark.

One day they had a visit from Wang. John felt a wave of despair pass through him when he heard the deacon tell his father that in Shangshi province there had been many missionaries murdered. Deacon Wang also warned that the folk in their local town had discovered they were hiding in the mountains.

'What're we going to do?' John asked his father, tearfully.

'We must stay here, and pray to God to protect us.'

John hated to see his father looking so pinched and pale, and he seemed to be always cross and edgy.

Later that day, soon after Mrs Wang had brought them food and drink, the peaceful countryside was disturbed by the fearful sounds of tramping feet, clanging of swords, and angry cries. The clamour drew closer and closer.

The little family huddled together in the cave, at the back of the house. John was paralyzed, too frightened to cry out. The angry voices grew louder, and sounds like the crashing of thunder reached his ears. Each slow minute was torture, and he expected to hear the scraping of the wardrobe, which would mean certain death.

His face muscles felt taut, his breath came in great gulps, his heart was thumping like a hammer; he was sure the noise it made would be heard by the Boxers.

Just then there was a terrible sound of banging of utensils. John's body stiffened, as an excited cry reached his ears.

'We've found the foreign devils,' came the blood curdling yell.

A strangled sound escaped John, 'Are they going to kill us now?'

His father's calm muffled voice was strangely comforting, but his words were like a bucket of cold ice being thrown over him. 'We'll all soon be with Jesus; now wait here children with your mother. I'll go out first.'

John sat huddled up to his mother and Amy, his breath locked in his throat, too scared to move. He watched his father grope his way along the passage.

As he reached the entrance, a savage cry rang out, then came a loud bang. His father plunged forward, spun round, gripped the wall for support, then staggered out of the cave, and disappeared from John's view. Father's dead, thought John, in a moment of panic. Then his father appeared at the entrance of the cave, blood streaming down his face. He cleared his eyes with his handkerchief.

'They've shot me; it's certain death for us all; it's only a matter of time now. You must come out, we can at least try to save Mr Wang and his family. We must not prolong this terrible waiting —' He bent to help his wife, and with emotion in his voice added, 'We're in God's hands.'

John's legs were stiff and painful as he crawled along the passage. He had to blink several times to adjust his eyes to the brightness of the sun. He took great gulping breaths which cleared his lungs and set the blood racing through his veins. Fear, solid, and strong, gripped the pit of his stomach.

His father led them out into the kitchen. Everything was in chaos – there were pots and pans all over the place, but not a soul to be seen.

As they stepped outside, John saw a man on each side against the wall. They were brandishing ghastly swords with wide curving blades.

A roar came from above him, and as he looked up his face froze – there were two men armed with guns.

A shot rang out; John covered his ears with his shaking hands, and closed his eyes. Rigid with fright, he held his breath. No one moved.

Slowly opening his eyes, he noticed that the pellets had left a hole in the doorpost. Amy began to cry, great hard, hurting sobs, that echoed around the courtyard. She was seized roughly by one of the Boxers, and John cried out in alarm, 'Don't kill her.'

They were all searched, one by one, and everything including his mother's wedding ring was taken from them, leaving them with just the clothes they were wearing.

After the Boxers had secured all their belongings, including their bedding, the family were ordered to start walking. John's father was too weak through loss of blood from his head and shoulder wound to carry Amy. One of the Boxers swung her up in his arms, slung his sword across his shoulders, and ignoring her cry of protest, set off on the long march back to Shu-lu.

Along narrow paths, through fields, over bumpy roads they were marched, each of them overshadowed by a couple of those awful swords, whilst those with firearms walked in the rear. The villagers turned out en masse on the surrounding hills, and watched as they passed by. The fields which had been so barren were beginning to turn green, and the ears of wheat were filling out.

The sun was beginning to set when they arrived in Shu-lu, weary, hungry, dusty and dishevelled. They were taken to their own home. A crowd had gathered but the Boxers would not allow anyone to enter, as they escorted them into the dining room and immediately fastened the door. John felt some of the horror of the last few weeks ebbing away as his eyes wandered around the only home he had ever known, where he felt safe and secure.

He noticed his father move furtively over to the heavy wardrobe in the corner of the room. Whilst the soldier on guard's attention was diverted, he opened a drawer with a false bottom, and removed a packet of what looked like brown bark. He slipped it in his pocket, only just in time, before the soldier returned. Under cover of the noise outside John whispered to him, 'What was that Father?'

'Shush,' his father, put a finger to his lips. Then when it was safe to reply, he explained. 'It's some bark I obtained from an Irish Jesuit I was friendly with in Shanghai. It comes from Peru, in South America. He told me it could cure malaria, and in this heat there'll be plenty of that about.'

The Boxers then left for their daily ritual and a policeman friend of the family said, 'Don't be afraid; the mandarin will be here directly.'

A Mandarin's official arrived, with an escort of 200 soldiers. They were told that the Mandarin had given orders that a lodging should be found for them within the Yamen* precincts, for safety. They were led to a small temple, where reed mats were spread on the damp floor. There they spent the night, thankful to be out of the hands of the Boxers.

Soon after daylight, they were assembled in the courtyard and told to wait for a cart, which would take them on to Cheng-ting. John's eyes lit up like a morning sunbeam when he saw Mrs Lin, his mother's helper. She threw her arms around him, and when she heard they were travelling on to Cheng-ting, she returned home and sent some fruit and cakes for the children, and thick wadded Chinese coverlets to spread on the bottom of the cart.

Eventually, after a long, hot, uncomfortable journey, they arrived at the east gate of Cheng-ting-fu. The cart was stopped, and they climbed down.

John's legs felt stiff and his head ached. Thoughts of food kept flooding his mind.

There was a stir in the crowd, and a military officer who knew John's father, said to him, 'Don't fear, you are being sent home to your own country.' To England, thought John, and his heart gave a little leap.

John felt himself roughly driven along the street by the soldiers. The crowd jostled and shouted abuse. His father grasped his hand tightly, as he pushed his way through, past the loitering coolies, and the empty rickshaws.

John tried desperately to keep his mother and Amy in his vision. The crowd pressed closer to them.

All was noise and confusion. John stumbled, but managed to keep his balance, and forced himself to keep up with his father's long strides. At last they were in sight of the Yamen.

*Mandarin's Administrative Centre.

CHAPTER II

The Flight

John looked around him; the huge doors at the entrance to the main courtyard were closed. They were given orders to wait. He was very tired and the minutes ticked by so slowly. 'Father, why're they being such a long time?' he asked, almost fainting with weariness.

'To keep people waiting like this is the Chinese way of emphasizing the supreme importance of the Mandarin. It's a way of saving face,' his father explained. 'We'll just have to be patient, that's all.'

Just then the great doors swung open and a man with a white beard, long silk robes, and a funny hat appeared.

'You'll have to leave immediately, the Mandarin won't allow you to stay here.'

Eric Aldcott protested. 'This is our home, and our work. We should be protected by the Mandarin's soldiers, just like any other citizen of China.' His words fell on deaf ears. The Mandarin's representative shook his thin wrinkled finger at them.

'Foreigners are no longer welcome in China. They bring bad luck wherever they are. We'll spare your lives and give you an escort towards the coast, but China does not need your religion or your aid. We have three thousand years of history behind us, we're a great nation, the centre of the world, and resent outside intruders trying to change our ways. We'll give you a cart, and letters of authorization to the next town.' Then with a swish of his robes, he turned and hobbled back through the huge gates.

They did not have long to wait for the cart. They were roughly bundled in. The afternoon light flickered between the houses as they set off for Pao-ting, escorted by Chinese soldiers.

The heat was unbearable as they travelled mile after weary mile. John felt light-headed, his mouth was parched and his lips cracking with the heat of the sun.

When at last they stopped to eat and rest, John's father talked to the soldiers about his vision for China. Then it was he noticed that one of the soldiers in the escort party was in great distress – it was obvious he had a fever. He was sweating profusely, and this was followed by severe shivering.

'You not feeling well?' Eric Aldcott asked him, sympathetically.

The soldier nodded his head, and the leader looked anxious.

'It seems to me you're suffering from malaria.' John's father had seen malaria many times during his years in China, and noticed the young soldier had the classic symptoms. He decided to approach the Boxer leader.

'I may be able to help the young soldier who is ill,' he said. 'I have some bark here which can make tea. This tea was found to have cured the Emperor of China of malaria in 1693, and I'm sure it will do the same for this young man.'

The Boxer leader hesitated. His eyes narrowed suspiciously as he did not want them all to fall ill, but was not sure whether or not to trust this strange foreign devil.

John's father saw his hesitation, and pressed his point. 'Why don't you boil up some water. You have a tin mug, and can make a fire by the side of the road, then you can drop these pieces of bark into the water and stir them well. You must then let it brew, as you would when making tea, and sip it slowly.'

'Very well,' replied the leader, and gave orders for the soldiers to proceed just as Eric Aldcott had instructed.

Thirsty again, John and Amy squatted beside the soldiers as they gathered kindling wood and lit the fire.

For the next hour, the children rested by the roadside, and the adults talked. They heated up the water in the mug, and John watched as his father dropped the bark into the steaming liquid, and stirred it round with a twig. Then he handed it to the sick soldier and advised him to sip it slowly.

'It'll take a while for it to work. He looks so weak I suggest he rides in the cart along with us.'

The young man smiled wanly, and grudgingly the leader gave his consent.

'We'll need to stop to brew up the medicine three times a day if it is to work,' warned Eric Aldcott. 'It'll take several days to become effective.'

At first the medicine made little impact, but after a couple of days the malarial sweats and chills left the soldier, and although he was weak and had to continue to travel on the cart, he began to recover.

'You're a good man,' the leader told Eric Aldcott reluctantly, when on the second day the soldier's fever broke. His manner was more respectful to the family. He began to talk about his hopes for China, explaining that he did not much like the Manchus and wanted China to become a republic.

As they travelled on, the leader walked alongside the cart. John's father realized that he was a well-educated man.

'Where were you born?' he asked, as they stopped for the second time to rest, and to administer the medicine.

'I was born in the Chih-li province, where my father was a magistrate.'

'If China is to become strong, it'll need educated people like yourself to bring in new ways,'

A profound silence followed – the leader was not sure he wanted all the new ways. Then he replied abruptly, feeling the need to break the silence, 'China must free itself from the sway of the foreigners, people who want to exploit China, and milk it of all its resources. We want to be masters in our own house,' his voice sank ominously. 'It's an affront to our filial piety that we should do things differently from our parents, and makes a mockery of our ancestors, who worked so hard to make China the central civilization in the world.'

'Yes,' John's father agreed, 'China has had a great history, and its civilization goes back to the time when we in the West were still cave dwellers. But any country must progress and develop. The ways of our ancestors are the ways that have served well in the past. My missionary society has not tried to exploit the Chinese people, but to help them. We have started hospitals all over China, where Chinese people are being healed of illnesses from which they would have died, had it not been for the treatment they received. Think of the effects on a family of losing the breadwinner.'

Suspicion clouded the Boxer leader's eyes, and he took his time over relighting his cigarette.

'I've heard rumours that Western Hospitals take Chinese babies, and use their eyes and other organs for experiments. Poor Chinese people have to sell their babies to the hospitals because they can't afford to bring them up.'

'I know about those rumours, but they're not true,' John's father said, trying to choose his words cautiously. 'We've certainly not experimented on babies. You should talk to people who've been in our hospitals, and who've recovered from their illnesses. You should ask them if they've been treated well. We've also started schools for the blind, so blind people can learn to read and write, and have a better life as a result.'

'That may be so.' An expression of guarded defiance had come on his face. 'But we must be free of the unequal treaties. China must be able to conduct her own trade, and particularly stop the opium trade, which has such a bad effect on our people.'

'My missionary society has always been against the opium trade,' John's father replied, somewhat forcefully. 'The government will not listen. They pay more attention to the greed of the merchants than to the needs of the Chinese people. I am greatly ashamed that my fellow countrymen engage in this trade.'

'I think you are a good man,' muttered the leader, as he turned away and hurried off to supervise his soldiers.

They travelled day and night, so sleep was impossible. Dropping with tiredness, they at last arrived at Pao-ting. They were taken by the soldiers to the Yamen, and their letters of authorization were handed over, but the only place available to them was the local prison. Clean straw was laid down. John slid from the soldier's arms, and fell into an exhausted sleep. He was totally unaware of the terrible conditions in which he slumbered. It was a flea-ridden, rat-infested prison. Their bedfellows were Chinese prisoners, half-starved, emaciated, their shallow waxy faces covered with a fine malarial sweat.

Early the next morning they were shaken awake, given a meagre meal of bread and tea, and told they were to be escorted to the railway station, and put on the train to Peking.

John felt refreshed after his long dreamless sleep. 'Will it be a real train, Father,' he asked excitedly, 'with steam, and a coal fire? Do you think they'll let me ride in the front and help shovel on the coal?'

'I doubt if they'll do that,' replied his father, 'but it's the quickest, and easiest way to Tien-tsin.'

'It's such a long time since I've been on a train. Come on, Amy, let's hurry,' said John, as he helped her finish dressing.

They once again clambered into the cart and bumped off toward the station. Relief was bubbling up through them – soon they would be on the train and off to safety.

As quickly as John's spirits had risen, however, they plunged. As they came in sight of the station, to their utter dismay the little train was puffing away. The roar was deafening in John's ears, pistons throbbing and smoke curling upwards into little clouds, as the train receded farther and farther into the distance. Great big silent tears rolled down John's grubby cheeks, his shoulders drooping with disappointment.

'What're we going to do now?' he sobbed, wiping his tears on his sleeve. The corners of his mouth twisted down, and the words sprang unbidden to his lips. 'It's not fair, I'm tired of riding in the cart, and I did so want to go on a train ride.'

His mother looked at him tenderly.

'Yes I know, darling, but we must be patient, and wait.'

'Waiting's the worst —'

'There must be a good reason why we missed the train. I think we should just talk to Jesus about it.'

She gathered the children to her, and there in the dust and dirt they all knelt in prayer.

John's father was almost fainting with weakness. There had been no opportunity for him to receive proper treatment – his clothes and hair were matted with congealed blood from his gunshot wounds. Pellets were embedded in his head, face, and shoulders, but fortunately they had not penetrated deeply.

Despondent and weary, they were returned to the Yamen, but their hopes of leaving Pao-ting rapidly were soon dashed when the Mandarin refused to see them. Then it was they learned that the Mandarin, not knowing what to do with them, proposed to send them back from where they had come.

The Boxers, with their swords and guns, continued to press around the cart. John's father decided to appeal to the Boxer leader.

'I'm trying to get to the coast with my family, where we'll take a ship back to England. If we're sent back to Shu-lu we'll all be killed. We've done nothing wrong, we've not broken any laws, nor harmed anyone. In fact we've helped many of your people with their illnesses. Can't you help us in our time of need?' he pleaded.

They were finally allowed to enter the Yamen, but learned that John's father was to be separated from them. Amid the noise and confusion, John's shrill cries rang out, 'Father, Father,' he screamed, 'where're you going? What're they going to do with you?'

'It's all right, John, they're just taking me to the men's prison. You have to stay with your mother, and Amy. Make sure you look after them for me.'

With a wail of despair, John threw himself into his mother's outstretched arms, and both children sobbed uncontrollably. She held them tight, and made soft, soothing noises. They watched with terrified eyes as their father was led away.

'What're they going to do to Father?' John sobbed, as they were led off to the women's prison.

His mother shook her head sadly and, stifling a sob, replied, 'I don't know, John, and I don't know what we will do without him.'

John had never seen his mother cry – he did not know what to do. He clung to her with a vice-like grip, and in a voice that trembled with lonely grief, suggested, 'Shall we say a special prayer for him?'

His mother's eyes softened as she gazed down at his earnest little face. 'Oh yes, John, let's do that.'

'God bless Daddy and keep him safe, and please, please God let him come back to us soon. Don't let the soldiers hurt him,' John prayed fervently.

They were given food, and just as the children were settling down to sleep, the door was opened. John sat up, rubbing his eyes. No, he wasn't dreaming. He jumped up and, flinging himself into his father's arms, felt himself held in a bear-hug. 'Father, is it really you?'

'Yes, John, it's me,' came back the deep, familiar voice.

Still staring at him, almost choking with relief, John cried, 'Jesus answered my prayers.'

'Yes, he has, dear,' said his mother, 'we mustn't forget to thank Him.'

'Father, you won't go away again, will you? Mother was so sad she cried.'

'No John,' his father replied, 'not if I can help it. I've asked that we might all be kept together, no matter where it is. The Mandarin has promised he will try to protect us.' Then laying him down gently onto his matting, he kissed John on the forehead saying, 'Now, young man, you must get some sleep, because tomorrow we may be going on to Tien-tsin by boat.'

Turning to his wife, in trembling tones he told her how the Boxer leader had gone to the Mandarin, and put their case to him. Their hearts were overflowing with thankfulness, as they too spread their coverlet on the damp ground, and went to sleep.

How glad they were to arrive at the riverside the next morning. They had been escorted by twelve runners, with gowns and dress hats, going on before the cart, while several Boxers with drawn swords marched alongside. They had been given food and money to help with their travelling expenses.

Their boat was flat-bottomed, with transoms made of a single plank, jutting above the water. It had one sail and two oars. Six Boxers came on board with them, and without delay the rowers cast off. Around them floated vessels as numerous as autumn leaves – junks, barges, sampans, crafts of bamboo tied together. John was fascinated with the sight.

'Can I sit and watch the boats?' he asked, appealingly.

'I'm afraid not,' his father replied, 'it's too dangerous. The fewer people who see us, the less likely we are to run into trouble.'

'This is like a game of hide and seek, but we seem to be hiding all the time,' John remarked, as he moved undercover of the thatched tunnel that formed the main shelter.

John's mother smiled. 'Well at least we're moving in the right direction, towards the coast. This boat gives a smoother ride than that dreadful cart.'

John tried to follow his father's conversation with the Boxers, but his Chinese was not really adequate. He could make out that most of them were farmers' sons, who were taking time off from working the land to help rid China of the foreigners.

'How's the wheat doing, now the rains have come?' asked his father. 'Will it be a good harvest?'

'Yes,' the young man replied. 'The rains came just in time. I want to get back for the harvesting,' he added wistfully, as he absent-mindedly drew on his cigarette.

John felt his eyelids drooping.

'It seems like a storm is coming on,' the young soldier observed, as John's father gently waved a fan over his sleeping wife and daughter. They were glad of the covering, which sheltered them from the relentless sun.

They had journeyed about thirty miles, when the boat came to a sudden stop.

'Are we there?' cried John scrambling up.

His voice was drowned by the loud booming voice of the Boxers' leader. 'It's impossible to go downriver any further. There are Boxers on both sides, at several points. They won't let us pass. The Mandarin in Pao-ting told us to kill you as soon as we are outside his jurisdiction. We're not going to do that as we see you are good people. We've no quarrel with you.'

John's father looked at him incredulously as the fan dropped from his hand. 'What are we to do now then?' he asked trying to keep his voice steady.

'You must leave the boat now. You're on your own, and must make the best of it.'

The Boxers helped them bundle up their few belongings and they stepped ashore. John's father thanked them for their protection.

Stunned, and moving as if in a dream, unseen, they edged away from the embankment and hid themselves in the reeds and thick undergrowth. Making sure they were hidden from anyone who might be passing along the bank, they spread their bedding and sat down to think.

'I believe it's the effect the children have on the Boxers which has saved us,' John's father said, turning to his wife. 'The Chinese have a great love for children, and the sight of John and Amy seemed to move them to pity us, and lessened their hatred of us.'

The afternoon silence was broken by the sound of voices, followed by shouts and gunshots. John felt the muscles tighten in his stomach, and set his heart thudding against his ribs.

'It's the Boxer's again,' he said quivering like a plucked violin string.

They held their breath and kept silent – it was clear that the Boxers knew they were in the area, but did not know the exact spot.

'I think they're just trying to frighten us into giving ourselves up,' whispered Eric Aldcott.

Eventually all was quiet, but they dared not move until darkness fell, then they were able to quench their thirst at the river. Sleep was almost impossible as they were plagued with mosquitoes, and to add to their discomfort, the storm which had been brewing suddenly broke. John clapped his hands over his ears as the hollow boom of thunder roared overhead, and the streaks of blue lightning lit the skies all around them.

'The wind seems to go right through me,' John shivered, 'and it's flattening all the reeds around us.'

'Yes, you're right, let us be thankful that it's dark, or we would be seen from the banks of the river.'

'I don't like it,' wailed Amy.

'It's alright, it's noisy, that's all,' her father comforted her. 'It won't harm you, but I'm afraid we're going to get dreadfully wet,' he said as the rain came cascading down.

'Eric, if we stay here in the open air we'll all catch pneumonia,' John's mother interrupted him.

'Yes you're right, my dear, I think we ought to try to find shelter. Now come children help your mother collect up your belongings.'

It was a very bedraggled little band which set off in search of shelter and safety. They had not been walking long when Mary exclaimed, pointing westward, 'Look, there's a light, Eric. Shall we make for it?'

'That seems a sensible idea, Mary, it's not too far now, come on, children.'

As they approached the house they met a young man in the yard.

'Can you put us up for the night? We'll pay you well for your trouble.' asked John's father.

'Certainly,' replied the young man. 'You must be chilled and wet. Come in and have a rest and a good night's sleep. Your clothes should be dry by the morning.'

After hanging up their wet clothes, they laid down thankfully in a small room, and were all soon fast asleep.

They were suddenly startled awake by an unearthly uproar outside in the yard. A great cry escaped John and Amy as a sword slashed the curtain of the room.

All was confusion as a crowd of Boxers burst in. They seized John's father by the hair, dragged him to the ground and started kicking him.

John screamed as he too was punched, pushed to the ground and held there. His hands were pulled behind his back and tied with a rope. Then his feet were bound, and he was hauled outside.

He rolled over, terrified he would lose sight of his parents. His mother was being wrenched by the hair to a kneeling position, and her head was being pressed onto a stone table. John's terror and despair were all locked inside him – he was too frightened to cry out. He looked up in horror as one of the Boxers shouted, 'Who'll strike first, and do away with these foreign devils forever?'

The atmosphere in the yard was electric; John had never known fear so intense – it caught him like a wave, drowning him in cold shivers. He closed his eyes and held his breath. This was the end.

Then there was silence, as the Boxers' leader arrived on the scene. His voice rang out loud and clear, 'We'll take these devils to our headquarters, and then decide what to do with them.'

As rough arms lifted him, John sensed that something had broken inside him. He could feel neither fear nor hope nor anything any more. He had reached the point beyond fear.

They were each carried between two men, and taken to a temple, just a short distance away. There they were left whilst the Boxers went off to confer amongst themselves.

'I've never seen the Chinese people so fiercely anti-foreigners before,' John's father said. 'I suppose we should have seen this coming, but it seems to have erupted all over the country.'

Just then the tall thin young Boxer leader returned. 'Where're you from?' he asked in Chinese.

'From Shu-lu in Chihli province. We're travelling to the coast to take a ship for England,' replied John's father.

'What were you doing in China?'

'We were missionaries.'

The questioning went on, but clearly the Chinese man did not believe his father. Eventually he told them, 'You can sleep now, but your case will be decided by the city council in the morning.'

When the Boxers returned they had more questions. Then John's father was taken away to the city council. The family waited anxiously for about three hours. When he returned their cords were removed, and they were given food. Sleep was impossible.

On the third night they slept from sheer exhaustion, and at sunrise

John's father was summoned again to the city council. The waiting was unbearable. Then there was a commotion outside – John's heart gave a little twist when at last he heard his father's voice, and saw his bruised, haggard face.

'What're they going to do with us, Father?' John asked, his voice soft and troubled.

A little light came into his father's tired eyes.

'I think its good news at last,' he said. 'At first they wouldn't believe I was not a Romanist, and then they realized I couldn't be as I have a wife and children. They told me the Governor had been very angry when he heard we hadn't been killed, and he was still issuing the same order to kill us. The civil body have overruled him and they're determined to protect us.'

'How is it they're going to spare us then?' John's mother asked.

He smiled wryly, 'They said I must have accumulated so much merit that Heaven itself has intervened on our behalf to save us, again and again. They're determined to protect us, and send us down to Tient-tsin when the way is clear.'

'Do you know what's stopping them then?'

'Yes, there's to be a large funeral procession for the two Boxers killed by the Romanists. The civil authorities aren't sure if they'll be able to hold their own against the Boxers who are expected to attend in great numbers.'

They waited. Some of the people who came to the temple gave them little gifts of food, and the children were given money. John's mother had fallen ill and could not eat solid food, so the money was spent on buying millet soup for her.

'Poor Mother,' little Amy comforted her, as she helped her father fan the flies from her mother's face. The injuries inflicted by the Boxers were turning purple, and her lips were swollen and beginning to ooze.

Two days later, when there were few people about and the guards were sleeping, John was surprised to see someone peering through the door. Then a crumpled piece of paper fell onto the floor. No one moved until the stranger motioned to them to pick it up. His curiosity aroused Eric picked up the paper, opened it out, and exclaimed, 'Well I never . . . '

'What is it, Eric?'

John was concerned to hear his mother's voice so tired and weak.

'Well, it's written in the idiom of an English-speaking Chinese. It says, "Don't be afraid, Peking and Tien-tsin belong to Europeans. Now I will go to Tien-tsin and tell your armies to protect you. You must tear this into pieces when you have read it."'

Eric Aldcott looked up, motioned his thanks and their unknown friend left and hurried away.

'Does this mean we are safe, and not going to die, Father?' asked John.

'It certainly looks more hopeful, John.' Eric turned away so that his son would not see the moisture in his eyes. Without proper food and medical attention, none of them could survive much longer.

Two more days they waited. Sick, cold, hungry and uncertain, the black pall of despair was beginning to settle on John's parents. They sang to try to keep up their spirits.

Then John's father was summoned to the meeting room and told they were to leave that evening by boat for Tien-tsin.

Reporting this news to his family he was full of foreboding, as he felt this meant going to certain death.

It was then that one of their captors told him, in a hushed voice, that the English Consul had heard they were prisoners in Hsin-an, and he had sent a message to the Mandarin demanding their protection, and a safe escort to Tien-tsin. A special Commissioner had been sent from Tien-tsing to fetch them.

At about midnight they were given food, and were told to prepare for leaving. In stunned realization John's father declared, 'It really looks as if we are safe at last. God's hand was upon us. He's protected us from the anger of the Boxers. Let's hope we are finally free of them.'

A large number of tradesmen came to see them off, having been impressed with what Eric Aldcott had said to them. Two boats were moored at the riverside. They embarked with an escort of seven men and the rest took the second boat.

Further down the river, the questioning began again.

'How did the Consul know you were in Hsin-an?'

Not wishing to give the messenger away, Eric replied, 'I think rumours must have reached him along the telegraph wire. It's unusual for foreigners to be held captive, and a large number of Chinese people knew of our whereabouts.'

They were again escorted to the Yamen, but now they were treated like honoured guests. The Mandarin sent them food from his own kitchen. John's eyes widened, and his mouth gaped at the sight of so much food.

'Is it all for us?' he whispered.

His father nodded. 'Yes, but don't eat too much at once, and eat very slowly, or you'll get colic.' Turning to his wife, he added, 'My dear the best news of all is that I can telegraph Shanghai to say we're safe.'

French troops arrived in the town a few days later.

It was then, worn out by strain, and illness, that Eric Aldcott completely broke down. He was unable to sleep but tossed and turned in his bed, his mind and body tortured. He was sedated with opium, placed on a stretcher, and taken to a field hospital. He was too ill to be moved.

Mary, too, was suffering from dysentery, and needed urgent medical attention. Though physically and mentally exhausted she declined to be placed in hospital where she would be separated from her shocked and bewildered children. Instead she gratefully accepted shelter in the beautiful compound of the China Inland Mission.

In the peaceful and quiet atmosphere, lovingly nursed by the senior missionary, she slowly regained her strength, but something had changed in her. The zeal for their mission to China had left her, and the call of her homeland was very strong.

It was many months before they were well enough to set sail first to Hong Kong, and then to England.

CHAPTER III

Schooldays

Eric Aldcott's health still gave cause for concern and he knew he would not be accepted again for the mission field. It was with some reluctance he accepted to take up a post as minister to a Methodist church in Wadhurst, a small market town on the borders of Kent and Sussex.

Prep school was a new and exciting experience for John. He was blessed with a good memory and was quick to learn. He also discovered a love of team games, and because of his sporting prowess he soon became popular with the other boys.

In his final year, all his energies were concentrated into passing his Common Entrance examination, in order to gain a place at King's Blackbury, the public school his parents had selected for him.

John's trunk was packed, and the horse and cart had been ordered to take him to the station. His destination was Blackbury, where he was to spend the next five years of his life.

He had used every argument possible to try to change his father's mind. He might just as well not have bothered, he told himself, as he struggled into his school uniform. For when Father made up his mind nothing on earth would change it.

He dreaded the moment when he had to say his 'Goodbyes' to his family. There was already a lump in his throat, which threatened to cause him to blubber. He shook himself. 'You are thirteen years of age, and behaving like a baby,' he told the reflection in the mirror.

'The idea of going to boarding school,' his father had argued 'is that you learn to develop a sense of independence and self-reliance.'

The first sight which met John's eye as the train steamed into Blackbury station, was the tall majestic tower of the cathedral ascending up into the heavens. The sight filled him with wonder, and despite his lack of enthusiasm, he could not help but be moved. His young patriotic heart swelled with pride at the beauty of it.

His trunk was put down at School House, in the Mint Yard. John gazed around him. The house was a distinguished-looking building made of flintstone, alternated with ragstone. On entering the huge doors, he was quite disorientated by the labyrinth of corridors, with rooms leading off them.

He was shown into a room full of swarming boys, all intent on their own affairs. No one spoke to him and he was overcome with loneliness and longing to be home in the comfort and security of his family. He wandered from room to room, wondering if he was doing the right thing. He forced himself to think of the happy times in his life and not show any signs of weakness.

At last a loud bell rang out, followed by a chorus of 'Supper'.

Somehow he managed to get through the meal, but every mouthful seemed to stick in his throat. He was thankful when eventually he was shown the dormitory. The room was large, containing fifteen iron bedsteads, each covered with a red blanket. Bravely he asked the boy in the next bed, 'Are you a new boy?'

'Yes,' came the reply.

'What's your name?' persisted John.

'Michael Weaver. What's yours?'

'John Aldcott.'

A head appeared round the door – John later learned that it belonged to the monitor.

'Does anyone want to say their prayers? You've got five minutes before lights out to do so.'

John was the only one in the dormitory to say his prayers. He was acutely self-conscious, and felt every eye was on him as he knelt on the hard, cold floor.

He climbed into bed and shivered as he drew the scanty bedclothes round him. The mattress was very thin and dipped in the middle from generations of use.

The next morning, John was woken by the clanging of a bell. He washed hurriedly and joined in the general chatter as he dressed.

'Just like the Ritz,' shouted one clown.

'Ugh, it's cold. I suppose it's meant to be character-building,' someone else groaned.

John did not recognize the voices. The next comment was drowned by the second clanging of the bell, and again John joined in the scramble for the dining hall.

He took his place at the long table. A monitor sat at the head and John thought how arrogant he looked. In a more receptive mood this morning, John looked around him. It was a large oblong room, hung with portraits of past headmasters and famous old boys. He ate hungrily.

The food was cold and greasy, but like everything else, he supposed he would get used to it in time.

After breakfast there were prayers which would last for twenty minutes. John took his place in the front row. The monitors filed in, followed by the masters, and finally the Headmaster, looking dignified and austere, his robes billowing out as he walked.

The hymn was announced but sung with less fervour than John was used to in the Methodist Church. Harper, John's house monitor, read the lesson. He was very athletic and good-looking. He was captain of the first fifteen, a 'Blood', and a jolly fine fellow, according to Weaver's brother in the third year.

After the head had welcomed the school back, and given a special greeting to the new boys, everyone filed out. John knew he had just enough time to study the noticeboard and fill in his timetable before making his way to the study of his Housemaster, Mr Maudsley.

The school routine left very little spare time. Sunday afternoons were the exception – after morning service in the cathedral they were free. Boys could visit the ancient town, go for walks, play some game of sport and see their parents on their monthly visit.

Mr Maudsley was perched on the front of his desk, legs crossed in front of him when he addressed the new boys. He was a very tall man with an oblong head and jerky movements. He had a long neck and prominent Adam's apple, which was very mobile. As he walked his head jerked back and forwards, rather like a chicken, thought John. Weaver, the source of all information, had told the dorm that he was nicknamed 'Jerk'. Now John could understand why. Mr Maudsley ran the confirmation classes in the house. He believed in God, School, King and Country, in that order.

John caught up with Weaver as they made their way to the classroom. He was just passing the Grange, where all the bicycles were kept.

'What a jerk, a real Bible basher, I'm told, a graduate from Pembroke College, Oxford,' Weaver puffed out his chest with an air of importance. 'Takes classics, you know. You'd better make certain you do your homework for him, otherwise it's a swipe across the shoulders with the cane.'

John was spared a reply because just then they were joined by Roger Bliss, a lad of medium height and stocky build.

'Well, trust me to get into a House whose main interest is sport – all I'll get is a reputation for being an arty-farty type. So go to it, and let's see School House top again this year.' A peal of laughter rang out as Bliss strutted ahead, his head jerking back and forwards, his mimicry of their Housemaster was him to a T.

'Oh, smack on,' chuckled John. 'You should be on the stage.'

After lunch, games were followed by more lessons. Supper at seven, two hours of prep, supervised by the junior monitors. At nine-thirty the bell was rung to call the house to prayers.

With the monitors' call of 'Lights out' at ten, the house would burst forth into a torrent of chatter. Everyone was together, and the gossip would flow, or grievances would be aired. Every topic would be discussed. John was glad of the darkness to hide his blushes, for not surprisingly, considering his background, he was often shocked by the language and vulgarity of the conversation. He felt certain that if his parents really knew what went on at school, they would withdraw him.

Bliss continued to be a constant source of amusement, but contrary to the impression he first created, he turned out to be a good sportsman as well. John and Bliss were thrown together by sharing the same form and house, and a friendship soon sprang up between them. John was writing a History essay one morning when Bliss burst into the study.

'What a splendid fellow Maudsley is.'

'Well that's choice coming from you. Why the change of heart?'

'You obviously haven't seen the noticeboard, old chap. The splendid Aldcott and Bliss have been chosen to play in the under-fourteens rugby team.'

'Whoopee,' cried John, throwing his book in the air. 'The greatest "Bloods" of all time are about to take their place in the annals of History on the Blores field.'

'I can see you won't be picked for the cricket team,' retorted Bliss, laughing, as John fumbled his catch, and the book landed at his feet.

Secretly John was thrilled to have been chosen for the rugby team, and even though he was too short to play prop, and instead was to play hooker, this did not diminish his delight. John knew, as every schoolboy knows, that the surest way to gain popularity is to have a real talent for sport. Honesty, integrity, hard work, academic achievements were not deemed to be so important.

One evening, just as John was filing out of the hall at the close of prayers, he was suddenly pulled up short by one of the monitors beckoning to him.

'Aldcott, I want to see you in my study. Pronto.' Prosser's voice was throaty, almost harsh.

John followed him, with no idea why he had been singled out.

'Shut the door, you fool,' was Prosser's first command.

John resisted the temptation to slam it. Never before had he taken such an instant dislike to another human being.

'Well Aldcott, I can constantly hear your heels clicking on the floorboards. For a new boy, you have far too many airs and graces. You may have been chosen for the rugby team, but that's no reason for making so much noise, and acting as though you're a "blood" already.'

'I wasn't aware I was making a lot of noise,' replied John, completely nonplussed.

'Well, believe me, you are, and I warn you just to be quieter in future.'

What a twit, thought John, but answered aloud, 'I'll ask my parents if they can get me a quieter pair of shoes next time I see them.'

'No, don't do that,' said Prosser. 'You just be careful how you go, I'll be watching you. Now get going, and don't come to my notice again.'

Bliss was waiting for John in the prep room. 'Well, old chap, what did Prosser want?'

'Would you believe it, he told me I was making too much noise when I walk, and that I was getting too big for my boots.'

'Oh really, I hope you told him to go to the devil.'

'No, not exactly,' smiled John. 'I told him I'd speak to my parents, and ask them to buy me some quieter shoes.'

'Oh, that was a good move. I bet he backed down.'

'Yes, he did. I guess thick as Prosser is, he had enough sense to know he was being petty.'

'Pompous ass. He was only appointed monitor this term. Power's gone to his head. Still, I can't wait to be in his shoes.'

Prosser continued to be a thorn in John's flesh. He seemed to have taken a dislike to him, and at every opportunity he tried to undermine him. One morning Prosser was in a particularly foul mood when he came across John cleaning his shoes in the tuck box room.

'Aldcott, my shoes could do with a clean too.'

John looked at him with scorn, and his jaw tightened. 'Clean them yourself, I'm not your fag,' he retorted, in a tone of contempt.

'Listen, you little upstart, if I tell you to clean my shoes, you clean them, and don't you dare disobey me. Now get to it and be sure to make a good job of them. Bring them to my study when you've finished.' Then, with a triumphant gleam in his eyes, he turned on his heel, and left John seething with anger. There was nothing for it but to acquiesce.

While John was applying considerable pressure to the hateful task, his temper subsiding with each stroke of the brush, Bliss sauntered in.

'What you doing, old chap?'

'Just cleaning Prosser's shoes,' John replied with a scowl.

'Since when did you become his personal fag?'

'Huh, he's the last person I'd fag for. He forced me to do it.'

'Oh hard luck, he seems to have it in for you. Still, keep your ears and eyes open, he's the type to come a cropper one of these fine days. Then revenge will be sweet. Come on, old chap, let's get going before you begin to see your ugly face in those shoes.'

'Thanks, Bliss, you certainly know how to cheer a fella up. I'll just go and throw these at Prosser, and I'll see you in "Cath".'

Prosser already had the cane in his hand, and a malignant gleam flared in his frosted eyes as John handed him his shoes for inspection.

'You're a cheeky little devil, and need to be taught a lesson. Now bend over that chair,' he ordered. John did as he was told, and steeled himself for the blows which were about to descend on him. Prosser lashed him hard six times.

John had to run all the way to the the cathedral – if he was late for morning service he feared he might get another beating. Breathless and panting, he took his place next to Bliss; he felt sore, but he knew better than to complain.

'Made it by the skin of your teeth,' whispered Bliss.

'Yes, it's been a close thing. Prosser gave me a beating; I didn't want another one for being late.'

'Really, old chap. Did it hurt?'

'It's a bit sore, not helped by these hard pews. A cushion would come in mighty handy this morning,' John grinned wryly, trying to make light of his punishment, though inwardly he felt humiliated and angry at a system which allowed such things to be done by one boy to another.

As term slowly drew to an end, there was an air of relaxation, mixed with relief. John said his last goodbyes to his friends, and without a backward glance made his way to the station, his first term at public school behind him.

He was free at last to return home to his family. He settled himself comfortably in his seat as the train pulled out of the station. School wasn't so bad, he reflected. His parents would be pleased with his exam results. Third overall, first in History, and second in Geography, but only tenth in Latin. How he hated Latin.

CHAPTER IV

Final Year

In his final year, John was working at full pitch. He knew he had to make up for a certain amount of slacking. Rugby had taken so much of his time that some of his lessons had suffered, and his examination results had not been as good as he had hoped for. He was a monitor, a rugby blood in the first fifteen, and he was popular. After the school match, along with his fellow team members, he would be clapped and cheered into prayers. Now, John sat at the head of the dining table. He remembered the arrogant Prosser, and determined he would not emulate him. He was firm but fair in his judgements, and the younger boys looked up to him, and grew to respect him. As a monitor he was rewarded with a smaller study, which he shared with Bliss. They had remained friends throughout the years.

Bliss was playful and easy-going, he acted the fool, but it was open and harmless, and he helped John to take life less seriously.

When, after a rather dirty rugby house match John learned that he had dislocated his finger and would not be able to play any more that term, he felt furious and frustrated. He was silent and sullen as he entered the school room the next morning, his arm in a sling. He did not look up, but kept his eyes on the ground when the school rose to clap the team into prayers.

'Cheer up, old chap,' coaxed Bliss, as they were making their way to the classroom. 'Think how much work you'll be able to get through – with no diversions you'll end up with a good matric result.'

'A fat lot of chance of that,' scowled John, completely missing the humour in his friend's remarks. 'Just as I was in top form, too,' he grumbled. 'The Tonbridge match will be tough, and I was really looking forward to it. Cheering from the touchline won't be the same.'

'Come on, you'll still get your first colours. Just think, you'll be able to walk on the green court, and sit under the lime tree, and dream of fame and fortune.'

Being unable to participate in sport, John sought to get down to some studying, and for a while his test results improved considerably. He would be taking his matriculation in his final term. Maths, Latin, and English were compulsory, and he was planning to add History and Chemistry.

While the rest of the House were out on the rugby field, John endeavoured to get to grips with Latin. It was on one of these quiet days that Maudsley discovered him in the library.

'I see you're working hard, Aldcott. What're you planning to do when you leave school?'

'My father wants me to go to Oxford, sir. I would like to study Chemistry there.'

'That's interesting. Why've you chosen Chemistry?'

John reflected for a moment, then answered, 'Well I think there's scope for innovation and progress, which could help people live better lives.'

'Em . . . it's certainly a bread-and-butter subject; not my line at all. I think you're right it'll gain in importance. Are you having any problems, with your work?'

'Yes, sir, Latin.'

'Well, your grammar's passable, but you need to widen your vocabulary. I'll hand out a book in class which I think will be helpful. You know there'll be a lot of competition for Oxford, but I applaud any boy who aims high. I'm glad you've started working seriously for your matriculation. Keep it up, you should do well.'

John flushed and, a little embarrassed by the compliment, stared after his Housemaster, as he strutted off. He certainly cut a strange figure, but for all that, John thought him a jolly fine master. He had come to respect him enormously over the years.

It was with very mixed feelings that John at last embarked on his final term. He enjoyed the sense of power which being a monitor and a blood afforded him. He did not abuse this power, and remained natural and unaffected.

With more time on his hands Bliss tried to persuade John to join the debating society.

'We discuss all sorts of topics, it's a good laugh.' Bliss coaxed. 'You'll enjoy it —'

'I doubt it,' John replied, but somewhat reluctantly he agreed to give it a try.

'Come on then before you change your mind. I'll stand you a round of hot chocolate before we start. Afraid the kitty doesn't stretch to anything stronger. If you've some cake left, bring it along, I'm famished.'

'Sorry, you're out of luck. You pinched the last bit yesterday with some other lame excuse, but I won't say no to some chocolate.'

Hardly before the steaming hot chocolate had cooled sufficiently to drink, John was summoned to the Head's study.

'I say, what you been up to old chap?'

'Haven't the faintest,' replied John, getting to his feet immediately and downing his drink. 'Though on second thoughts, old "Greasy" has probably just realized what an asset I am to the school, and has decided to make me head boy.' John stuck his thumbs behind his lapels and puffed out his chest. 'Modesty was never my strong point,' he grinned.

'Ass, mind your head or it will get stuck in the door. Much more likely your sins have been found out at last,' chortled Bliss. John made a face at him as he left the room.

'Come in' was the response to John's knock.

The Head was seated behind his desk, but he stood up, walked towards John as he entered and moved a pile of books off the chair, indicating to him to sit down.

'Aldcott, I have some bad news for you,' he began. John's heart missed a beat. 'I'm afraid your father is seriously ill.' He placed a hand on John's shoulder. 'I'm very sorry, I do hope he will make a good recovery. Your mother has requested that you return home. I have had all the necessary arrangements made for you. You can leave immediately.'

John was stunned. He felt the blood draining from his face, and for one dreadful moment he thought he was going to faint. He somehow managed to say, 'Thank you, sir,' groped his way to the door, and with a heavy heart collected his coat and a few personal belongings. He made his way to the station just in time to catch the train to Tunbridge Wells, where his grandfather was to meet him.

John could not remember the walk to the station, nor the journey. He thought only of the Head's words. 'Your father is ill, and your mother has requested you return home.' It must be serious, or she would never do that, John said over and over again to himself. He could not envisage his father being ill. He was always so alive, so vital. He knew, of course, that the China experience had taken its toll, but he was only in his early fifties, and had always seemed so strong and invincible.

His grandfather seemed to have aged. He gripped John's hand and they embraced.

'We will go straight to Wadhurst,' he said, as soon as they had greeted one another. 'I must warn you, your father is very ill. Your mother and Amy have been at his bedside all night. They will be pleased you've been able to get here so quickly.'

John noticed his Grandfather's steps had slowed, and there was now a stoop to his shoulders. The journey seemed interminable.

At home John's mother rose from the bedside to kiss him and Amy gave him a tearful hug.

John looked down into the face of the man who had always been such a tower of strength to him, the man he loved and respected above all others, and recoiled with shock. His father seemed wasted and deathly pale, gasping for breath and unable to speak. His hair, once so dark, was now streaked with grey, and his hands lay on the coverlet, bony and lifeless. His sunken eyes registered recognition, however, and he tried to talk, his voice faint and weak. John bent his head to catch his words.

'Good to see you, Son,' he panted. 'Take care of your mother and Amy. I'm very proud . . .' His voice trailed away, he gave a gasp and his eyes closed.

'Don't die, Father,' John whispered, his eyes swimming with tears, 'please don't die.'

He felt rather than saw his mother move to the head of the bed and softly cradle his father in her arms. She was crying softly, 'It's all over, oh my darling, we are going to miss you,' she crooned brokenly, the tears falling slowly onto the pillow.

The tiny church was packed for Eric Aldcott's funeral, the gallery had been opened to take the overflow, such was his popularity. The Rev. George Taylor was to conduct the service. He had met John's parents in Hong Kong, where John was born. He and his wife, Esther, were John's godparents. Both families then went on to serve in China, but working in different provinces.

The service began and the congregation rose. They had chosen one of his father's favourite hymns 'Rock of Ages, Cleft for me, let me hide myself in Thee'. The choir led the singing. John was surprised to hear his mother's voice, clear and sweet, beside him. He glanced at her – she was pale, but composed and serene. His heart went out to her and he marvelled at her faith, that even at this time, when she must have felt sad and alone, she could remain calm and courageous. He himself was too shocked and numbed to sing, the lump in his throat was threatening to choke him. Any minute, he expected to see his father walk up into the pulpit and announce the next hymn. He could not believe he would never see him again.

He tried to concentrate on the words of the hymn, but could find no solace in them. He was angry, but he was not sure who he was angry with, and so blamed God. John was not ready to grasp the finality of death, nor accept the reality of loss.

His mother found comfort in the hundreds of letters of sympathy which she had received from the congregation and friends as far afield as China, Hong Kong and South Africa. They had read them all as a family, and he knew how much his mother would treasure them.

For several weeks, after his return to school, John felt as though he was lost in a fog, and could not find his way out. It was difficult to concentrate on his work. There were times when he felt life would never be the same again, the pain was too great. He was so totally unprepared for life without the guiding hand of his father. He could not pray, the words would not come. So he gave up, but as he gradually began to throw himself into his work, the numbness wore off and the ache in his heart began to subside.

There were exams to get through – this was something he could do for his family; he would work hard and if necessary provide for them; his father would not expect anything less of him.

At last it was all over, the speeches, the drama, the prize-giving, the customary cheering as the visitors rose to leave. Soon the old athletic heroes would be forgotten, and new ones take their place.

John looked around him for the last time – all was quiet, their farewells done, the shouts and laughter died away. He passed through the quadrangle, then through the school gateway, along the narrow streets, wending his way to the station.

Then he turned and looked back to the beautiful cathedral – it still gave him the same sense of wonder as it had on his first day.

CHAPTER V

University

'It's the postman,' Amy cried, and returned a few minutes later, waving an envelope towards John. She thrust it into his hand.

'Come on, open it,' urged his mother.

'Oh dear, I'm almost too scared to, you open it, Mother.'

'Alright, I'm sure you've done well, hand me my glasses please, Amy.'

John was not so certain – he expected the worst. He realized he had spent too much time on the sports field, and thought his exam results would have suffered as a result.

'Well dear, you have done extremely well, but I'm afraid not well enough to get into Oxford,' said his mother looking at him tenderly.

'Oh dear,' sighed John, his face taking on an anxious frown. 'I've let you and Father down. He would be so disappointed in me.'

'No, John, he knew you always did your best. I think your results are good enough to get you into University College, London.' Noticing John's doleful expression she quickly added, 'It has a very good reputation.'

'Hard luck, John,' exclaimed Amy,' but cheer up, it's not the end of the world. Just think, if you go to London, we'll see much more of you. Besides,' she added shyly, 'you'll be near to James.'

'Yes, Amy's right. James has decided to take digs in London. You could either stay up there during the week and come home at the weekends, or you could travel up daily. It'll be much easier when we move to Tunbridge Wells. Grandpa and Grandma too will be so pleased to have you nearer.' John's mother rose from her seat, hugged him, and added, 'John, always remember your father loved you dearly, and was very proud of you both. Whatever you choose to do, I'll be behind you one hundred per cent.'

John bent to kiss his mother. 'Thanks Mother, you're the tops.' He gave Amy a playful peck on the cheek, and absent-mindedly cleared his crockery from the table, as he thought of the happy times he and James had shared over the years. James had befriended him on his first day at prep school, and they had remained friends, sharing so many secrets. He had missed him sorely when he went to King's.

There was a decided autumnal nip in the air as John set off to catch the train to London on his first day. A new life was about to open up for him, and John had a feeling of exhilaration, mixed with uncertainty.

From Charing Cross, he took the underground to Goodge Street, and set off to walk the last bit of the way. He gazed around at the impressive buildings, the dome and steps at the front of the college. It looked like an archetypal place of learning, he thought. He entered the building through the South Cloisters, and stopped to look at the fully dressed, embalmed body of Jeremy Bentham, which was displayed in a glass box. A bit macabre, thought John, and he wondered what sort of man would want to be displayed like that, rather than be buried like everyone else. As he had arrived early, he stopped to read the plaque before making his way to the Slade wing, on the north side, where he knew the Chemistry department was situated.

John discovered the laboratories located in the basement. The one he attended was filled with working benches and looked very crowded. The students began to drift in. There were about twelve men and four ladies, and conversation was rather stilted. John found himself sitting next to a short, sandy-haired student wearing heavily rimmed spectacles.

'Where are you from?' enquired John as they introduced themselves.

'I live in Ealing,' replied Duncan, 'and you?'

'Tunbridge Wells, close enough to travel in every day.' Just then the door opened, and the professor entered. He was a man of medium height, with dark hair greying at the temples, and mournful brown eyes. His distinguishing feature was a thin, sharp nose, which gave his face an inquiring look; his shoulders were rounded, from years of bending over books.

'I'm glad to welcome you to the Chemistry department of University College,' he began, his face lightening up as he spoke. 'My name is Sedgewick, Professor Sedgewick. I have two assistants, Messrs Williams and Fox. I'm afraid the department is rather cramped, student numbers have increased steadily year by year. The present laboratories are scattered and inconvenient and also overcrowded.'

As they dispersed after the professor's speech, John felt a tingle of excitement. He resolved to make the most of his opportunities. Every day of his school life had been planned and busy. Now he had a great deal of spare time, and he had to organize his own days. The discipline learned at King's, and the need to manage his time well, stood him in good stead, for at University College real self-discipline was needed to get through the work.

John loved his chosen subject. He immersed himself so deeply in his studies that the uncomfortable surroundings never bothered him. He had a vision of the undiscovered universe, the mysteries of which he felt he was helping to unravel, and he dreamed of the benefits this research would one day bestow on mankind.

In the summer term of his first year John saw on a noticeboard that the Philosophy Society had a college philosopher speaking on 'God and the problem of evil'. I'll go along to that, he promised himself. Since his father's death, he had been consumed with doubts about the existence of God. He had felt unable to talk to anyone about it other than James, his friend from prep-school days. James had been sympathetic, and suggested several books he might read which would help him think things out for himself. Yet they did not seem to offer an explanation for what was troubling him. He reasoned that either life on earth is a preparation for something greater and more lasting, or it is meaningless, dark and dreadful. He became more determined to discover the truth for himself, made up his mind to attend and invited James to come along to.

John suggested they meet in the students' common room. Arriving first he ordered two coffees, knowing James was always punctual. Sure enough James appeared just as the waitress brought their order.

'Well timed,' he greeted his friend cheerily.

They exchanged news, and views, and sipped their coffee companionably. Then they made their way to the lecture hall.

The lecturer came in. Mr Cohan was a handsome man, with dark brown hair, and clean-cut features. He had a good voice which carried well, but John found his manner somewhat pompous. He expounded his theories for twenty minutes, and quoted various passages of the Bible to show that God is omnipotent, omniscient and all loving.

The key points of the lecture concerned the Nature of God. He summed up: 'If we accept this as a premise of God's nature, we must follow through logically what this nature entails. In my view if we accept the biblical account of the nature of God then evil would not be able to exist in the world. For if God is omniscient, He will know evil exists; if He is omnipotent He will be all powerful, and be able to change evil. If God is all loving, then He will want to wipe out evil. Yet we know from our experience of the world that evil is present. Wars take place, people murder and torture their fellow men, natural disasters such as hurricanes, famine and earthquakes occur. I would argue that as evil exists then God cannot exist.'

Mr Cohan looked up from the lectern and glanced round at his audience. 'I have reached this inevitable conclusion through reason and logic, and I would like at this point to open up the subject for debate.'

Several hands shot up, but a young man in the front row was the first to rise. 'In my opinion the reason evil exists in the world is because God has given man free will, with which he can make good or bad moral choices and decisions. We read in Genesis, when Adam tasted the forbidden fruit, he fell from a state of moral perfection to one where he could choose to perform evil if he so desired; God would not intervene. Since the fall there has been a struggle between good and evil in the human heart. I believe too, that man was not alone in the fall from grace, but that nature also fell from perfection in the Garden of Eden, and this explains why there are natural disasters.'

'An interesting theory,' observed the philosopher, 'but you still have to prove that God exists, and I guarantee that I can refute any argument you might put forward.'

The arguments flowed back and forth. John's mind was still tormented with doubts and uncertainties. He continued to mull them over with James until the small hours. John often dossed down on the floor of James's room, if he had to remain in London overnight.

Having started on his quest, John was determined to see it through. As soon as he had some free time he requested an interview with the University Chaplain, the Rev. Hamilton. It was a four-storey climb to the chaplain's office. John took the stairs two at a time.

The door of the chaplain's office was open; Martin Hamilton jumped to his feet to greet him with hand extended. He hung an 'engaged' notice on the door, then closed it quietly and turned to John.

'Now we won't be disturbed,' he announced cheerfully.

John guessed that he was in his late thirties, a tall man with premature grey hair and a ready smile. Lowering his lanky frame into his chair, he swivelled it round and leaned back. 'Now, what's on your mind? How can I help you?' he enquired.

John warmed to him and felt immediately at ease, as he explained about his background – how after the death of his father, his childlike, unquestioning faith had been of little help to him. He told of his doubts, and how, because of his need for some kind of intellectual 'proof' that God does indeed exist, he had gone to the seminar, but had come away even more confused. Finally he asked, 'Can you explain what the cosmological argument for God's existence is all about?'

'Certainly, but first let me say "thank you" for being so honest. It is refreshing to hear someone openly admit to doubts. We all have them of course, but we seldom speak of them.'

He crossed his long legs, and thought for a moment, seeming to choose his words carefully. 'Before we get onto philosophical theories I would like to make an observation. In my opinion in the case of the average Christian, belief is in part the result of tradition and upbringing coupled with some experience of the felt presence of God.

'Then comes the reasoned conviction of the existence of God, and lastly comes an act of will. Acting on the belief, one find's the theory works.' He paused for a moment to let John reflect on his words, then went on, 'What you have told me suggests you have not lost your faith, but got a bit stuck.' He smiled encouragingly. 'Don't get too downhearted – this happens to a number of students, and you have had two very difficult experiences. Losing your father, and the institutional religion of your school, have combined to dampen your spiritual vision a little, but I can say with complete sincerity that you are taking the right course of action. You will come through this experience with your faith deepened and enriched, because you are working at it; but remember, John, a living faith in God involves the heart and will, as well as the intellect.'

John nodded, and Martin continued, 'So now to the cosmological argument. It derives from Aristotle's conception of a first cause or unmoved mover. Aquinas argued that every event in nature has a goal towards which it is aimed by someone. For example the arrow speeding towards it's target requires an archer to set it in motion. Someone must have caused the archer, and so we can go back in history from any event to work out it's causal history, if necessary back to the beginning of time.

'Someone must have set all the causes in the universe in motion. Someone powerful and knowledgeable enough to understand the natural laws, and create the energy which set the cause and effect relations in motion. This must be someone omniscient and omnipotent, and this for Aquinas was God.'

'I think I'm beginning to get the idea,' John interjected.

Martin nodded, then continued, 'Some modern philosophers have argued that this theory is flawed. The atheist Bertrand Russell argued that not all series of events have a first mover. The series of natural numbers go on one, two, three, four, five etc., off into a never-ending infinity, the numbers growing, with no end or first cause in sight. Have you read any of his works?' Martin enquired.

'Yes, I have,' replied John, 'he claimed that the Universe has always been there. It did not require a creator. He says the universe just is, and that's all.'

'Yes, but I find Russell's argument unsatisfactory as it does not address the question – How? or, Why is the Universe there?'

'Hm, I can see it's a lot more complicated than I thought,' the puzzled expression was back on John's face.

'The key thing to remember about arguments for and against the existence of God is that they are not conclusive,' continued Martin. 'Philosophical debates are not like scientific debates, where empirical experiment about the natural world is the final decider as to which of two theories is correct.

'A good theory in philosophy is one that starts from reasonable premises, then follows the laws of logic to their conclusion. Human logic and limited intellect are not enough to conceive the enormity and purposes of God, and what He is like.'

'So belief in God is a matter of faith?' observed John.

'It is faith based on a reasonable, rational foundation. You are not illogical or irrational just because you are a Christian,' pointed out Martin.

'Yes, I see that,' replied John, 'but how in Christian terms can you explain evil, human suffering, disasters, man's inhumanity to man etcetera? These make it very difficult to believe in a loving God.'

'Yes, so many people get hung up on this, and it's difficult to know the answer. However I believe that hardship and sorrow are often the consequence of the sin or injustice of others, and not the direct will of God.'

'In other words, because God has given man free will, he can chose between good and evil,' observed John. 'You are referring to the the fall of man from grace, driven from the Garden of Eden. But many people today do not take the Bible literally.'

'It makes no difference whether we treat it as literal history or just as a quaint parable. Whatever the actual facts may have been, sin exists, as you have pointed out.'

'So therefore if we take the story literally, Adam and Eve were faced with a choice, and they chose to disobey.'

'Yes, that's right, but I feel there was progress in it.'

'Progress?' John looked bewildered for a moment, then he said a trifle hesitantly, 'You mean they passed from innocence into that of moral progress, if man had not sinned he would have remained innocent and harmless, or a puppet in the hands of God, to do with as He willed.'

'Yes, exactly, and if God had not given man free will he could never have been able to reach the heights of goodness. You know, John, I believe the universe is one of law and order, and I don't think God would intervene to alter the natural succession of events, even though his heart must ache continuously with the way man mars his creation, and inflicts pain and suffering on each other.'

They continued to discuss this point until late into the evening. Martin Hamilton was a true believer that knowledge can only be imparted to those who are eager to receive and willing to do their part in the work of receiving it. He thought John was truly seeking after the truth, and he delighted in encouraging his students to think for themselves.

At the close of the interview, he went to his bookshelf and selected a slim volume. 'Here's something to get your teeth into,' he said earnestly.

Rising to his feet, John thanked him for sparing him his time and for the book. There was a reflective expression on John's face, as he returned to James's digs, to spend yet another night bedded down on the floor.

During a free Wednesday afternoon, when John had nothing in particular to do, he decided to take the tube to Perivale, the college sports fields. There, to his delight, he found a game of rugby in progress. He joined the handful of spectators and cheered as loudly as the others.

'Who's playing,' he asked a student, who looked to be at least six-foot-four.

'UCL versus King's College,' the 'giant' replied. 'Oh, well played, Taylor! You new here then?' he queried, all in the same breath.

'Yes, started in September, reading Chemistry.'

'Interested in rugby then?'

'Yes, I used to play for my old school.'

'We could do with some new players – what position?'

'Hooker.'

'Any good, were you?'

'Passable,' replied John modestly.

'How about joining us then?'

'I'll think about it. I wasted so much time playing at school that my matric results were not as good as I'd have liked, so I came here determined not to make the same mistake. I'm very tempted though. I could do with the exercise,' John responded, laughingly.

'Good, that's settled then. Come along to the union building tomorrow, at two, and I'll introduce you to the Guv.'

John soon found himself back in the scrum and the mud. He couldn't, of course, help comparing King's with the college team. In his opinion, the college team were ragged and lacked polish, but they were enthusiastic, they did not take the game too seriously, but let themselves go and enjoyed it.

John enjoyed the comradeship of the rugby team. Off the field, however, he found it hard to identify with them, as they would go off, as soon as the pubs were open to drink heavily and many of them would stagger home afterwards, bawling rugby songs.

It was after the rugby match with Bart's Hospital, when they were all crowded into the Jolly Roger, celebrating their unexpected victory, that the captain of the team, Gregory Barns, slightly the worse for drink, invited John, derisively, 'Come on, you played a good game, have something a bit stronger.'

'No thanks, this is fine,' John replied good-humouredly, raising his glass of lemonade.

'Oh, a bloody sissy, can't hold your drink then,' jeered Barns.

'Never tried,' said John beginning to feel rather uncomfortable, as all eyes were focused on him.

'Never tried? Where've you come from, the nursery school?'

'Oh give it a rest, Greg,' chipped in Allen Chapel, the scrum half. 'He's a fine player, a great asset to the team, we don't want to lose him. Anyway, we ought to be making a move.'

'Come on then, drink up everybody, let's get going.' said Greg.

They all staggered out of the pub, and made their way northwards towards the river, singing as they went, oblivious to the stares of onlookers. As they approached Waterloo Bridge, a challenge went up.

'Dare you to walk along the parapet, anyone not doing so is a fart.'

Singing at the tops of their voices, Gregory leading the way, they mounted the parapet, and started to walk unsteadily along it. Reaching the middle of the bridge, Greg lost his footing, and to everyone's horror, keeled over the side and plunged into the icy cold water.

John looked over the bridge in time to see Greg being swept along by the swirling tide. Without a second thought, he tore off his shoes and coat, and jumped in after him. He was a strong swimmer, but as he hit the water he felt its icy grip dragging him downwards. He could see Greg floundering in the distance, crying for help. The sound of his terrified voice mixing with the eddying water seemed unearthly.

'Hold on,' yelled John, 'I'm coming.' He started to swim as fast as he could towards Greg, but his limbs felt heavy and cold, and the fast-flowing tide churned around him.

God help me, he cried in his head. It flashed through his mind that he had not prayed for months, except in church, and he was ashamed.

With these thoughts pulsing through his head he made a determined effort, and struck out powerfully. Only a few more strokes and he would reach Greg, he told himself.

The tide was flowing upstream as he passed under Hungerford bridge. Greg had disappeared, then in the half light he saw him resurface. He was gasping and spluttering. John grabbed for him, but missed. Greg disappeared again. John dived and groped around helplessly; his lungs were bursting. Then his fingers touched something and he grasped it. It was Greg. John held on tightly and kicked for the surface. As they both surfaced, Greg began to retch and choke.

John was exhausted by his efforts. 'Don't struggle, just go limp,' he screamed at Greg. 'I'll make for the pier, hold on.'

With an almighty effort, his breath coming in gasps he managed to cling on to Greg. In his mind he repeated over and over again, I mustn't give in. He was swimming for life now, his and Greg's.

He tried to get his mind to focus on his breathing, but that too felt numb. The Angel of Death seemed to be hovering around them, and a feeling of hopelessness began to engulf him.

Then at last, the pier appeared in the shadows. They made it there but John did not have the strength to heave Greg out of the water.

A figure loomed out of the darkness and strong hands gripped Greg and John, and hauled them to safety. They lay spent and panting on the floating pier.

'Well where did you two spring from?' asked the unknown rescuer.

'We were larking about,' replied John, his teeth chattering, 'and Greg here slipped on the bridge and fell in. I could see he was struggling, so jumped in to help him. The rest you know. Thanks so much for your help.'

'We'd better get you both to the hospital as quickly as possible, before you catch a death of cold. You'll need to be checked out – these waters are somewhat polluted.'

At that moment panting and looking extremely worried, their mates came dashing towards them.

'Thank God you're safe,' it was Allen Chapel who was first on the scene. 'You OK?'

'Yes, I'm alright,' John gasped, 'but our good friend here thinks we should go to hospital to be checked over.'

'Yes, sure, good idea,' said Allen decisively. 'I'll call a cab, you look all in, both of you. Here, take your coat, John, I've got your shoes too. Greg, you'd better have mine.'

'Thanks.' Greg had at last found his voice, and by now was cold sober and feeling rather sorry for himself.

Allen managed to persuade a cabbie to take them to University College Hospital. They were lucky that they happened on one with a sense of humour. He ribbed them unmercifully, but did not seem to mind the mess left in his cab.

'Just so long as I gets me money, that's alright by me,' he said cheerfully, when John apologized for the second time.

Greg had to remain in hospital for three days as he developed a high temperature. John suffered no ill effects and was allowed home the following day, but he was advised to take a couple of days' rest.

John had been surprised at the total absence of any religious observance in the college. He learned that the college had been founded for Nonconformists, Catholics and Jews at a time when, to go to Oxford or Cambridge, students had to be practicing Anglicans. The fundamental principal of the new institution was that religion in any form should neither be a requirement for entry, nor a subject for teaching, and so the college had become known as one for the 'Godless students of Gower Street'.

John had not been unduly bothered by this because his faith had been badly shaken. Now, following his close brush with death and his desire to discover more of the fundamental truths of life, he set out to find out what, if anything, the college had to offer.

He discovered that there was a Christian Union, and on the noticeboard was an invitation for new students to join. John did so, and found that there was a membership of fifty people who were studying the Gospel of St Mark.

John, as a newcomer was welcomed warmly and asked if he would like to introduce himself to the group. His words were hesitant at first, but his nervousness quickly wore off. He explained a little of his background, and then told his listeners how he had turned his back on God, but that he was now seeking to find a balance in his life between the intellectual and the spiritual.

All work was abandoned on bonfire night as the students gradually filled the front quad. In excitable mood preparations were made for Rag Day. Phineas Maclino, the college mascot, was being made ready for the annual procession.

'It's a fine mascot,' John said, turning to Allen Chapel, his rugby club friend. 'I wonder where it came from? There must be a story behind it, surely.'

'Yes, you're right, there is. As you know, these figures are a common sight outside tobacco and snuff shops. A few years ago, I think it was in 1900, news of the relief of Ladysmith in South Africa reached the college. One of the more daredevil students was exploring in Tottenham Court Road, spied Phineas, seized him, and paraded him back to Gower Street, where he was placed in a position of honour on the portico.'

'So he's been the mascot ever since.'

'Yes, and much envied by other colleges. He's quite an integral part of student rags.'

'Come on, the parade is starting.'

John, and Allen joined their fellow students, and with Phineas at the head, paraded down Tottenham Court Road, bringing all the traffic to a standstill. The banner held aloft proclaiming the Rag Day informed all who turned out to watch the procession that money was being raised towards equipment for University College Hospital. The crowds gave generously, as the students excitedly shook their boxes.

As the day progressed, the students became wilder. A lot of cheering for Phineas went on and a challenge was issued to their arch rival, King's College, London, to do battle with them. About one hundred students bought a lorry-load of soot, which they mixed with water and flour. Soon the forecourt of University College was the scene of good-humoured battle.

John noticed that one of the King's students, becoming over enthusiastic, found himself detached from the main body and was quickly surrounded. He struggled to get away as he suddenly realized their intention was to debag him. His efforts were useless – they over-powered him and his captured trousers were triumphantly displayed and whirled above their heads as a trophy.

The night ended with a bonfire and a lot more celebrating, but poor old Phineas, now propped up on the bar of the Union building, was a sorry sight. In an unguarded moment he had been captured by the enemy, who had covered him from head to toe with soot.

University College decided to take revenge for the undignified assault on Phineas. The plan was to borrow a lorry, break into King's College Union, and capture Reggie, their copper lion mascot. As John walked into college the next morning, he was surprised to see a crowd gathered, all looking upwards to the Union Building. When he saw what they were staring at, he hooted with laughter. There was Reggie, tarred, and feathered.

'Three cheers for UCL,' John cried, 'the best college in London.' A great cheer went up, amid much clapping and laughter.

John learned to love London, with all its noise and bustle. The theatres lent a new dimension to his life. He revelled in the dramas of Shakespeare, Ibsen, Strindberg and a host of other plays. His mother, Amy and James often accompanied him, when time allowed. His young eager mind was quick to absorb these new experiences. Yet he was mindful that he had family responsibilities. So it was, in his final year, that he sought the advice of his tutor.

Mr Foster, a graduate from Cambridge, was a Mancunian. His untidy red hair and freckled face made him fair game for ribald comments. Yet he was well liked and respected by the students. He was always in a hurry, yet he was patient and considerate with his students, and his inordinate common sense made him a good advisor for those students who were fortunate enough to be in his tutor group.

'Well, John, how're you finding things?' his tutor asked encouragingly, as John seated himself.

'I've almost completed my paper on valency, and would be grateful for your comments. It was quite hard going, and I'm not certain if I've picked up the main points,' John replied.

'Yes, sure, leave it with me, or would you like to use the time now to peruse it.'

'I would really prefer to leave it with you, as I rather wanted to ask your advice. You see, I'm interested in doing some kind of research in Chemistry when I leave university, and for that I need to get an upper second in my finals paper.'

'Well, it won't be easy, but it's evident you've worked hard throughout your time here. I'd suggest the first thing you need to do is to look at past examination papers, which you'll find in the library. You'll see that certain questions appear at regular intervals. Try to spot which topics are likely to come up in this year's papers. Choose the six or seven most topical ones. I used to make notes of the key points on cards for each question, so I could revise them easily. They would trigger off in my mind further ideas.' He paused thoughtfully, running his fingers through his hair. 'Do seminar papers on the areas you think need revision, and discuss the topics you think will come up in the finals. Try to read up on the recent articles published on the subjects you've chosen for your finals, so that your knowledge is bang up to date. It takes a lot of work, but I think it pays off in the end. Besides, it'll be good training for you in the future, as research requires thorough and painstaking effort.'

As the time for John's finals drew nearer he was exceedingly grateful for the advice given by his tutor.

'You're working hard, dear,' his mother remarked, her brow creased in anxiety. 'Why not have a break? You've been working six days a week non-stop now, for months. You look very tired.'

'I'm fine, Mother, and it's not for much longer now. I just need a last push to get through the finals papers.'

John heaved a huge sigh of relief, and a sense of elation stole over him as he completed his last paper. All he longed to do now was to get home as quickly as possible, and to luxuriate in the wonderful sense of freedom which was washing over him. Once home, he flung his books in the air and sank into the comfort of his grandparents' well-worn armchair, while the family gathered round him.

'Well, come on, tell us how it went.' Amy, never lost for words, spoke for them all.

'Oh, not so bad, most of the questions I anticipated came up, but there were a few surprises. I had to improvise a bit, and stir up some general knowledge of the subject to get me through.' John sat back in his chair and stretched out his arms. 'Oh, it's good to have that behind me. I'm so looking forward to my holiday with James in Scotland. After that I must look for a job.'

CHAPTER VI

The First World War

Towards the end of the month, the eagerly awaited letter arrived offering John a post at Acetate Chemical Works, in Hertfordshire.

He had been at Acetate for just a year when war broke out. What should he do? His mind was torn between his work, and joining up to fight for his country. He still received the Blackbarian, his old school magazine, and read there that some of the old boys had volunteered, and were fighting over in France. He felt he ought to join them.

His employers, however, persuaded him the firm still needed him, and that his work producing the diphtheria serum was helping the war effort. So John stayed on.

He read the newspapers avidly to learn of the latest happenings on the Western Front. His thoughts were in turmoil as he read about the terrible slaughter the machine-guns were inflicting on the soldiers in the front line. He felt an overwhelming sense of despair on learning that several of his schoolfriends from King's had been killed.

Then, in 1916, all those who were not in reserved occupations were called up. John made up his mind he must volunteer. Having gone through the usual form filling and medical checks he was accepted for the Royal Army Medical Corps.

The weather had turned gloriously fine, with hot summer days and moonlit nights. The front was very quiet. They had been moving stretchers, and other equipment into the front line for two days. John decided to scribble a quick line home.

Dear Mother,

There is every indication that there is going to be an attack quite soon. Give my heartiest congratulations to Amy and James on their engagement. My thoughts are always with you, and I know you are praying for me. God bless you all.

Your ever loving Son John.

He quickly folded the letter, and with a heavy heart sealed the envelope. He was just addressing it when his mate Cookson rushed in. He looked flushed, and was panting, breathless. His usually smiling face was sombre.

'The tanks are being prepared,' he announced. 'I was just taking a stroll around, and got chatting to one of the blokes in 'C' Company. They're moving the tanks from the orchard where they've been camouflaged. He reckons they'll be on the move by midnight. So, chaps, this is it, real war at last.'

John's stomach did a somersault, but he finished addressing his letter and stuffed it in his pocket. They waited expectantly for their orders. They did not have to mark time for long before they were summoned to the Advanced Dressing Station. John followed Cookson and the rest of his unit out along the trenches to where Captain Dr Powell was awaiting them. Without preamble, he addressed his men.

'There's going to be an attack tomorrow. I expect you've seen that the tanks are moving. Tonight they'll move up further to take their places at the start line. Our division is to go in behind the tanks. The ground we are covering is dry and not too badly shell-holed, so the going should be ideal. This is the first time tanks have been used en masse, and we have great hopes for them. They should be able to cut the wire, and with the use of their fascines they can cross the enemy trenches and eliminate the enemy machine-guns. The infantry will be able to shelter behind the tanks as they advance. We'll go forward with the second wave of troops, pick up the wounded from the first wave, and bring them back.'

As darkness fell, the whole countryside became filled with quiet noises – tramp of hoofs, the rattle of wheels, the voices of men passing orders and warnings.

John slept fitfully that night, his mind racing at the thought of the battle tomorrow. Early in the morning, he again heard the noise of tank engines moving towards their start lines. He prayed that the weather would remain dry and that the war would soon be over. At five a.m. he roused himself, washed and shaved, and prepared his equipment.

'What the hell's going on up there?' came a cheerful voice behind him.

'Oh, morning Cookson, you look fit and ready for action.' John's words were almost drowned out by an appalling crash of sound, as a torrent of shells whined overhead. 'Jerry must be deep in his dugout, I wonder how he feels when that lot hits him.'

'Let's hope it doesn't churn up the ground too much, so the tanks can't get through,' replied Cookson. 'Gosh, it's jolly misty out there.'

'At least the ground is dry and will enable them to make a good advance. Oh look.' cried John, 'there's a tank crossing our front line. It looks like some monstrous prehistoric monster.'

'It sure does, and the infantry are beginning to follow, and what's more, I think Jerry has been taken completely by surprise.'

'Yes, there's the coloured SOS lights going up over their trenches. At least the tanks will crash their way over the wire and make a way for our infantry,' added Lane, a giant of a man, well over six foot, broad shouldered and muscular.

John edged his way further over the trench parapet, so that he could follow the course of the attack more clearly. He could just pick out the enemy field-gun shells bursting around the tanks and infantry as they advanced. Just then a shrill whistle was heard.

John felt a tightening of his jaw and stomach. Fear gripped him by the throat and a sense of unreality swept over him. Cookson's voice boomed in his ear. 'Right, old mate, it's our turn to advance, and God help the poor blighters out there.'

With the blood pumping through his veins, John clambered over the parapet, and Cookson and he went forward, their medical equipment straddled in a satchel over their shoulders, carrying a stretcher between them. The rest of their section followed closely behind.

The first tanks were now across the main and reserve trenches of the Hindenberg Line. There was the swish-swish of bullets passing all around them. Shells followed the slow progress of the tanks with uncanny accuracy. The atmosphere was tense, the guns were making an earth-shattering noise. Suddenly, in the light of the early dawn, John spotted smoke pouring out of one of the tanks.

'Come on, over there,' he shouted to his unit. 'There may be someone needing our help. Looks as though it's taken a direct hit.'

'Oh crikey, yes, let's go.'

They sprinted across the field, through the barbed wire. Cookson slipped, cursed, then righted himself, as they clambered up a slight bank. The noise of war was all about them. They had almost reached the burning tank when they were stopped in their tracks.

'Look out,' hissed John, as he threw himself down, every nerve and muscle at full stretch. The shell screamed down towards them. There was a tremendous thud which shook the ground. John covered his ears with his hands as the shattering blast of the explosion rocked his brain.

'Phew! That was a close one,' gasped Cookson, as pieces of shrapnel zinged through the air. Their hands were shaking as they brushed away the earth from their tunics. Drawing a deep breath of utter relief, they retrieved the stretcher and raced on.

Billowing smoke and blood-red flames were now engulfing the

machine's fuel tank. One of the side doors was open. A gunner lay sprawled beside the tank, blood oozing from his shoulder. He was deathly pale, but conscious. Another body was blocking the entrance.

'We're too late to be of help to that poor fellow,' sighed John, as he moved him aside. He clambered into the tank. A body was slumped in his seat in the front. He heaved, then half lifted, half dragged the unconscious man out. Eager hands grabbed him, and John went back for a second body.

'That's four accounted for,' he yelled at Cookson. 'Looks like the commander.' Cookson and Lane helped to drag him free of the tank and lay him on the ground. By now the tank engine had caught fire. 'You can't go back inside there', yelled Cookson.

'We can't leave them to that inferno, I must try,' John yelled back, his breath coming in gasps. 'I've got to try again.'

'Don't be a fool, it's suicidal to go back,' both Cookson and Lane screamed at him. Cookson jumped up, and began to pull at John's coat. Abruptly, John came to his senses and realized he could do no more. It would mean putting them all in jeopardy. With a heavy heart, he escaped through the door, and fell exhausted to the ground. He took two or three great gulps of fresh air into his lungs then, coughing and sputtering, looked around him.

'Well, how are they?' he at last managed to spit out, indicating the bodies lying on the ground.

'Three alive, just . . . good work, Aldcott. You OK?'

'Yes thanks, I'm fine. We'd better get —' John's words were interrupted by a groan from one of the prostrate figures lying on the ground. Lane was trying to stem the flow of blood from a gash on the man's forehead. John leapt to his feet as though he had been prodded by a pitchfork. 'Roger, would you believe it it's my old schoolfriend Roger Bliss.' There was a tightening in his throat almost choking off his breath as he fell to his knees and grasped his friend's hand.

'My God, would you believe it . . .' gasped Cookson. 'He's still breathing, the sooner we get him away from the battle zone the better.'

In a voice which shook with emotion, John murmured, 'Hold on, old friend, we'll soon have you in hospital, safe and sound.'

Leaving the others from their unit to attend to the less seriously wounded, John, Cookson and Lane very gently loaded the semi-conscious Bliss onto a stretcher. As carefully as they could, so as not to jolt him too badly, they made their way through the pock-marked landscape of no man's land.

It was quieter overhead now, just the occasional burst of artillery shells, as they crossed the exposed open ground, to the next relay of stretcher bearers. They would take over and carry Bliss on to where the motor ambulance would convey him to the base hospital.

'Nearly there, Roger, sorry it's such a bumpy ride —'

John's words were lost for suddenly a shell came shrieking down out of the blue and burst three yards in front of them.

John hardly felt the flying fragment of red-hot steel that hammered into him – he keeled over, and lay as one dead.

CHAPTER VII

Claire Gordon

John lay racked with wave after wave of agony. He was sometimes conscious of shadowy white figures around him, and concerned faces looking down on him. Then he would wander away again. At times he felt he was dead, but his mind was playing tricks on him. He imagined he was floating through white clouds, and then looking beyond them he could see a long tunnel, and at the end a brilliant light. Passing through the tunnel he walked into the most incredibly beautiful garden. Everything was perfect, and the peace was almost tangible.

'John,' faint though it was the sound of his name reached down to pierce the mist of his unconsciousness. His eyes fluttered open and he blinked his lids as he tried to get them focused.

Gradually his mind began to clear and he looked up into a pair of sparkling eyes, which were of a green he had never seen before, almost emerald with gold flecks. The voice that spoke to him was gentle, with just the trace of a Canadian accent.

'Nice to see you've woken up, you've certainly taken your time about it.' A faint smile touched her lips, revealing even white teeth.

'What happened?' The effort to speak was almost too much for him; his mouth and throat were parched.

'You were knocked out by shell shrapnel, you lost a lot of blood, we thought we might not be able to save you. The doctors have had to remove shrapnel from your legs and arms. Then on top of that, you went down with a fever.' John looked around him and noticed that he was in a long low building, with rows of beds on either side.

'Where am I?' he asked, his head beginning to swim again.

'You're in the Canadian military hospital, near Calais,' replied the nurse. 'Now, no more questions, you must rest.'

'I'm thirsty,' he whispered.

'Good, I'll fetch you a drink.' She bustled off, returning a few minutes later with a glass of water. John sipped it, then fell back exhausted. His arms felt like lead. A little later she returned with some hot soup; she had to prop him up in bed with pillows. The contact sent little shivers down John's spine.

'What's your name?' he asked shyly, between spoonfuls of soup.

'Staff Nurse Gordon —'

'Yes, and a very proficient one too,' burst in a voice which John immediately recognized. The nurse blushed and flashed her warm smile.

'Reg Cookson, for heaven's sake,' exclaimed John. 'What're you doing here?'

'Jerry nearly got us all, but we were fortunate. Your friend Roger is on his way home. Lane, lucky beggar, got away with just a scratch.'

'And you, were you badly hurt?'

'No not really, I'm on the mend now, and after a few weeks' leave I'll be right as rain.'

'Now then, you must not tire Mr Aldcott,' commanded Nurse Gordon gently but firmly. 'You'll have plenty of time to catch up on all the news later.' She busied herself rearranging John's bedclothes, and then turned to attend to another patient.

Reg glanced smilingly at John. 'It's good to see you back with us again, you gave us quite a fright, old chap. Still, I'd better obey orders,' he added, his eyes boring into the back of the retreating nurse. 'Sweet dreams, see you tomorrow.'

Three days after this, John felt strong enough to get up. With the help of Nurse Gordon he swung his legs out of the bed and tried to stand, but they buckled under him and he would have fallen had the nurse not been on hand.

'Steady on, you mustn't try to do too much, you're still very weak,' she chided him. 'Now, lift your legs, one at a time, and do a few exercises before you let them take the weight of your body. That's right, lift, and bend it under, good, now try again . . . Well done, now your arms.'

John groaned as the pain gripped him, but gritting his teeth he tried again, and again, until the perspiration ran down his face.

'OK, that's enough for now. It looks as if you've been fortunate, you'll be able to walk again. Lots of the men who come through here never even get near that stage.'

'Yes, I realize how lucky I am, but I think it was more than luck. Do you believe in divine providence, Nurse Gordon?'

'Yes, I most certainly do. I'm a daughter of the manse. My father is a Methodist minister back in my home city of Toronto. He works in the downtown area.'

'What a coincidence,' said John, surprised. 'My father was a Methodist minister, first as a missionary in China, and then in Wadhurst, a little market town in Sussex. He died a few years ago, but my mother and sister still live near there. What's Toronto like?'

'It's very cold in winter, the temperature gets down well below freezing, the winds are piercingly cold as they blow straight off the prairies. There's snow on the ground often from mid-November until April. In July and August it's very hot.'

'I guess we have less extreme weather in Britain.'

'Yes, plenty of rain, and not much sunshine,' Nurse Gordon laughed, and John noticed the dimples forming in her cheeks.

Their eyes met and locked. John felt a wild desire to reach out and touch her. His emotions were churning inside him. 'You must rest now, and we'll have another session tomorrow.' The nurse donned her professional voice, and then abruptly turned her attention to the other patients. She was getting too close to this patient, and it worried her.

John's gaze followed her, as she stopped to speak to each of her patients, giving them her full attention, or so he thought. He did not know how difficult it was for Nurse Gordon to concentrate. It was so out of character for her to be swamped by such fierce, overpowering feelings. All John knew for a certainty was the profound effect she was having on him – he had never felt like this before. Whenever he closed his eyes, a picture of Nurse Gordon swam before him.

She was not pretty in the accepted sense, but when she smiled, her whole face lit up with a warm radiance. He had found himself liking her instantly. What was it that was so attractive about her? he asked himself. Then suddenly it hit him. He had never felt so comfortable talking to a woman before. It was as if he had known her all his life, as if there was an affinity between them. He tried to pull his mind away from the image of Nurse Gordon, but his thoughts persisted in returning to her. He wanted to get to know her better, but how, was the big question.

As the days went by, John slowly regained his strength. He missed Cookson badly, he could have done with his friend's buoyant presence – he was always so cheerful.

Not one to be idle for long, John soon made himself useful on the ward, but he tired quickly. There was a deep wound in his calf muscle which caused him considerable pain. He was provided with a stick, but quickly dispensed with it as it made him feel like an old man.

Between shifts one day he plucked up courage and sought out Nurse Gordon. He was somewhat relieved to find her sitting alone, enjoying the last of the evening sunshine. He studied her for a few moments and a strange excitement arose within him. 'May I join you, Nurse?' he asked, trying to keep his voice casual. She was startled, her green eyes, widening in momentary surprise.

'Yes of course,' she said, smiling, and immediately made a space for him to sit down beside her.

'Can I get you a drink of something?' he enquired, a little awkwardly, feeling less sure of himself now.

'Oh no, thank you, I've just had some tea.' She pointed to the empty cup on the ground. 'I'm enjoying the last of the sunshine,' she went on breathlessly, 'it's been quite a day.'

'You look tired, Nurse, you work too hard,' he said, in a tone of concern.

'Well yes, I guess we all do . . . sometimes it all seems so hopeless . . .' Her voice broke, for a moment she was wrapped in sadness. She took a deep breath. 'Those poor guys . . . I fear sometimes I have lost my faith in the goodness of God. All that carnage, the pain and suffering. If there is a God, why oh why does He allow all this?' She spread her hands indicating the suffering and pain all around them.

'Yes, I know, Nurse, I thought that when my father died, and other times too during this terrible war. It's a difficult problem, and one which gives non-Christians as much trouble as Christians.'

'Yes, I must confess it has baffled me for a very long time,' admitted Claire.

'You're tired out,' John observed. 'Perhaps we will just have to accept there's no real answer this side of the grave. I have come to believe, though, that the injustices of this life will be redressed in the next one.'

Claire gave a weak little smile, and shrugged her shoulders.

'It can't last much longer,' he tried to sound optimistic, but what he really wanted to do was to put his arms around her and comfort her. He had never seen her looking so tired and vulnerable – on the ward she always appeared so calm and efficient. Instead, he turned to her and asked. 'What are you planning to do when the war ends?'

'I don't really know. I'd like to travel, but my parents aren't too keen on the idea of me doing so as a single person. And you, Mr Aldcott . . . ?'

'Well, it's strange but since I joined the R.A.M.C., I've decided that what I really want to do more than anything is to train as a doctor.'

Nurse Gordon turned her head and fixed her gaze full on him. 'You'd make a good one,' she told him confidently. 'You're a great help on the ward, we'll miss you when you leave.' She glanced reluctantly at her watch. 'I'm afraid I must report back on duty, thank you for your company. It's been good to talk.'

John politely rose to his feet. He felt a complete idiot asking her the next question, but he had to. 'Is there any chance I can see you sometimes? I mean . . . other than on the ward, and like this . . . and could you possibly call me John . . . ?'

'Well, yes to both, so long as you call me Claire . . . off duty of course,' she added, giving John a brilliant smile.

After that they formed the habit of spending their coffee, and lunch breaks together. John managed to persuade Claire to swop her duties and accompany him to one of the concerts put on by the hospital staff and some of the soldiers. It gave him great pleasure to see her relax and enjoy herself.

One morning, John observed that Claire was unusually glum. When at last they were able to take a break, he turned to her and asked sympathetically, 'Why the long face, Claire?'

'Oh dear, am I so transparent?' she sighed. 'As a matter of fact, I received a letter from home this morning, and I guess I'm feeling a little homesick. Nothing more.'

'Tell me about home then, it may help,' said John hoping to coax the dimples back to her cheeks.

'You won't be bored . . .'

'No fear of that. I've never been to Canada, but it sounds great. How did you spend your spare time?'

'I often went swimming off Toronto Islands Park in Lake Ontario, when the weather was good.'

'Do you sail on it as well?'

'No, but many families do.'

'I'd love to visit Canada sometime, it's such a huge country, with tremendous opportunities. The Rocky Mountains and Great Lakes must be quite a sight.'

'Well, the best time to visit Ontario is in the Fall. Out in the countryside all the leaves on the Maple trees are turning red and yellow. I've been canoeing up in the north at that time of the year. It's so beautiful, with the autumn colours reflected on the water.'

'What made you volunteer for the Canadian Army Nursing Service?' asked John.

Claire looked thoughtful for a moment, and pushed a stray curl away from her face. 'I guess I wanted to travel and see a bit of Europe, and this seemed a good way of doing it. I also wanted to serve my country, and help the men who are fighting in this terrible war.'

'Do you like travelling?'

'Oh I haven't done much, just a trip down to New York once, on the train, to visit a cousin who was working there. Ever since I was a little girl, I've wanted to go to China.'

John looked at Claire over the rim of his cup. 'That's interesting, but why China?'

'I had an uncle who was in the Canadian foreign service, and he worked in China for a while. He told us all sorts of interesting stories of what it was like there. I was also fascinated by the work of Doctor Hudson Taylor.' Claire cast a shy glance at John. 'Well, actually I really wanted to go to China as a medical missionary, but my parents were against it. They think it's too dangerous.'

John leaned back and stared at her incredulously. 'There's one place in China which is quite safe,' he said, 'and that's Hong Kong. That's where I was born.'

Claire's eyes widened in surprise. 'Were you really.'

'Yes,' he replied, smiling at her warmly.

'I remember you saying your father was a missionary in China. Oh, you must tell me all about it!' Claire leaned forward eagerly.

'I can't remember much, as I left when I was eight. We had a terrible time getting out during the Boxer Rebellion.'

Claire noticed the pained expression which passed fleetingly over John's face. She was immediately concerned, and impulsively reached out and placed her hand on his.

John almost jumped, as her fingers on him felt like an electric shock passing through him. He gazed at her, and the look of tenderness and concern on her face almost overwhelmed him.

He recounted all he could remember of his time in China and of their dramatic escape.

They continued to talk about their families, telling each other things they would never have dreamed of discussing with anyone else. They talked about their hopes and plans when the war was over. Finally, John told her of his discussion with the hospital doctor. He watched her closely as he explained that he was to be honourably discharged from the R.A.M.C, and was due to leave hospital in two days' time.

Claire kept her eyes downcast. Since learning this news from the doctor, she had dreaded this moment. Not able to trust her voice, she nodded.

John seized his chance. He had been longing to know for days whether his feelings were reciprocated, for now he was certain without a shadow of doubt that he was in love with Claire.

'Claire, would you miss me?' he asked, his dark, intent gaze not leaving her face.

Without hesitation and with complete honesty, she met his eyes. 'Oh yes, John, yes I would, very much.' It was then that John recognized the meaning of the radiant smile on her face. He jumped to his feet and stretched out his arms. She seemed to melt into his embrace.

As John bent to kiss her, for several giddy moments his senses spun and whirled. Slowly they pulled apart, and looked at each other long and tenderly. John was the first to break the silence.

'I've two weeks leave to go home to see my family and recover from my injuries. I can't bear to be parted from you Claire. Is there any possibility of you getting time off?'

'I'm sure I could, as I haven't taken any since being posted here.'

'That's wonderful, I know my family will love you and make you welcome. Say you'll come Claire, please.'

Claire beamed at him, her green eyes dancing merrily. 'Yes of course, if you're sure your family won't mind. I'd love to.' She paused, then added shyly, 'I thought I would never see you again, once you were well enough to leave hospital.' Her voice faltered, and a blush spread over her pale cheeks.

'That's settled then,' said John drawing her into his arms again.

They caught the train from Dover to Tunbridge Wells three days later.

'It's all so different from anything in Canada,' Claire exclaimed excitedly, gazing through the train window as they sped along. 'It looks more cultivated than the fields in Ontario. Nearly every scrap of land seems to be hedged off and there are far fewer woods and forests. Ontario has large towns and in between not much else but forest and fields.'

'Yes, Kent is a small county, with lots of little towns and villages. I'm so happy to be sharing my homeland with you, Claire, but this isn't Kent at its best. It looks most beautiful in early May, when all the pink blossom is out, and the leaves are beginning to burst.'

'I think it's quite beautiful,' Claire sighed. 'Oh I can't wait for the war to end, then I can show you my country. You will come, won't you?'

'Oh yes, I'm longing to meet your family.'

Claire was thoughtful for a moment, then observed, 'Ontario is more of a melting pot. There are Scots, English, Irish and Welsh people living there, as well as lots of other nationalities. Toronto has a good university, a good orchestra and a good ice hockey team. My Dad loves to watch the ice hockey.'

'Your father sounds quite a personality,' John remarked. 'Did he ever play ice hockey?'

'Yes, he did when he was young. He gets more excited about the matches at the Toronto Maple Leaf ground than anything else on earth,' laughed Claire.

'He must feel the same way as I do about rugby,' said John, flashing

Claire a grin. She loved the way John's dark eyes lit up in his handsome face when he smiled. It was a strong face, full of character.

The journey passed without incident. It had been cold but sunny. As they alighted from the train in Tunbridge Wells, however it began to drizzle.

'Well, at least the weather doesn't change,' John laughed, as he lifted his kitbag onto his back. He was too weak to carry Claire's case.

'Welcome to Tunbridge Wells,' he said breathlessly. The joy on John's mother's face was plain to see when they arrived home, having taken a cab from the station.

'Come on in both of you, you must be famished. Your letter only arrived this morning . . . Oh it's so good to see you after all this time.' Tears were streaming down her face as she hugged John. Then she turned to Claire as John led her forward and protectively placed his arm around her. 'John has told us so much about you in his letters. It's a real pleasure to meet you,' she said, her face glowing. The two women embraced and obviously immediately warmed to each other.

Just then there was a clatter of footsteps and Amy came flying down the stairs. She leapt at John and hugged him, almost knocking him backwards in her eagerness.

'Goodness me,' John exclaimed, trying but not quite succeeding in swinging her off her feet. Then he held her away from him and studied her for a moment. 'My little sister has grown into a very beautiful young lady. I can see now why my best friend has fallen in love with her,' he remarked, smiling at her affectionately. 'Congratulations Amy, I hope you'll be very happy.'

Amy blushed with pleasure at the unexpected compliment. 'Oh thank you, John. I think I'm the happiest person in the world.'

The two weeks passed all too quickly. There was so much news to catch up on. They made the most of their time visiting the famous Pantiles, where they tasted the spa water from the spring. John laughed at Claire as she screwed up her face and shuddered. 'Ugh! It's horrible.'

They walked in the countryside, well wrapped up as there was a nip in the air, and the leaves on the trees were beginning to turn golden. They took the train up to London, and visited St Paul's Cathedral, the Tower of London and the Houses of Parliment. They had to queue to go into the Strangers' Gallery to listen to the debates about the war.

'I've never been to Ottawa, to see Canada's Parliament buildings,' said Claire, 'but I'll make sure I visit them when I get home.'

On one of their walks around Tunbridge Wells from Eridge station into the countryside, they stopped for a rest on a grassy knoll. It was a beautiful day for mid-October, crisp and sunny. John had been unusually quiet and thoughtful. He suddenly took a deep breath, and a wave of emotion washed over him as he turned to Claire. His voice was very gentle as he took both her hands in his.

'Claire, I've never known anyone I felt so happy and contented with. I love you with all my heart, and I want to be with you for the rest of my life. Will you marry me, my darling?'

Trembling with emotion, Claire returned John's gaze. 'I love you too John. It's the most beautiful and wonderful feeling which has ever happened to me.'

John was so overcome with his feelings for her, that at first he couldn't speak. Then he reached out and caught her hands in both of his, heart pounding as though it would burst with passionate excitement. Claire's eyes told him all he wanted to know as he held her from him. He looked deep and tenderly into her face and drew her once again into his arms.

They walked on in silence, hand in hand, until John's limp became more pronounced. Turning to him, Claire reproached herself. 'Oh John, I shouldn't have let you walk so far, you've tired yourself out.'

'It's nothing, it's been so lovely and peaceful that I almost forgot about my war wounds. Still, I guess we should be getting back.'

John immediately sought out his mother in the kitchen.

'It's good to have you all to myself for a while,' he said as he bent down and kissed her cheek.

'Yes, John.' She returned his kiss, and smiled up into his face, thinking how much better he looked. 'I've missed you too. Sit yourself down . . . it's wonderful to have you home . . . now tell me what's on your mind.'

'Its hard to know where to begin. Before joining up I was happy in my work at Acetate, but the war seems to have changed me. I've been face to face with so much death and suffering, and at times felt so useless. Yet I've never felt so contented with life as when I was helping in the hospital. I feel my vocation is in medicine.'

'Oh John, I'm sure it's important that you fulfil yourself in a way that is honouring to God as well as other people . . .' she paused for a moment, her eyes hooded with memories.

'Mother, you've already spent a lot of money on my education, and I'll never be able to repay you for that.'

'My dear, your uncle was responsible for that, as you know. We all have him to thank for the provision he made for us, which has been more than adequate. Your father invested it well, and he would want it to be used to help you with your future studies. Amy never wanted to go on to further education, so I've decided to give her her share of your uncle's money when she gets married.'

John nodded his agreement. 'I've already written to Acetate, to ask if I can return there,' he observed. 'I had a reply this morning and have been accepted back.'

'That's wonderful, dear,' replied his mother.

'The work there has expanded. It looks as though I'll be able to put in quite a lot of overtime. The extra money will help finance me at medical school, if my application is successful.'

Mary Aldcott rose from her chair to peek into the oven. 'Well, who knows, perhaps one day you'll be able to use your skills on the mission field. Your father was always disappointed he couldn't return to China —' Tears blurred her eyes.

John sprang to his feet, took two strides and threw his arm around her. 'You're still missing him too —' he whispered into her hair.

She nodded, and then twisting her head, she looked straight up at him and said, smiling through her tears, 'There's no time like the present, so you'd better write off to Medical School right away. Have you decided to apply to University College Hospital?'

'Well, yes, I guess I'd stand a good chance of getting in there,' John replied, with a great surge of relief.

'That's settled then. Now what else is on your mind?

Taken aback, John stared at his mother, then laughed heartily. 'You must be a mind reader, Mother... I've never been able to keep anything from you.'

'Well, I'm glad nothing has changed between us,' she answered swiftly.

'Mother, I know it's a bit soon, but I've asked Claire to marry me.'

'Oh John, I'm so pleased. I like her very much, she's a very sensible and charming girl, and will make a wonderful wife.'

Giving his mother a hug he exclaimed, 'Oh it's good to talk to you —'

She laughed, 'That's what Mothers are for.'

CHAPTER VIII

Hong Kong

John's years of medical training were over; it had been a hard slog. John and Claire, who had been happily married for two years, were thrilled at last to be realizing their ambition to work as medical missionaries in the Hollywood Road Hospital.

It had been a terrible wrench parting from their families. For the first few days on board the *Empress of Asia*, a sense of homesickness threatened to overwhelm John as he thought of all he was leaving behind.

The weather was fine and the sea calm, until they reached the Bay of Biscay, then a violent storm blew up. Claire felt so ill she just wanted to die, and lay in her cabin for days, unable to face food. John ministered to her very tenderly – it was the first time he had seen Claire unwell. He wiped her brow and brought her cool drinks. Sailing on through the calm waters of the Mediterranean, she was soon restored to her usual robust health.

The days settled down to a routine of study, exercise and getting to know their fellow passengers. They were determined not to waste their time on the long sea voyage, and when they met a young Hong Kong Chinese student, they persuaded him to help them learn the complicated language. With much laughter, their attempts at speaking Cantonese very slowly improved.

At last the scenery began to change as they passed along the desert shore, on to the Indian Ocean, down the coast of Ceylon, on to Singapore, and finally Hong Kong.

'Oh, come and look Claire, we're approaching Hong Kong harbour.' John's eyes were shining, and he was breathless with excitement and trepidation as he grasped Claire's hand. Claire's first glimpse of Hong Kong left her speechless. Myriads of small islands, with hills rising steeply around them, rose out of a sapphire sea. The great white and grey mansions of the mid-levels looked quite majestic. The Peak seemed to tower over the town of Victoria, and a multitude of ships, junks and sampans filled the sheltered harbour.

They rounded the tip of the Kowloon peninsula and headed towards Wanchai.

'It's beautiful,' breathed Claire at last catching her breath, 'but its not such a hustle and bustle as I was expecting. It's so much more peaceful and quiet.'

'Yes, you're right,' John agreed 'Its very strange. So different from what I remember when I arrived with my parents after our escape from China. I was only eight then.'

'I guess it's because of the strike,' said Claire.

As the ship's ladder was lowered down the side, there were no steam launches to take them across. Everyone on board ship had to hire a sampan to row them. There was considerable haggling at the bottom of the gangway over how much it was going to cost. John looked into the tired sad eyes of the shabby coolie, in his tattered blue trousers and torn shirt, and his generous heart went out to him. They were just so grateful to get ashore with their luggage that they willingly paid the price asked.

They were to be met by David Schom, the London Missionary Society representative in Hong Kong. They eagerly scanned the smiling faces waiting at the wharf. Then John caught sight of his name on a poster being held aloft by a Chinaman of medium height. Even from that distance, John could see that he was immaculately dressed in a dark pin-striped suit. John waved in his direction, and continued to wave until a broad smile lit up the Chinaman's face. They quickly made their way towards him through the milling crowd. When the introductions were over, with a broad grin and in excellent English, David Schom observed, 'Welcome to Hong Kong. You have come at a very difficult time. You see, there is a seamen's strike, the first strike to ever have affected Hong Kong.'

'Yes, we guessed that was the reason the harbour seemed so quiet,' said John.

Thankfully, they left all the negotiations to David. He had hardly finished speaking when, with what seemed to be just a click of the fingers, rickshaws had been hired and he was bundling John and Claire inside.

'You go, I'll see to the luggage,' he ordered, and they gratefully obeyed.

Everything seemed so strange, and the pungent smells were having a strange effect on Claire's internal organs. There were so many new sights and feelings to absorb as they rattled along – Chinese banners hanging on poles from houses; festooned, congested streets with shoppers buying wares from open markets; the noise was unbelievable with the clanging of tram bells, and the chatter of swarms of people all going about their business or eating at the street restaurants.

For the first time, Claire saw people eating from exquisite bowls and using chopsticks adroitly. Leaving the flat areas, they were then transferred to sedan chairs as they began to ascend the Peak.

'You'll have to travel this way, because of the strike the Peak tram isn't working,' David Schom informed them.

It was a rough ride, the bamboo poles creaked under the strain. The coolies were sweating profusely when at last they were deposited outside their new home on Bowen Road.

The flat was small and sparsely furnished. John looked a bit crestfallen, but Claire smiled at him. 'Don't worry, darling, we'll soon brighten it up and make it more homely.'

The door swung open, and a tiny wizened-faced Chinese women padded towards them, clad in a floral jacket, black baggy cotton trousers, and wearing felt slippers. She bowed in greeting and smiled warmly, showing a mouth largely devoid of teeth.

'This is Lily Kwok,' said David, as Claire and John returned her smile. 'She used to work in the hospital. She doesn't speak any English, but she understands some pidgin. She will do all the housework, and help you with the shopping and cooking Mrs Aldcott.'

'How much should we pay her,' asked John.

'She's a very good Amah. I think it would be fair to pay her twenty-five dollars a month. For that she will arrive at eight in the morning and leave at eight at night . . . Is that all right for you, Mrs Aldcott?'

'Yes, that would suit us very well,' said Claire, and John nodded agreement.

'I'm sure you would like some tea now. Yes?'

'Tea would be most welcome, thank you,' said Claire, flashing a smile in the direction of Lily Kwok.

Turning to David Schom, John thanked him for his help. 'It's all very strange at the moment,' he added. 'Everything seems to move at such a hectic pace.'

Claire sank down thankfully into the only comfortable chair. 'I think it will take us quite a while to adjust,' she remarked.

'Yes, that's Hong Kong for you, Mrs Aldcott. We Chinese are taught from an early age to work hard, and in conditions Westerners are unable to survive in.'

'We're delighted to be here. It has been a dream for Claire and for me through the long years of medical school to return to my birthplace to work.'

'Oh, you were born here?'

'Yes, I was, but my parents moved on into China, when I was still quite a baby.'

Lily Kwok entered with a tray of tea, smiled her toothless smile again, poured the tea, and departed.

'We've so much to learn,' John exclaimed sipping his tea.

'Yes, the gulf between the British and Chinese is enormous. You'll find, though, that the British taipans who live on the higher altitudes of the Peak try to preserve their way of life as it was back in England.'

'Maybe, but we've come to live and work with the Chinese, and we want to learn your customs and get to know your people,' replied John.

David nodded, 'Quite so, but you're followers of Christ, and that makes all the difference. You do not think of yourselves as being in any way superior to us.'

'No, of course not,' replied John and Claire in unison.

'You'll find that ninety per cent of the Chinese patients are Buddhists, and most of them retain the customs of old China. For instance, you'll still find women in China who bind their feet.'

'I saw many women like that in China, when I was a boy.' John recalled.

'So you'll know about arranged marriages.'

'You mean marriages that are arranged in the traditional way, with the bride being selected by the bridegroom's parents.' replied John.

'Yes, but also in consultation with astrologers and fortune-tellers. Sometimes the couple won't have seen each other until the wedding day. Lily Kwok ran away from her home because she didn't want to marry the man chosen for her by her parents. You see, she used to work at a missionary station. There she met and fell in love with another Christian worker. They came to Hong Kong and got married, and they've remained here ever since.' Seeing Claire and John exchange looks, David added, 'Very different in your country, huh?'

'Oh yes, it's all a bit of a culture shock,' affirmed John.

Claire just nodded. The journey had make her feel quite queasy, and she was longing to lie down in a cool room.

'Arranged marriages are rarely objected to. You see, filial piety is so strong in Chinese families. You understand that Chinese think of a marriage as an alliance between families, rather than as a personal bond between individuals.'

'I guess it was similar in the old days in Europe, when parents used to have a big say in who their children married.' said Claire.

'Yes,' added John, 'in medieval times marriages were arranged by the nobility to cement alliances and end feuding. That's how the Wars of the Roses ended, with Henry VII, as Duke of Lancaster, marrying a Yorkist princess.'

'There's plenty of that going on in China today as well, with families and clans trying to forge alliances to gain wealth and power,' said David. 'Now I'll tell you a bit about the hospital.'

'That would be helpful,' replied John. 'I've had some literature sent out to me. I read that it opened in 1887, and that a wealthy Chinese businessman who had been educated in England helped to start it.'

'That's right, Dr Aldcott. You must be aware then that it was set up as a training hospital.'

'Yes, and I've read somewhere that Sun Yat Sen, the Chinese president, was trained as a doctor there.'

'Yes, he was a brilliant student, and he graduated from Hong Kong with high distinction.' David smiled. The smile broadened. 'But now, after all these years, he has become president of China . . . we are so proud.' He paused, apparently trying to find the right words, then he went on, 'We hope it will be the end of all the feudal customs the Manchus, and Empress Cixi imposed on the Chinese people. We want China to become a modern industrial country, ready to take its place in the world . . . but you're too kind, you let me talk too much,' he chuckled. 'You need to rest, I'll leave you now. Tomorrow I'll accompany you to the hospital, and introduce you to your colleagues.'

'May I come too?' Claire asked. 'I'd love to see the hospital. As I'm to help with the nurses' training, I'd like to get involved right from the start.'

'Your enthusiasm will be welcomed, I am sure, Mrs Aldcott. A trained nurse with your experience will be quite an asset. There's plenty of work to be done.'

They all shook hands formally, and John showed David out. Closing the door behind him, he turned and took his wife in his arms, saying softly into her hair, 'Well, darling, we've arrived, how does it feel to be in Hong Kong?'

Claire, returning his hug, smiled up into his face. 'Oh I wish I could say wonderful, but it wouldn't be true. I feel so hot and sticky at the moment. I'd just like to take a long cool shower.'

'Let's go and see if that can be arranged.' John's eyes twinkled with amusement as he added, 'And we can try our hand at communicating with Lily Kwok.'

John and Claire rose early the following morning. John was due to commence work at eight, but needed to be at the hospital by seven-thirty for prayers in the chapel. Every day began like this, and every Sunday evening a service was held in one of the general wards, conducted by one of the Pastors. The staff firmly believed that the Christian message was the greatest thing given to them, and regarded the healing of the body and of the spirit for each patient to be of equal importance.

After morning prayers, John accompanied Dr Grayson, the medical superintendent on the ward round. He learned that the doctor had been in Hong Kong for many years.

'It has taken us a very long time to overcome some of the suspicion of the Chinese people about Western medicine,' Dr Grayson observed, as they strolled through the ward. 'Their first resort when they are sick would usually be to a traditional herbalist. I'm afraid that the overcrowding, poor diet and the heavy smoking of opium helps to produce a great deal of disease. I feel certain we could eradicate a lot of illness if only we could impress on these people the necessity for better hygiene . . . if we could just stop them spitting in the streets, it would be a start . . . by lessening the prevalence of TB,' he muttered. The doctor walked so briskly through the hospital, pointing out the various departments as he went, that John had to lengthen his stride in order to keep up with him.

'The sanitary conditions in the Colony are appalling —'

'Yes, I've noticed,' John broke in. 'Can't the Government do something?'

'They've tried, but it's difficult to get the majority of people here to co-operate, or to change their way of life.'

'They work such long hours, for so little money —'

'Oh yes, they work to survive, but it's as natural to them as breathing. Idleness is unthinkable. They believe that leisure is only for the rich,' said Dr Grayson.

'I've been told that some smoke opium to escape their misery.'

'That's right, and suffer the consequences in bad mental and physical health. No, I'm afraid the Government does little to help the plight of the poor, though they know how desperately they need assistance,' sighed the doctor. Just then, he stopped by a bed and motioned John to do the same. 'Well, what do you make of this, Dr Aldcott? Have you seen anything like this in England?'

John looked down into the lined face and glassy eyes of what appeared to be a very elderly man, but before he could comment Dr Grayson continued. 'No, I'm sure you haven't, as this is a classic example of an opium sufferer. He smoked it to relieve his pain, which is quite a common practice amongst the coolies. You see if he didn't work he wouldn't be paid, and as he has no family to support him, he would have to steal or starve. He was picked up from the gutter and brought in, half dead.

'Now here, we have several cases of malaria, dysentery, typhoid fever and beri beri.' They continued the ward round. Then John was shown the operating theatres and X-ray departments. 'These are badly in need of modernizing – in fact we desperately need a new hospital. You may have heard that there are plans ahead for this, but money is short. Oh dear, there's so much more we could do if only we had the resources.'

John's head was swimming as he took his leave of Dr Grayson. He felt as if he had been hit with a hammer, they had moved so rapidly through the wards, and his new colleague had talked as rapidly as he walked. He was wound up like a spring and looked ready to snap, John thought, a worried frown creasing his forehead.

As the weeks and months passed, John began to feel more confident in this strange, pulsating land. Once a week he held an out-patients' clinic on Bowen Road. At the end of one very busy day, John was tired and longing to get home. He was just packing his bag when outside the clinic he heard a car screech to a halt. A well-dressed European jumped out from the back of the gleaming chauffeur-driven Rolls Royce.

In a loud angry voice, which sounded strangely familiar, he began yelling obscenities at the retreating figure of a shabby rickshaw coolie.

'Where've I heard that voice before?' John wondered. Just then the man turned, walked to the front of the car, and began to scrutinize it closely. He looked up as John drew alongside him – John found himself gazing into the angry face of Prosser. Oh no, he thought, not him of all people, here in Hong Kong. He tried to hurry by.

'I know you, don't I?' the all-too-familiar voice stopped John in his tracks. Prosser was scratching his head, and staring straight at him.

'Yes, I believe we were at school together,' replied John, somewhat reluctantly.

'Well, I'll be damned if it isn't Aldcott! How are you, old fellow? Fancy seeing you, here of all places.'

John noticed a warm smile replacing the previous angry expression, and remarked as casually as he could, 'I work in the hospital.'

'I always knew you had brains, Aldcott, you've obviously done King's credit.'

'It's good of you to say so,' answered John, but he could not help glancing at the gleaming Rolls, and wondered how on earth Prosser had made so much money in his short lifetime as to be able to afford such a car.

Prosser noticed the look and smugly commented. 'Not bad, eh?'

'It's beautiful . . . is it yours?'

'Yes, one of the little luxuries of a successful business career. I don't know how I would have managed during this strike. The Peak tram is out of order —'

'So you live on the Peak then?'

'Yes we're fortunate we are able to avoid the worst of what can be a very trying climate.' Prosser paused for a moment, then added. 'This really is a pleasure, you must come for dinner... yes, dinner. My wife will be delighted to meet you. Are you married?'

'Yes,' said John. 'Claire and I have been married for nearly four years.'

'Well, bring your wife – she'll be company for Virginia. She's always pleased to meet people from home.'

'That's very kind of you,' replied John trying desperately to reconcile Prosser's charm with the arrogance of the schoolboy he had known. 'I'm kept pretty busy you know.'

'I'm sure you are, but now the strike is over you can get the tram to the Peak terminal, the house is only a short distance from there, you can't miss it, it's the second one on Lugard Road . . . how about Saturday evening at eight?'

John could not think of an excuse, and as the invitation was also extended to Claire, he accepted as graciously as he could and they parted.

So Prosser has made good, thought John, and he appears to be a changed character. Yet he still remained wary at the prospect of spending any of his precious off-duty time in the company of Prosser.

Claire was busy in the kitchen when John arrived home.

'Had a good day?' John enquired, kissing her.

'Yes busy, but interesting. And you?'

'Hectic . . . but would you believe I bumped into an old boy from King's today.' John then told her about the dinner invitation and his inability to make Prosser out. Claire listened in silence, then burst out laughing.

'John, you look so hangdog. I've never known you be so unsure of anyone. Do you really hold such unpleasant memories of him?'

'Yes, he made my life pretty miserable at school, but I must say he seems to have changed – he's quite friendly now.'

It was the first time John and Claire had been beyond Bowen Road. The ride on the Peak tram was spectacular. To reach the summit the tram was pulled up by a steel cable, while the descending car acted as a brake.

As they began to ascend, Claire turned to John whose face was bleak – he was too immersed in his thoughts to enjoy the view.

Claire nudged him. 'Oh John, it's so beautiful, do look.'

John gave himself a metaphorical shake and turned to stare out of the window. It really was a magnificent view, with all the lights of the City below.

The tram shuddered to a halt and they stepped out. Beside the upper terminus, the Peak Hotel loomed majestically. They followed the road round as Prosser had instructed. The roads leading from one level to another were lined with palms, ferns and flowers. It was a breathtaking sight, looking down on the harbour and all the twinkling lights.

Prosser's house was indeed easy to find – it was palatial. A servant, immaculately dressed in black trousers and white jacket, opened the door.

'You are very welcome,' he said, giving a slight bow, 'please, who shall I announce?'

'Dr and Mrs Aldcott,' replied John stiffly.

They were shown into a huge hall, the highly polished mahogany floors were set off to perfection by thick, beautifully patterned Chinese carpets. Prosser came hurriedly towards them, with hand extended.

'Good to see you,' he greeted John, giving Claire a long, curious stare, before going on, 'and this must be your charming wife.'

John introduced Claire and they were ushered into a spacious room.

'You certainly have a beautiful house,' John remarked, without envy. 'You must be doing very well to have acquired it.'

'Well, let's just say my trading operations have been successful. Do sit down, Claire, my wife will join us shortly.'

John and Claire sank down into the most comfortable of chairs, and admired their surroundings. The furniture was European, with deep sofas arranged around a huge fireplace, an intricately carved Chinese table, on which a large candelabra sparkled, beautifully carved camphor-wood chests, silk drapes, and a glass case full of the most exquisite ceramics. Prosser waved his hand, deliberately casual, but could not refrain from saying, boastfully, 'Mostly Ming.'

'Oh really,' murmured Claire, while John could think of nothing appropriate to say.

'When I came out to Hong Kong in 1910, I joined the biggest company, Lane Mclery, worked for them for eight years, and then broke out on my own. As you can see I've done pretty well. Now, my dear fellow, tell me what brings you out here.'

'I'm a doctor with the Hollywood Road Hospital. I came out after joining the London Missionary Society.'

'Ugh,' Prosser shuddered, 'Hollywood Road is right in the middle of the coolie district. All that filth, disease and disgusting living conditions. I'm surprised you haven't caught some terrible disease.'

'We're very careful about hygiene, and so far we've kept well,' replied John.

'Most Europeans live on the Peak, from fear of disease, and it's five or six degrees cooler than the lower levels at night. If we let the Chinese live here they would soon start building those awful Chinese-style tenement houses which on the lower levels are notoriously filthy.'

'Yes, the need for medical help is certainly greatest on the lower levels,' declared John, determined to stand his ground, but at the same time thinking this was the old Prosser showing himself.

'I find trading with China very difficult. The warlords fighting each other for power all the time, and ragged, ill-disciplined armies ravaging the land. They may have had a great civilization in the past, but their present set-up is absolutely hopeless. It's very disruptive of trade as well, and you're always having to grease the palms of corrupt officials —' Prosser broke off as there was a knock on the door. 'Come in.' he called out. The door opened and a servant entered, carrying a silver tray. 'Champagne?'

'Thank you,' replied Claire.

'Would it be too much trouble to have a soft drink, I've never got around to drinking the hard stuff, and I find a soft drink quenches the thirst better in this climate.' said John.

'Oh sure, whatever you like.' Prosser snapped out an order, and the servant departed. Prosser handed Claire a glass, quickly downed his own, and was pouring a second one when the servant returned with a flagon of orange juice. He poured a large glass and left the jug for John to help himself.

They sat sipping their drinks and making polite conversation until Prosser's wife joined them.

'My wife Virginia,' he announced not troubling to rise to his feet.

She was quite stunning, with raven black hair, high cheek bones, fair skin and very dark eyes. Her long, close-fitting emerald green evening dress accentuated her slender waist. Studying her, Claire thought she should have looked graceful, but something seemed wrong.

She had entered very slowly, holding her head to one side. The right side of her face was in shadow, and it was not until she turned to shake hands with John that Claire noticed a black and yellow bruise. Claire was about to comment, then thought better of it.

John thought what a lovely smile she had, but quickly changed his mind when he realized the smile did not reach her eyes. They were sad and listless.

'Pleased to meet you,' said Claire. 'Have you been in Hong Kong long?'

Virginia opened her mouth to reply, but before she managed to get more than a couple of words out, Prosser took over.

'Virginia came out to Hong Kong with her mother on the milk run in

1919.' He smiled smugly and Virginia blushed furiously. 'Her father died when she was a kid and her two brothers were killed in the war.'

'Oh, I'm sorry,' sympathized Claire.

'Her mother had to sell the family shoe-making business when her husband died. Virginia went to a good school though, Cheltenham Ladies College, so there should be some grey matter between her ears.' He smiled at Virginia mockingly.

A slow tide of colour suffused Virginia's passive face. Claire wondered what lay beneath the surface of the marriage. Prosser seemed to have little respect for his wife. Claire had a strong desire to say something positive about Virginia.

'I'm sure Virginia's a great support to you,' she blurted out.

'Support? Oh yes, she's a good companion and hostess, and very helpful in my business activities, aren't you, dear?' A loud muffled clang interrupted Prosser in full spate. 'Ah, the dinner gong. Thank God for that, I'm famished.' He ushered Claire and John into the dining room. Virginia followed behind and took her place at the foot of the long table.

The food was brought in by a number one and number two boy. They kept their eyes down as they served at the table, entering and leaving discreetly. They dined on roast beef, served with crispy roast potatoes, vegetables of various kinds, with the lightest of light Yorkshire pudding.

'My, what a wonderful meal. I haven't tasted anything so good since leaving England,' Claire said, turning to Virginia. 'How ever have you managed to achieve this here in Hong Kong?'

'In my business dealings I eat a lot of Chinese food, so when I'm home I like to have traditional British food. I hired an English chef to show them how to cook. Besides they're much cheaper to keep . . . and, er . . . easier to get.'

'So you don't have any difficulty keeping them?'

'Good Lord no, it's quite a privilege for them to work here. Don't you find that?'

'Well I wouldn't really put it like that. Our Lily Kwok is quite a treasure, and we're the ones to feel privileged, as it enables Claire to work too.' replied John.

'You only have one servant?' Claire noticed the look of surprise which flitted across Virginia's face.

'Oh yes, we live in a tiny little flat next to the hospital, so we don't need any more help.'

'You need to be careful of all the diseases down there. There have been plague and cholera in the coolie districts.' Prosser's voice held a note of contempt and John felt the irritation gathering within him.

They were spared having to reply as the dessert was brought in. Claire wisely steered the conversation into calmer channels. Claire and John declined the brandy and port, and after congratulating their hosts on the delicious meal, they managed with almost indecent haste to make their excuses to leave.

'Phew,' Claire slowly let out her breath as the door shut behind them. 'There's something very wrong with their relationship. Poor Virginia, she looks so unhappy . . .' She took John's arm and they hurried towards the tram.

'Yes, she seemed unable to assert herself at all —'

'And Prosser continually cut across her attempts to enter into the conversation,' Claire jerked out. 'I felt so sorry for her, I wonder she puts up with it.'

'You know, Claire, there's something very fishy about his business connections. He cleverly evaded telling us what line of business he's in.'

'Gee, something shady, I'll be bound.'

'Opium, is my guess.'

'Do you really think so, John?'

'Yes I do, it's the quickest way to make money out here, or so I'm told. My bet is that he's smuggling opium into the French concession in Shanghai. The French use their police force as a means of distribution throughout the whole Yangtze river valley. They're the pushers. I bet you anything Prosser is one of the middle men.'

'Middle men? What do you mean?'

'Between the growers in Siam and the French. The French don't admit to the trade openly but everyone knows it goes on, and it provides a huge income to the French Exchequer, so they turn a blind eye to it.'

'I thought it was the British who introduced opium into China.'

'Yes it was, but the French have taken over where we British left off.'

'Oh John, the more I hear about the Far East, the more corrupt I think it is.'

They were both immersed in their own thoughts on the Peak tram and were almost home when Claire turned to John. 'John what did Prosser mean by the milk run?'

'It's the system in the Far East where eligible women come out to the colonies from Britain, usually with some close relative, in search of a husband. It's a bit more civilized than a cattle market, but the ones that don't make it are always known as the "returned empties".'

'What a humiliating idea. John, did you notice Virginia's bruises? Do you think Prosser beats her up?'

'Oh no, Claire, Prosser wouldn't be such a cad.'

Claire wasn't so convinced.

CHAPTER IX

Mui-Tsia

'John,' Claire's voice sounded strained over the line, and John felt himself freeze.

'What's the matter, darling, is the baby coming?'

'No John, No . . . No I'm fine. But . . . er . . . I've found a little girl of about eight. She's in a terrible state . . . John, John, are you there?'

John let out a sigh of relief – he had been afraid something had happened to Claire. She never phoned him at work, and since they had known she was pregnant he had been anxious every time he left her.

'Yes, Claire, I'm listening. Go on, darling, what's the problem?'

'John, can you come home and take a look at her? I'm so worried.'

'Well, tell me more about it. Was she involved in an accident, or what?'

'No, I don't think so. It looks as though she's been beaten, and . . . er . . . she's been burnt quite badly, on her arms. At least it looks like burns.' There was a slight hesitation, then Claire went on. 'I was just going out for a little exercise, as it had stopped raining, and I heard this crying. It was coming from the old hut behind the house, and I found this little Chinese girl. I wasn't sure what to do, so I ran back to fetch Lily Kwok. She . . . she thinks she's a runaway servant.'

'Alright, Claire, I'll soon be finished here. I'll get home as quickly as I can.'

John whisked through the last of his patients, locked up securely, and set off for home. The rain had been almost continuous for over a week. The streets were like muddy rivers. The noise and violence of the downpour swelled to a great splashing crescendo as John ran the last few yards. His feet were soaked and his shirt steaming from the heat of his body. Lily Kwok met him at the door, looking very uneasy.

'Little girl awful bad.' She shook her head, as she relieved John of his dripping umbrella. Hearing John's voice, Claire looked up and smiled thankfully. The little girl was crying pitifully. John looked at her small, battered face and crumpled form, and anger flared in him at the person who had done this. Then, as he began a thorough examination of the tiny body, his heart ached with compassion.

He straightened his back and looked into Claire's anxious face.

'You did right to call me . . . she's in a bad way. She'll need a blood transfusion, but meanwhile try to get as much liquid into her as you can – she's dehydrating. The skin is severely damaged around her left ear, and there's extensive blistering on her arms. The burn areas need to be covered and kept germ free. I think we'll have to get her into the isolation ward.' John's professional manner had now taken over, and for the time being his emotions were controlled.

'I'll see to it straight away. Do you think you can cope for a bit? The bruising is bad, but I don't think there are any broken bones. Still, let's deal with the burns first, before they become infected.'

The child was still muttering and crying out incoherently, like someone in a nightmare. John took hold of her little hand, and looked down into her glazed eyes and expressionless face.

'It's alright, little one, you are safe now. We'll look after you, and make you well again.' The gentleness in his voice must have touched something in the child. She stopped crying and a curious stillness came over her face.

'What has she told you, Claire?'

'Very little, she's so terrified, poor little mite. When Lily Kwok asked her name, she just screamed, "Missee . . . don't beat me, don't beat me".' Claire seemed to be trying to find the right words, then blurted out. 'Lily Kwok thinks she's a mui-tsai.'

For a stunned second John looked at Claire. 'Well if that's the case, then I'll be moving heaven and hell to get something done to stop this sort of thing,' he vowed. Claire knew he meant it.

Little Storm, Claire's name for the child, slowly responded to treatment. Claire was free to visit her each day in the hospital now she had given up work to await the birth of their first child. John, true to his vow, lost no time in contacting the police. It had been agreed that the child would be kept in hospital until the court hearing.

Buoyed up by her concern for Little Storm, and now with more time on her hands, Claire was determined to find out more about the mui-tsai system.

'I suggest you go to see Mrs Pickering – she used to be a doctor, now she's a member of the child Labour Ordinance.'

'That's rather a grand title, what does it mean?' asked Claire.

'I think she makes inspections of factories, and gathers information about the exploitation of child labour.'

'Oh, she sounds just the right person. I'll go tomorrow.'

'She's a very busy women, Claire. It may be better to ring her first.'

'Yes, of course, I'll do it right away,' Claire heaved herself out of her chair.

'Oh, John, I'm getting a size,' she remarked, glancing down at her enormous bulge.

John laughed and sprang to his feet to assist.

'Not much longer now, darling.'

Claire had to wait two days before Mrs Pickering, their Pastor's wife, could see her. She greeted her cordially, and with a smile Claire accepted her offer of tea.

'Well, what is it you wish to see me about? I take it this isn't just a social call.'

'No, you're right, and thank you for sparing me the time,' said Claire. She went on to explain about Little Storm, and her concerns about the system which she felt led to exploitation of girls like her.

'Well, it's a system that started many years ago in old China,' Mrs Pickering said. 'As you know, there's a lot of poverty in China and Hong Kong, made worse by floods and famine. A poor family might not be able to feed its children. The male children were preserved at all costs because they could perform the family rituals of ancestor worship. So important, you know, in Chinese religion. Some of the female children were drowned. As an alternative to drowning, these girls often, while very young, could be sold to rich people, and still are. They are expected to treat them like one of the family.'

'And I expect many of them do,' replied Claire.

'Well yes, and that's why it's so hard to get the Government to act. But it isn't only poverty that leads to girls being sold, they can also be sold to finance a gambling or opium habit. You see, in hard times it was accepted as normal for an individual to be sacrificed for the sake of the family.'

'I'm sure there's some merit in the system, but there's also a lot of abuse too.'

'Yes, Claire, of course you're right. They're often expected to work long hours. Some are interfered with, and others, as in the case of the little girl you mentioned, beaten and ill-treated.'

A snort of indignation escaped Claire. 'It's immoral for a British colony to continue this practice.'

'Yes, that's what I think,' Mrs Pickering sighed, 'but it's difficult to bring any change here, because it's such an ancient custom, and the

Hong Kong Government has always said it would respect Chinese customs. But many westerners regard it as a form of slavery.'

'I suppose there's no poor law system in Hong Kong to help these families?' said Claire, a small knot of perplexity settling between her eyebrows.

'No, they're dependent on the goodwill of the rich. In theory, by the age of twenty-one, they should be found a husband, and of course some are. But as you say, the system is open to abuse. That's why we've formed a Society to try to have it abolished.'

'Yes,' Claire agreed, 'and meanwhile, children like Little Storm suffer. They have no rights or liberties, and many end up as prostitutes . . . all those poor girls we treated in the clinic with sexually transmitted diseases. Each must have her own story of cruelty, neglect and seduction by their masters —' Claire paused for breath.

'I can see you'll be quite an asset to the Society,' Mrs Pickering commented with a confident smile.

Claire left, totally committed to joining the anti mui-tsai Society.

She hurried home eager to share with John all she had learned. That night baby Luke made his rather hurried arrival into the world.

Claire resumed her daily visits to Little Storm, as soon as she could after Luke's birth. She sometimes took him along to the hospital, pushing him in his pram.

Little Storm's eyes would light up as she saw them enter the ward. Claire was relieved to see the terror and sadness had completely left the child's face. With skill and care from the medical staff, her bruises were healing, but Claire knew she would remain scarred for life by the dreadful burns which had been deliberately inflicted on her.

Claire and John had to give evidence at the court hearing. Little Storm's mistress was sentenced to twelve months' imprisonment. Her excuse that the child had fallen into the fire was not believed by the magistrate. The Secretary of State for Chinese Affairs took over the care of Little Storm and decided she should be placed in a Salvation Army Hostel.

On the day before she was due to leave hospital, Claire and Lily Kwok visited to say their goodbyes. Claire's eyes filled with anguish as the child clung to her. She had come to care deeply for Storm and dreaded the parting.

'Don't send me away —' implored Little Storm, tears scalding her eyes.

'You'll be alright, little one,' Claire soothed her. 'You're going to live with kind people who'll love and protect you.'

They sat with her for over an hour, trying to reassure her. Little Storm's sobs wrung Claire's heart as she left the ward.

Two weeks later, Claire was setting out to give Luke his daily airing. She had not gone far when she had a strange feeling that she was being followed. She stopped and turned, but there was no one in sight, so she walked on, but the feeling persisted. She turned again, and could not believe her eyes. She shook her head, fearing that she must be day-dreaming. A girl, the image of Little Storm, was following her.

'Little Storm,' she called, hesitantly.

The child shot forward, almost knocking Claire off balance. She fell to her knees and clung to Claire's leg.

'Don't send me away . . .' she sobbed.

'But, little one, I must . . . you . . . you can't live with me.' Claire spoke slowly and quietly to the child, but her thoughts were tumbling over themselves as she wondered what on earth she should do. She could not leave her there, so she decided to take her home for the time being. Lily Kwok's eyes nearly popped out of her head when Claire returned home with a jubilant Little Storm clinging to her skirt, her face wreathed in smiles.

'Oh my . . . my,' was all Lily Kwok could think to say. Little Storm was duly returned to the hostel that same evening. John and Claire told themselves over and over that there was no way they could keep her. They had to harden their hearts to her sobs.

She was very quiet on the journey, but held John's hand tightly all the way, not letting it go until they reached the hostel. After explaining to the matron, John said goodbye to the child. She stood looking at him, mute, the silent tears sliding down her cheeks. His own eyes moist, he turned away abruptly and left without a backward glance. Little Storm stood at the window and watched until he turned the corner out of sight. The tears turned into a secret smile, which was not lost on the matron.

'Little minx,' she said, under her breath. 'We're going to have to watch this one, or she'll be off again.'

Two days later, Little Storm was back.

'Why can't we keep her?' John argued, dreading having to return her again to the hostel. Claire was adamant. 'No John, it would not look right.'

Again, John had to return her to the hostel. This time Matron asked, 'Couldn't you make a home for her? We can't keep her tied up all the time, and as far as I can tell, that's the only way we would be able to force her to stay.'

'It's not that simple,' John replied.'We're very fond of her, but my wife has been working closely with the anti mui-tsai Society. She thinks it would look very strange if we took her into our home.'

'Well, I don't know what I'm going to do with her, she's not a bad girl. In fact we all love her, she's such a happy, sweet-natured child. She is quite obviously devoted to you and your wife.'

'How did it go?' Claire greeted him.

John recounted his conversation with the Matron.

'What're we going to do, Claire?' he finished with a tired sigh.

Claire had agonized over the problem for days and shook her head sadly. 'I really don't know what to do for the best, John.'

'Her actions are telling us she wants to live with us . . . ' he mused, 'and we both love her dearly . . . ' his words trailed off.

Claire was thoughtful as she went on feeding the baby. Presently she looked up, and John smiled as he recognized the determined expression in her eyes which he had come to know so well.

'John, I'm going to talk to Mrs Pickering about it, and if necessary all the members of the Society.'

'Good idea, darling,' he agreed, 'Do you want me to come with you?'

'Yes, John, would you?' She reached out and touched his hand, and the baby went on contentedly sucking.

The women were sympathetic when Claire and John discussed the problem of Little Storm with them. They were divided in their opinions, however. So it was, when Little Storm ran away to them for the fourth time, they made up their minds that they would not send her back, but would make all the necessary arrangements to adopt her legally.

The adoption process, with the Department for Chinese Affairs, was quite a lengthy one. 'If the Judge refuses our application to adopt, I dread to think what will happen to her.' Claire had said despairingly at breakfast on the day of the final hearing.

After studying the legal documents thoroughly, the Judge asked a few relatively minor questions of John and Claire. Then he turned his attention to Little Storm. She was so buoyed up with excitement that her words tumbled over themselves as she replied to the Judge's questioning.

Happiness flowed through John's veins when a quick smile spread across the Judge's heavy face, and with a smothered laugh he said, looking straight at John and Claire, 'She has made it perfectly plain – a young lady who knows what she wants, and I suspect will stop at nothing to get it. In my opinion, she's very fortunate to have found you. All that remains for me to say is Good Luck.'

'Thank you, your Honour,' said John solemnly. Claire and Storm just smiled gratefully at the Judge.

Outside on the street, John whistled with relief, while Claire said, 'Phew I'm glad that's over.'

'It's been quite a memorable year. Our family has doubled —'

'Yes, don't I know it,' cut in Claire. 'Now perhaps I can get down to some serious work for the Society.'

It was two days later, the children were in bed. Claire was in the kitchen making a hot drink, and John had slumped wearily into his armchair with the newspaper. Claire returned with their drinks on a tray. John smiled his thanks and continued to read. Suddenly a broad smile crossed his face. 'Claire, oh Claire, have you read this?' he waved the paper in front of her.

'Goodness, John,' she spluttered, almost choking on a mouthful of tea. 'Whatever is it? I . . . I've not had time to read the paper today.'

John handed her the *South China Morning Post*, and perched himself on the arm of her chair. He read aloud, 'The British Government, stunned with the revelation that child slavery continues to exist in a British colony, has put pressure on the Hong Kong Government to abolish the system. The Chinese representatives on the legislative council have debated the matter and the Hong Kong Governor has reached a compromise. It falls short of abolition, but no new mui-tsai are to be engaged, and existing ones are to be registered.'

Claire was triumphant. 'Thank God,' she exclaimed, giving John a hug. 'That's great news.'

'It looks like all your hard work is paying off, but the trouble is,' added John, 'registration is going to be difficult, with Chinese people moving to and from the mainland in their thousands . . . surely it will be impossible to keep a check on families bringing in mui-tsai.'

'Never mind,' replied Claire, 'it's a start. The next step we must campaign for is the establishment of a Society for the Protection of Children.'

'I'm sure that will come too, eventually. If my wife has anything to do with it,' he said, with a wry grin.

'Well, we certainly need some good news to cheer us up,' said Claire, 'the National Strike is having a devastating effect on the colony.'

By mid-July, the strike and boycott had worsened. Workers from most trades had left their jobs. Schoolchildren had to start their summer vacation early for fear of being beaten up by the older students. Many government hospitals had to close for two months because the male nurses and dispensers left their posts. However, the missionary hospitals remained open at full strength.

John was arriving home even later than usual. He was working too hard and the stress was beginning to show. Nightmares still plagued him spasmodically, but were now happening more frequently.

'You look tired, darling. Had a bad day?' Claire greeted him with a kiss one particular evening.

'Yes, and on top of that we've had to call an emergency committee meeting.' John slumped wearily into the chair. 'Because business is so bad, donations have fallen drastically, and the hospital's heavily in debt. Now we've been told that the building is unsafe.'

'Oh John, how dreadful, what's going to happen?'

'We've decided to borrow the money and rebuild, but with a modified scheme.'

'I guess you have to have faith that things will improve,' said Claire.

'Yes, and meanwhile the British Government is determined to maintain a policy of inaction because they're hoping that events in China will eventually sort themselves out.'

'That sounds rather a defeatist attitude to me,' said Claire with tight annoyance.

'Perhaps things will change with the appointment of Cecil Clementi as Governor,' said John. 'I'm told he understands the Chinese well. Let's hope he can promote better relations between the two races.'

On the day the boycott ended Claire had her own good news to tell. She was pregnant again.

The new hospital took two years to complete. It was a four-floor building next to the existing one.

'It's been worth all the noise and disruption,' John told Claire. 'The operating room is well equipped, and it has a nurses' lecture room and some private wards. It also has an out-patient waiting room.'

'So now all the work can be concentrated in one building.'

'Yes, and make for greater efficiency, I think.'

'I hope we'll be able to set up ante-natal care, and also post-natal and infant welfare clinics, too, before long.'

John nodded, 'Yes, darling, they're badly needed here, but much work will have to be done to convince the Chinese that better care will lead to safer deliveries.'

'Well, things are changing.'

'Yes, slowly, but,' John went on sadly, 'the mortality rate of children is far too high, and we still have a long way to go to stamp out malaria, typhoid fever, and pulmonary diseases.'

'Give it time.' Claire smiled. 'It took years, but at least the Plague has been virtually wiped out.'

CHAPTER X

Changing Times

Life in Hong Kong was changing fast. The narrow roads could not cope with the steadily increasing pace of motor traffic. Rickshaw coolies used to taking the centre of the road caused frequent accidents, and were being slowly squeezed from their trade.

The Wall Street Crash was at first just headline news, ignored by many in the Colony. Then the Hong Kong Stock Market took a dive. David Schom's usually beaming face seemed now to wear a habitual frown.

'We're almost out of funds. I hope this depression doesn't go on too long,' he complained to John and Dr Grayson.

'It seems to be worldwide,' interjected John. 'Perhaps the countries of the League of Nations will be able to get together to do something jointly, to stimulate their economies all at the same time.'

'Well, I don't know about that. I know Germany has been hit very badly. They've had very high inflation, and now six million unemployed. Doesn't look good, not good at all,' mumbled Dr Grayson.

'What we need are politicians with vision to sort out these difficulties. The trouble is a lot of good people of my generation died in the war, so the politicians of the previous generation, like Stanley Baldwin, are getting a second innings, with their old-fashioned ideas and outdated concepts.' John was just warming to his subject when he was suddenly called to attend a very sick patient who had been admitted the previous evening. 'Have you time to come and take a look at him, Dr Grayson?' he enquired. 'I'm very concerned. I fear he left it too late, and we're going to lose him. I'd be glad of your advice.'

'Yes of course. Lead the way.'

John went ahead, acknowledging with a smile greetings from many of his patients as he passed through the ward. He stopped beside a bed at the far end, then stood back for his colleague to do an examination. The patient, a man of indefinite age, had been brought in by a distant relative. He was deathly pale and emaciated, in an extreme state of starvation, being unable to keep any food down.

After a thorough examination Dr Grayson looked up, his face grave. 'Obstruction in the alimentary canal,' he grunted.

'Just as I thought. What are his chances?' John asked, with concern.

'I'm afraid he's had it,' Grayson replied grimly. 'Even if we did go ahead with surgery, he'd be too weak to make it. If only he'd been diagnosed earlier we could have saved him.'

John nodded gloomily, every line of his face registering dejection. 'It's the same old story. I just don't know how we can prevent the influence of these herbalists. True, they have a few good remedies, but their claim that their herbs can heal typhoid, malaria, syphilis, leprosy, and even cancer, is wildly exaggerated. There's just no scientific evidence that they have the slightest effect on these major illnesses.' A sigh of indignation escaped him.

They returned to the office, their white coats flapping as they walked. Grayson scratched his head. 'Just give it time, we'll get there in the end. When I first came out to Hong Kong, malaria was very prevalent; now it's been totally eliminated from the urban areas.'

'Yes, due in the main to the Government setting up the malaria bureau,' replied John.

'That's right. They had to use heavy tactics to ensure that adequate drainage works were undertaken, so that mosquitoes couldn't breed in accumulated still water, but it's paid off.'

'Yes, but not in the countryside. How do we reach these people?' asked John. 'Health standards there are abysmal. The farmers just manage to scrape a living, but it's barely at subsistence level.'

Dr Grayson let out a modulated snort, but did not reply.

'I think what we need are more Chinese trained doctors and nurses, to help break down the barriers.'

David Schom was flicking through a file and looked up as the two doctors entered.

'We were just discussing the problem of how to overcome the Chinese suspicion of Western medicine,' John explained to him.

David Schom smiled knowingly. 'The Chinese believe that because they've had knowledge of medicine for over three thousand years, tradition makes it hallowed.

'Chinese pharmacologists, two thousand years ago had many herbal drugs, such as iodine for goitre, and mylitta lapidescens for tapeworm, which are still very effectively used today —'

'Hippocrates is just as ancient as any Chinese pharmacologist,' interrupted Grayson. 'Western medicine was based on herbalism too. Where Western medicine is more effective is in the application of scientific method to its understanding of the human body. By careful dissection, and understanding of the anatomy, physiology and biochemistry, we have arrived at far better medicines and methods of preventing disease through inoculations than herbalism ever could.' John listened intently, for he loved a good debate. He found it mentally stimulating. Grayson had a brilliant mind, but could seldom be lured into discussion. John winked at David Schom, who continued enthusiastically:

'Chinese doctors also stress the prevention of disease, by regular habits, proper diet and suitable combination of work and leisure to maintain a calm mind. Two thousand years ago, this aspect had not occurred to practitioners of Western medicine.'

'No, that's very true.' Then Doctor Grayson added, with unusual dry humour, 'Even in the Bible, in New Testament times, we find illness being thought of as a punishment for sin.'

'Yes, China was very advanced in many ways, not just in medicine,' John conceded. 'But sadly, it went into a sort of time warp.'

'I suppose the time warp, as you call it, was caused because of an exaggerated respect for tradition, and filial piety towards parents and elders.' David Schom's voice was wistful, as he added, 'There was no innovation for generations, as a result.'

'At the moment, they still won't allow autopsies to determine the cause of death, and therefore ways of avoiding it,' Doctor Grayson pointed out, with an edge to his voice.

'No, Chinese regard it as sacrilegious to investigate the human body after death,' admitted David Schom.

'We've got to overcome this superstition somehow, and persuade the average illiterate Chinese of the importance of science,' said John. 'Perhaps it all goes back to what we were saying earlier about the need to train more Chinese doctors and nurses.'

'Yes, and better general education —' The telephone rang, drowning out David Schom's voice.

John was needed on the ward. It looked like being another difficult day.

Arriving home late again, he found that Claire was faced with a different but no less important problem. Luke had been attending the local day school. It was dominated mainly by children from Army and Civil Service families, who were preparing for the Common Entrance Examination. All through his primary school years, Luke had shone academically, but he had no real interest in sport. His skills did not match his competitiveness.

'Luke seems to be rather unpopular at school.' There was bewilderment as well as concern in Claire's voice. 'He seems to be getting into a lot of fights. I wish you'd have a talk with him. He came home in tears again today.' She paused and gave John a stricken look. 'As far as I can make out, his teacher asked him to captain the soccer team, and they lost five-nil. Luke seems to think they all blamed him for losing.'

'Oh, poor Luke, he's a bit sensitive about things. I'll go and have a chat with him,' John replied.

'I hated sport at school,' said Claire flatly. 'I expect he takes after me. It's a pity you haven't been around more to encourage him.'

'I know, Claire, don't rub it in, I feel guilty enough as it is. I just hope I can spend more time with you and the children when we go home on furlough.'

'I can't wait.' Claire's eyes lit up. 'I'm so looking forward to seeing all the folks back home.'

'Won't be long now, only another six weeks before we sail.' John uncurled himself from his chair, and went off in the direction of Luke's bedroom. Luke was deep in a book.

John pulled up a chair, straddled it, and smiled at his son. He came straight to the point. 'Hello, Luke, Mummy has been telling me you're having a bit of trouble at school.'

Luke nodded his head.

'Yes, it's not fair, Dad, all the boys blamed me for losing the match.'

'Well, I agree that's unfair – it should be a team effort, where everyone should be working together.'

'I hate soccer anyway,' Luke scowled.

'You can't be good at everything, you know. You're good at cricket, and swimming, and if you like I can teach you how to play squash when we get back to England. That's a game of individual skill, where you won't have the rest of the team judging you. The real purpose of sport isn't just to win, you know, Luke, but to help you develop a healthy body. Why don't you practice with some of your friends in the park?'

'Don't want to – it's bad enough having to play at school without doing it in my own time.'

'Surely it's better for him to concentrate on the things he's good at, like art and music,' Claire intervened, as she poked her head around the door.

'Er, yes, from the point of view of Luke's talents, but at this stage of his school life he needs to have well-rounded interests. He can specialize more when he gets to senior school.'

'I think the problem is, Luke doesn't have much ball sense,' said Claire.

'That would come with practice, but it's not the end of the world, old chap,' declared John, noticing the mutinous glance Luke shot towards his mother. 'When we go to England we'd better look for a school that doesn't accentuate sport, but concentrates more on the arts, and music.'

'I hate school . . . they, they call me a swot,' Luke blurted out, scrubbing at his eyes.

John ruffled his son's already tousled hair. 'Yes, I know, son. School can be pretty grim at times . . . ragging and bullying can be hard to take.'

The boy looked up miserably at his father. 'I want to run away sometimes,' he admitted, then gazed down at his book again.

John studied his son for a long moment 'As bad as that.'

Luke just nodded, still keeping his eyes down.

'There's nothing wrong with being academic you know, Luke. Your last report was excellent, far better than any I ever got.'

'Was it really, Dad?' he gaped at his father.

'Yes, I often had remarks like, "Could have done better in this subject if he had tried harder". You see, Luke, I spent too much time playing rugby, and as a result my academic work suffered. I wanted desperately to go to Oxford, but failed. You stand a much better chance if that's what you want.'

'Really, Dad?'

'Yes really, Luke. Now, how about putting that book down, and getting some sleep.'

'Thanks, Dad —' his voice trailed away, but he managed a wavering smile. Claire bent to kiss him, and they both left the room. They peered in at Storm and June, who were both sound asleep. Claire tidied June's garments which were strewn around the room. She tutted, 'Really, she's the limit. Have you ever met anyone as untidy as this young madam.'

John's chuckle was fond and indulgent as he replied, 'Yes my sister Amy, she's the spitting image of her.' He bent, and planted a resounding kiss on his daughter's flushed cheeks. 'She's growing into a real beauty,' he murmured, swelling with pride.

'You spoil her, you know, John.'

'No I don't,' he retorted quickly, giving Claire a playful smack.

'Oh you,' she laughed, as she shut the door quietly behind her, and followed John into the sitting room.

June, at the age of eight, still attended primary school. She seemed to sail through life, quite undaunted by anyone or anything. To Claire's intense relief she had grown out of temper tantrums, but still had a will of iron, and a natural sense of curiosity. Claire, at times, found it difficult to find answers to her probing questions.

Storm, now seventeen, was an apprentice to Jackie Wong, the prosperous owner of a flourishing fashion house in Queen's Road

Central. She loved her work, and it was clear from her reports that she was quite gifted in needlecraft and design. It had been difficult for John and Claire to obtain Jackie Wong's permission to allow Storm to travel with them to Britain, but with perseverance they had overcome her reluctance.

For John and Claire, it had been a long ten-year haul. Both, in their own ways, had missed their families, and were looking forward to the reunion.

'It won't be all holiday,' John warned his disappointed children. 'Mummy and I will have to travel around to various churches in England and Canada to make people who support us financially, and prayerfully, more aware of the sort of work we do in Hong Kong.'

'Pity we have to go to school,' grumbled Luke.

John looked down the table at his son. 'It won't be so bad. Think on it as a new beginning.'

Claire laid a hand on Luke's arm. 'Don't look so glum,' she said. 'You'll have a lovely time, getting to know your grandparents, your aunts and uncles, and all your cousins.'

CHAPTER XI

War Clouds

'Good to have you back.' Dr Grayson's smile was warm and welcoming, but John was shocked at his pallor and listlessness. 'Yes, I'm afraid I've been unwell for some weeks,' he admitted when John enquired about his health. 'Now you've returned I can have a break. I'll go to Scotland – I'll soon feel better there. Firstly, though, I must tell you of all that's been happening in your absence.'

John pulled up a chair and for almost an hour they talked. Then finally Dr Grayson said, 'Unfortunately, we're still in the red. The opening of the new hospital will have to be postponed.'

'I'm sorry to hear that – any idea when we can start?'

The doctor shook his head, and the tired lines stood out more prominently. 'No, not really. Money is slow in coming in, but we're going ahead in faith.'

It was not until five years later in 1938 that the new hospital was officially opened.

No sooner had the hospital opened its doors than the flood of refugees from China, fleeing from the Japanese armies, poured across the frontier. Many were in very poor health. John and his staff were kept exceedingly busy. To John it was a godsend as he was missing his children badly. Luke, having passed his Common Entrance Examination, had sailed off to school in Tonbridge two years previously. June had followed him a year later.

Claire was beginning to get very anxious about John. His working day was getting longer. All he wanted to do when he returned home at night was to sleep.

'The number of patients has almost doubled.' he said to Claire.

'Can't you take on more staff?' she asked anxiously.

'It's funny you should say that; in fact we have a new nursing sister arriving from England next month.'

'Oh good, perhaps you'll get home a bit earlier then.' There was a harsh note in Claire's voice. Then immediately repentant she added,

'Oh, we had a letter from June today. She's arrived safely, and enjoyed her first week . . . ' Claire produced the letter, and sat in the armchair whilst he read it.

'Sounds as though they're having the time of their lives,' John smiled up at Claire.

'Well, you know your daughter, nothing seems to bother that one.'

'I'm pleased they've settled alright, but I miss them so much . . .'

'I know, the house is so quiet without them . . . and tidy . . .' Claire agreed laughingly. She thought of them every day, and wondered what they were doing. 'I miss them too,' she acknowledged. 'It's left a huge gap in my life now they've gone.'

'James and Amy will take good care of them, I'm sure,' John murmured reassuringly.

When the Americans cut off oil supplies to the Japanese to prevent their continued war against China, the people of Hong Kong expected trouble. But life went on much the same as usual.

'We need to be prepared,' John told Claire. 'Though I don't believe for one minute there'll be war with Japan. They've too much to lose, whilst if it remains peaceful, they'll make huge inroads into British trade in the Far East, just as they did in the First World War.'

'I hope you're right,' replied Claire. 'It's bad enough having the children in Britain at the moment with the worry of the Blitz, without having a war on this side of the world as well.'

'I wonder if we did the right thing in sending them to England. Europe is in such turmoil.'

Claire noticed the anxiety in his voice. Her face reflected her understanding 'Yes, perhaps after all, they would have been better off with my parents in Canada.'

'If we had acted before war was declared I would have agreed, but now there are U-boats in the North Atlantic I think it would be very dangerous to move them.'

Claire nodded. 'I suppose it's easy to be wise in retrospect,' she said listlessly. 'It's so hard sometimes, though, to know what is the right action to take.'

John smiled sympathetically. 'If the Japs take on Britain and America, our greater industrial strength will see them off. They must know that. Plans have been made, should Japan dare to attack us. Defences have been set up on the "Gin Drinkers' Line", starting from Gin Drinkers' Bay.'

'Where's that?' asked Claire.

'In Tsuen Wan, across the Jubilee Reservoir, along the line of Kowloon hills to the sea at Shatin, and then south-east to Port Shelter,' replied John.

'I heard today that two battalions of the Indian Army have arrived to help defend the Colony; also two Canadian battalions. We'll be alright now,' said Claire, patriotically. 'Those Canadians will be tough, and battle hardened, and they'll put up a good defence in the event of trouble.'

'I hope you're right,' said John, somewhat concerned.

For some time there hung over Hong Kong the uncertainty of war, but they continued to pray for peace.

On Sunday, 7 December 1941, John, Claire and Storm were in their usual seats in Union Church. That morning they listened intently as the Pastor, his face grave, announced that Japanese troops were massing north of Fanling on the Chinese border. An audible gasp resounded around the church. John met Claire's troubled eyes over Storm's head. All the servicemen were ordered to battle stations by five o'clock that evening.

The next morning John was driving his small, newly acquired Austin to the hospital, when he heard the air-raid sirens going. He put his foot firmly down on the accelerator and finished the journey in record time. He plunged out of the door and pounded up the steps at top speed. Entering the building, he spotted Grayson just a few steps ahead of him.

'Dr Grayson,' he shouted, but his voice was drowned out by the crumping sound of bombs. Grayson turned abruptly and they both dashed to the window.

'Sounds like Kai Tak airport – just look at that smoke.'

Grayson's voice quivered and his face seemed to John to have turned three shades whiter. John's heart was banging as he hung between disbelief and fear.

They rushed to the door. Crowds of walking patients, nurses and orderlies were gathering, puzzled at the sound of the siren and the planes wheeling overhead. Anti-aircraft guns were booming in the distance.

Contingency plans in the hospital, which had been set up months previously, were rapidly put into action.

'There's no time to lose,' said Grayson. 'We'll have to be ruthless and clear as many beds as we can to receive casualties.'

'How about using the next door church as a ward as well?' suggested John.

David Schom nodded. 'I'll contact the Pastor right away, to see if he is agreeable. I'll also contact the head of Ying Wa Girls' School – their classrooms and hall would make excellent nurses' quarters.'

'Good idea, we'll need all the staff you can contact to report for duty, and as many volunteers as you can muster. I'd start with the medical students – nothing like throwing them in at the deep end.'

'Right,' agreed David Schom, 'I'll see to it. I think we're going to be in for a busy time over the next few weeks.'

'I'll give my wife a ring,' said John. 'She'll come in to help out, I know.'

Before he could get to his feet the phone clanged. Grayson, sitting nearest to the phone, lifted the receiver. 'Grayson speaking,' he said, gruffly. Then his stern face lit up, 'Oh good, good. Yes, he was just about to phone you. I'll hand you over.' Turning to John, he wiped the perspiration from his forehead, and held out the phone. 'Your wife . . . beat you to it,' he said with a smile of admiration.

John sprang to his feet, 'Hello, Claire, your timing was perfect. You alright, dear?' he asked worriedly.

'Yes, I'm fine.' Claire's voice was calm at the other end of the line, but John was spared from seeing the anxiety in her face. 'I phoned to let you know I'm coming down to the hospital.'

'Oh good,' John exclaimed, 'we'll need all the help we can get. The number of beds is being increased from one hundred to one hundred and seventy, so we're going to be stretched to the limit. I think you'd better pack a few things for us both. We'll have to be prepared to stay several days, until the situation clears. We're hoping to set up temporary quarters in the girls' school.'

'Yes, right John,' Claire's voice faltered. 'The news is pretty grim.'

'I'm afraid so, Claire, take care, see you soon.'

The first casualties of the bombing began to arrive at the same time as Claire appeared, laden with bedding and clothes. Disposing of them in the nurses' quarters, she went in search of John. She found him with David Schom, organizing the wards.

'Great to have your help, Claire,' John managed a wry smile. 'We are cramming in as many beds as possible, leaving just enough space for the nurses to work, and no more. Can you take over, dear?'

'Yes, of course,' Claire replied, with a swift, reassuring look as she recognized the concern in John's eyes. She immediately pitched in, glad to have something to occupy her mind.

John returned to the receiving room and joined Dr Grayson in the difficult task of sorting out the patients according to urgency. Those requiring immediate surgery were moved to the operating theatre, those in serious condition were given saline solutions and dextrose injections, until they were strong enough to undergo surgery and the operating theatre was free to take them.

The main blood groups were soon completely exhausted. Everyone who could be persuaded to give blood to help with transfusions did so. The less urgent cases were given morphine to alleviate pain, had their wounds dressed, and were sent home with instructions to report daily for redressing.

'The Japs must be much better soldiers than we've been led to believe,' John remarked to Claire when, in a brief lull, they managed to snatch a few moments together. 'They have complete air superiority, and with all the bombing and artillery they're going to blast Hong Kong off the map. I can remember the effects of heavy artillery when I was in France during the First War. There's not going to be much left of Hong Kong Island by the time they've finished.'

'I just hope the hospital will escape the bombardment,' replied a tight-lipped Claire. 'With all the wounded here, it would be dreadful if we were to suffer a direct hit.'

John looked into her pale face and his heart went out to her – he knew what she was going through. The last war was to have been the one to end all wars, and here they were, once again in their lifetime, facing another.

'At least we're not in the direct line of fire,' he observed.

'They'll try to get through the Gin Drinkers' Line first, and hopefully that'll last about six months. Time enough for us to be relieved by the Royal Navy. If the Japs reach the hospital in their invasion we'll have to hide you and the nurses somewhere.' They exchanged worried looks.

Claire shivered involuntarily, but with a toss of the head, she replied, 'We'll think about that when we come to it,' then added, 'It's a good job the Government ordered all the women and young children who weren't working to leave Hong Kong, and go to Canada or Australia.'

'Yes, it is, there were a lot of complaints at the time, but with hindsight it was obviously a wise decision.' Then swiftly, he added, 'Claire, as much as I love having you with me, I wish you were safely away from all this.'

Claire stared up into John's face, and murmured softly, 'I love you, John, and whatever comes we will face it together. Besides,' she went on defiantly, 'I'm needed here.'

Four days later, the Army was evacuated from the mainland. The Gin Drinkers' Line, which was expected to hold up the enemy for six months, had fallen in one night. The shelling and bombing continued day after day and the number of casualties in the hospital, mainly from shrapnel wounds, increased.

Everyone in the hospital worked flat out, with a remarkable degree of calm. Morale was high, but tiredness and exhaustion were beginning to have an effect. Orders were issued that all staff should have six hours' sleep in every twenty-four hours.

Coping with hospital emergencies occupied John's mind, but during the relative quiet of the night he found that fear and doubts kept him awake. He remembered the stories he had heard of the Japanese atrocities and rapes in Nanking and other Chinese cities they had invaded. He feared for Claire, and Storm, and all the nurses on the wards.

One night he awoke from a restless sleep with a start, his clothes drenched with perspiration, his mind racing. He dressed hurriedly and reported for duty, where he was to relieve Dr Grayson.

'Busy night?' John asked, by way of greeting. Then, seeing the strain on Grayson's face he queried, 'What is it, what's wrong?'

'Things are getting pretty drastic.'

'Any news getting through . . . ?'

'Not much, and what we do hear smacks of propaganda. Seems that the Japs have gained control of the reservoir area in the New Territories. They've turned off the main source of water supply. The water situation is now desperate, and electricity has also been cut off. It's been quite a night . . .'

John gaped at him in astonishment. 'So that means we can't X-ray either, and the lift will be inoperable.'

' 'Fraid so, still I guess it could be worse – at least our Chinese helpers have stayed at their posts, most of the other hospitals report that their domestic staff, orderlies and others have failed to turn up for work, due to fear of the shelling.'

'Yes . . . but you look all in . . . I'll take over. Go and get some rest.'

John worked non-stop with the assistance of the university students. They had to use oil-lamps to operate by, and firewood and coal to boil the water for sterilizing their instruments, which slowed their work down. Then to add to their troubles the supply of rubber gloves ran out.

The shelling by day was constant, then on the eve of the 18th, the Japanese invaded the island around the eastern end, at San Kai Wan and at North Point, crossing over from Kowloon in rubber boats, sampans, and anything else they could commandeer.

By the morning, they had made a deep penetration into the Island, almost cutting it in two, and isolating the defences. There followed a week of intense fighting, and Hong Kong Island began to fall, inch by inch – yet the troops were urged to hold fast and fight on. By Christmas Eve, cases of malaria and cholera were being admitted to the hospital.

Conditions on the Island were deteriorating. Stagnant pools of water, dirty tin cans and cesspools where mosquitoes could breed, were everywhere. The night soil coolies were unable to work because of the bombardment. Rubbish and filth accumulated all over the place, which bred great numbers of flies. The swarms fed on the decaying bodies on the hillsides and brought with them typhoid, dysentery and diarrhoea.

Christmas Day 1941 dawned – it was a beautiful day, warm and sunny. With forced cheerfulness, John and Claire wished each other a Happy Christmas. As they gathered with staff and patients for the early morning Service, they could hear the guns booming outside. There was to be no peace on earth for them, even on Christmas Day, and the Japanese certainly had no goodwill to dispense. Only a short distance away they were involved in an orgy of slaughter, rape and looting. As the morning drew on, all was strangely quiet.

The hospital had been saving two turkeys for Christmas lunch. John, Claire and Storm gathered in the rather uncomfortable nurses' quarters for some Christmas cheer. Dr Grayson, performing the ceremonial carving, called for three cheers for the cooks who had performed something of a miracle in producing a wonderful meal under such difficult circumstances.

News did not reach the hospital until Boxing Day that the battle for Hong Kong had been lost. The Governor had signed an unconditional surrender, the white flag was flying over Government House. They were now a Japanese colony.

For three days after the fall of Hong Kong the Japanese held victory celebrations. There was a triumphal march from one end of Hong Kong to the other, with trumpets blaring and with great shouts of 'Banzai' echoing down the empty streets.

Inebriated Japanese soldiers began to loot shops and houses at gunpoint, and looted, murdered and raped at will.

A steady stream of rape victims began to report to the hospital, ranging in age from their early teens to their sixties. Women came in with broken teeth and noses, from being hit with rifle butts, bodies showing bayonet prods and scars.

'We must act quickly to protect our nurses,' John told Dr Grayson and David Schom.

'Oh, surely the nurses will be safe,' a weary, dispirited Grayson replied.

'They certainly will not,' John retorted heatedly. 'Look what happened in Nanking.'

'Well then, any suggestions?'

'Yes, we must send all the nurses home, and replace them with elderly amahs —'

'Really, and where do you propose getting these elderly amahs from?'

'Well, I've thought about that and I'm sure our Lily Kwok will be able to organize it . . . she's been with us for years, and is devoted —'

'I think you're overreacting, Dr Aldcott —'

'No, he's right, Dr Grayson. They're doing the most atrocious things under the influence of drink. Our nurses are in grave danger —' said David Schom, sharply.

'Oh, very well, do what you think is right, but how you imagine we're gonna manage without them is beyond me . . .' Still muttering, Grayson stepped towards the door, fumbled with the handle and stomped out, slamming the door behind him.

John stared at the closed door in stunned silence, then flashed a quick glance of enquiry at David Schom who was wiping his forehead with his handkerchief. He shrugged his shoulders in a gesture of uncomprehending helplessness.

'He's tired out,' John said dully, as if to himself.

David Schom nodded, then promised gravely, 'I'll see what I can do.'

'Thank you, I'll contact Lily Kwok. As soon as we can get help, I'll send all the young nurses home. We're dealing with a ruthless mob.'

While David Schom contacted the churches, the indomitable Lily Kwok lost no time in rounding up several of her friends and acquaintances. Barely had they been set to work, when the calm of the hospital was shattered by the sounds of heavy boots thundering through the corridors.

How ludicrous they look, was John's first impression, as he stepped out of the office with Dr Grayson at his side, to confront the intruders. Most of them were short and squat. They carried bayonets on their rifles and clearly knew how to use them. With the schooled placidity of the professional doctor, John stepped forward.

'Good evening, this is Bonham Road Hospital. What can I do for you?' He was surprised at the calmness of his voice, whilst fear, cold, solid and strong, caught at his breath.

'Where are the nurses?' demanded one of the Japanese soldiers in broken English.

John, fighting down the panic he felt, replied, 'We've sent them home.'

Pushing John roughly aside, they marched on, closely followed by the Indian nightwatchman, who stuck to them like glue. Having thoroughly frightened the patients, they left as hurriedly as they had arrived. A little later, Dr Jones, the Hong Kong medical superintendent, arrived with a Japanese officer and an interpreter. The officer had closely cropped hair and his uniform was covered in decorations. He wore white gloves, highly polished black boots and carried an unwieldy Samurai sword at his side.

'We need to use this hospital for Japanese wounded,' the interpreter repeated after the officer.

'You should give him all the help you can,' said Dr Jones.

John stood erect, his breath locked in his throat, as Dr Grayson almost snarled his reply.

'Well, of course we'll help anyone who is sick, that is our duty. We'll make as much space as we can, but the efficient functioning of the hospital depends on the nurses returning safely, and not being molested. You must give me the assurance that my staff will be protected.'

'I will put up a proclamation on the entrance to the hospital,' said the officer, via the interpreter. 'It will say that the hospital is now under the protection of the Japanese Imperial Army. This will keep unauthorized people out.'

With a click of his heels, the officer and interpreter departed. The poster was duly erected. Whenever Japanese soldiers came prowling at night, the gatekeeper had only to flash his torch on the poster and the soldiers would leave without causing any trouble.

The nurses were promptly reinstated and the hospital returned to a semblance of normality. Soon the wounded Japanese soldiers started to arrive. The Western doctors and nurses continued their work in caring for the Chinese patients, but a Japanese doctor was sent to supervise the treatment of the Japanese soldiers. Chinese doctors and nurses were forced to work under him.

With no news coming in, they felt very isolated from the rest of the world. Storm was still at the hospital. John and Claire, determined to ensure her safety, enrolled her as an auxiliary nurse. She slept in the nurses' quarters. Storm hated nursing, but she was too terrified to go home alone. She was thankful that she could remain close to the two people she loved most in the world, and tried her hardest to learn and to conform to the hospital discipline.

The atmosphere was strained and tempers short, as each day they wondered what would happen next. Then on 14 January, a proclamation was issued by the Japanese that all enemy nationals, which included Dutch, Belgian, Norwegian, British and American, should report to the Murray Parade barracks in Central. The only other instruction given was that people should carry with them such essentials as would be needed for overnight use.

Storm clung to John and Claire. 'What'll happen to you?' she cried.

'Darling, I don't know,' said Claire, striving to stay calm. 'But promise me you'll be careful. Don't do anything without discussing it with Lily Kwok. Remember you can trust her implicitly; if you are frightened or in trouble go to her. Promise me, Storm!'

'Yes, yes of course, I promise.' Tears were scalding her eyes, and she was shaking uncontrollably, as she kissed each of them in turn. John and Claire gathered together as much medical equipment as they could, packed a bag, and provided themselves with a bedroll each. They squeezed themselves and all their belongings into a car provided by Colonel Enguchi, and drove off.

They were bundled out at Murray barracks, where hundreds of other British and Americans had already collected. All around were Chinese coolies swarming down the street staggering under loads of loot and firewood. At Murray barracks Japanese guards, with bayonets fixed, were strutting up and down. The barracks was full of shell and bomb holes. Several burned-out cars and Bren-gun carriers were strewn around the parade ground, as well as thousands of drums of petrol which still had not been destroyed.

There was total confusion. Japanese officers and interpreters were milling about trying to get some semblance of order and to register the prisoners. Finally, all effort at registration was abandoned.

They were lined up six abreast, a rough count was made, and they were forced to march down Des Voeux Road, past the Hong Kong and Shanghai Bank building, which John noticed was pitted and scarred where heavy shells had hit and bounced off.

Thousands of Chinese lined the curb to watch the woeful procession. It was all part of the Japanese desire to humiliate the allies and to show themselves as conquerors, John thought with disgust. As they struggled through Central towards Wanchai, John noticed Japanese flags flying from all the buildings. After about an hour of marching, they were halted outside a three-storied hotel with a veranda and flat roof. John grabbed Claire's hand so as not to be separated from her. They were herded into a narrow dark hallway, and made to climb the stairway to the upper floor.

Claire stumbled and winced as she felt the butt-end of a rifle being dug into her. They were pushed roughly into rooms about six feet by four feet, four persons to a room. It was very dark, hardly any light penetrated beyond the small veranda. There were no chairs in the room, only a bed.

Claire was very close to tears as she surveyed their accommodation. 'Ugh, it's filthy dirty . . .' she shuddered, then let out a piercing scream as a rat scuttled across the room. Trembling, she clung to John, who held her close. 'It's alright, darling, it's gone now.'

Rather shamefaced, Claire tried to smile at the other couple who had been pushed into the small cubicle with them. They were in their late sixties, John surmised. The woman was about five foot in height, her hair was turning grey and her face was quite lined. Her husband stooped a little; John reckoned he was over six foot.

John was the first to recover his composure. 'It looks as if we're to be room-mates, we'd better introduce ourselves. I'm John Aldcott, and this is my wife, Claire . . .'

'What a strange way to meet. I'm Gordon Barnes, and this is my wife, Alice.' Gordon Barnes's handshake was firm.

'One bed between four. No offence meant, but I hope it won't be for long . . .' he went on.

Alice Barnes smiled, a smile which softened her rather severe face. 'I guess we'll have to take it in turns to sleep, and keep a watch out for the rats and cockroaches.'

Claire shuddered again, 'Oh I can't bear the horrid things, but surely they won't leave us here for long.'

There was nothing to do, it was too dark to read, even if they had had the inclination. For the next hour they chatted politely. No food was brought to them, but Claire had packed a few sandwiches which she shared amongst them. Around seven in the evening, under the escort of an Indian guard, they were allowed out to a restaurant. Their meal consisted of just a bowl of fried rice. They were given only twenty minutes to eat, and were then herded back to the hotel.

'It's a former brothel,' Gordon Barnes informed John.

'Really? I never thought I'd frequent such a place,' John replied with a grin.

'Well, not with your wife,' Gordon grinned back.

Alice Barnes, they soon discovered, unlike her husband, lacked any sense of humour. She shot a disgusted glance at Gordon, who turned his back on her and winked at Claire. John and Claire wondered how these two completely opposite characters could have remained together for forty years. Alice ruled, and her indulgent husband tried to grant her every wish. She moaned constantly.

'She has every reason to moan,' Claire confided to John, 'but if only she realized what a depressing effect she has on us all, she might stop.'

'I doubt it – she's a born pessimist,' replied John wearily. The strain of their situation was getting him down. They had to draw water from a well, and lug it up the stairs, as the lift did not work.

'Not for long,' they tried to console themselves, still believing in an Allied victory.

'Even though the Japs beat us, we'll win in the end,' Gordon scoffed. 'The Chinese armies will march south and drive the Japanese out.'

'The Japs are going to be a lot tougher enemy than we first thought,' John predicted. 'They're highly trained and disciplined. They've a good deal of high technology, as we saw from the operations of their air force. Britain has the Indian Army behind it, as well as the Canadians, and all the other Commonwealth countries. I fear it'll take the British and Americans quite a while to defeat them, but I'm certain our industrial strength will triumph in the end.'

'I'm sure you're right,' Claire tried to sound cheerful. 'This is probably the worst situation I've ever been in, but we won the First War, and I'm darn sure we'll win this one too. In the meantime we have to sit tight, and make the best of things.'

Alice just snorted.

The prisoners decided to have a chairman and floor representatives. Every day they held a meeting, at eleven o'clock, with the Chinese liaison officer of the house.

As John could speak Cantonese, he was elected chairman. The main topics of discussion were complaints about food, insufficient light and heat, the inability to get bedding, lack of milk for the children, lack of medicines, and poor sanitation.

'These meetings are useless,' John confided in Claire, and Gordon and Alice. 'It's clear that we're going to be powerless to improve our situation. The Japs are insistent that we pay fifty cents a day for our "supplementary rations". We've complained that we're only getting two meals a day, of rice and stale fish or buffalo, so it's hard to see how we're being supplemented.'

Claire was aghast. 'How on earth are we going to be able to pay? Our bank accounts have been frozen since the beginning of the war, and we don't have a lot of cash left.'

'Well, we had quite a heated discussion about it, and the committee have recommended payment so as not to anger the Japs and cause a reduction of food. Our diet is badly lacking vitamin C as it is, and if we have to stay here long, there'll be a lot of illness like scurvy, and beri-beri. So we'll be asking for a donation from each internee towards purchasing fresh vegetables.'

Day after day, John came back with news of fresh demands from the Japanese.

'What do they want today?' Claire would greet him with on his return from the committee meeting.

She nearly exploded when he replied, 'They now want us to pay for the wood to boil the drinking water and cook the food.'

'What —' three horrified voices exclaimed.

'We've decided to draw the line, and have refused to pay.'

'Oh, good for you, we must stand up to the blighters,' growled Gordon.

'Pah!' sneered Alice, 'we'll be sorry, you mark my words.'

Alice's predictable 'I told you so' grated on John and Claire when, two days later, John reported that the Japs had immediately withdrawn the woodpile.

The situation became so serious that the committee had to rapidly change its mind. The hotel manager then wanted his cut to pay amahs and houseboys. It became clear that the manager was pocketing all the internees' payments.

The committee organized relays for drawing buckets of water from the well for sanitation purposes. It was heavy going, as it had to be carried up to the roof tank. People with medical knowledge were given the job of supervising the boiling of the drinking water, and also of carrying out the Japanese order that everyone must be inoculated against cholera and typhoid. Claire and John helped set up a dispensary in the open air on the veranda. A wood chatty was used to boil water to sterilize the needles.

'There's not going to be enough needles to go round,' John told the committee. 'If we have to use blunt needles, it'll be very painful.'

Before they could give the second shot of typhoid inoculations the serum had run out, and they were told there was no more available. There was some relief, as most people naturally disliked the blunt needles.

The committee protested vigorously about lack of fresh air and exercise. Eventually, they were given permission to open the roof of the hotel. Half of it was shut off to bar the prisoners from looking at the harbour, and barbed wire was erected to prevent them reaching the adjacent roofs.

John and Claire were glad to be kept busy, and when time permitted, they would go up on the roof and watch the world going by beneath. People passed along in an endless stream day and night, as the Japanese evicted Chinese families from their homes and sent them back to their villages on the mainland. Old, young and sick were all wearily struggling with what they could carry.

Because there was no electricity, night time became a looters' paradise. From their room in the hotel, John and Claire could hear shots being fired at the looters, and gongs being beaten to summon the Japanese gendarmes whenever there was trouble. Sleep for them became difficult as Alice and Gordon both snored so loudly.

For sixteen days they existed in the verminous hovel. While Alice complained John and Claire tried to think of all the happy, exciting times they had enjoyed in order to keep up their morale.

A ripple of excitement spread through the building when they heard the news of a pending move. 'We're going to be moved to Stanley,' John told his eager listeners.

His news was greeted with smiles and cheers. Alice did her usual snort. 'If it's anything like this, it won't be much. I bet we'll be crammed in like we are here.'

John thought of the times he had taken Storm, Luke, and June to the beach at Stanley. Luke had learned to swim there. It was situated on the south of the Island. In his mind's eye, he could picture the tranquillity of the bay. It had lovely sandy coves, where the peninsula jutted into the sea. The nearby hills formed a natural background. For the first time in sixteen days, he felt his heart lift.

The next day, they were told that half the group in the hotel were to be moved by bus to Stanley. All their baggage was to be taken by trucks. John volunteered, along with three other men, to go with the baggage to avoid looting.

'If you get there early, you may have a choice of accommodation. Choose the smallest room, just big enough for the two of us, that way we will get more privacy,' Claire whispered to John as she kissed him goodbye.

Claire was to follow the next day, or so she thought. All day they waited, but nothing happened and Claire's spirits dropped as rapidly as they had risen. Alice was becoming unbearable – Claire bit her lip, fighting the temptation to tell her to shut up. Then at last news came through that the bus had broken down.

'Now what're we going to do? We'll die in this hole if they don't soon get us out,' wailed Alice.

'I'll see if I can find out what's happening,' volunteered Claire, thankful to escape Alice's company for a while. The toilet queue was always the best source of information. She reported back twenty minutes later. Alice had been persuaded by her husband to take a nap, but opened her eyes as Claire stepped through the door.

'Well, have you heard anything?' she immediately enquired.

'Yes, do you want the good news or the bad news first?'

'Well, there's never any good news . . .'

'Of course there is,' snapped Claire. 'The bad news is the bus has broken down, but the good news is we're going to be transported by cargo launches to Stanley.'

'You call that good news. I bet they all leak, and we'll all drown —'

'Now, now, dear, don't distress yourself,' Gordon tried to comfort his wife. 'I'm sure we'll get there alright, and it certainly will be better than being cooped up here.'

Stupid woman, Claire thought, but was immediately contrite, when she realized just how scared Alice was. When the time came, instead of deliberately leaving late so as to avoid being with them, she took Alice's arm and talked to her gently, coaxing her into the launch.

Even the level-headed Claire's heart gave a lurch when she saw the launches in which they were to travel. They were decrepit and top heavy, and it took much rearranging of people to make them seaworthy for the two-hour trip to Stanley.

Between them, Gordon and Claire managed to get the distraught Alice on board. Concern for her helped Claire forget her own fears, but it was a nightmare journey. Claire was not a good traveller at the best of times, and nausea threatened to overcome her. Taking deep breaths, she managed to refrain from being sick.

Junks which had been towed behind the launches were used to take them ashore as the water in Stanley Bay was very shallow. The advance party helped them land.

Once ashore, they were herded around by the squat Japanese soldiers, lined up, counted and segregated into American, British and Dutch groups. Claire looked anxiously around for John, but he was nowhere to be seen. Panic momentarily constricted her throat. Then suddenly his tall figure emerged through the crowds and she almost flew towards him.

The steep climb up the hill from the jetty seemed too much for some of the weary, hungry prisoners. Alice soon tired and had to stop and sit down several times. Claire and John stayed behind to help her.

When the last exhausted traveller arrived at the camp, the order was given that the British were to go behind the barbed wire. Some remained sitting, but others rushed around trying to find old friends and acquaintances. John led Claire to a tiny room, which was completely bare. As they had been unprepared for a long stay, they had brought very little luggage with them. Even if they had it would have been impossible to fit it in. Their bedrolls would have to remain rolled, John decided, and their cases would have to double for chairs. Claire's shoulders drooped and choking tears crept into her voice. The pent-up emotions of the last few weeks overcame her, and she sank down onto her bedroll and sobbed.

John held her close and whispered into her hair, 'It's not much, but we'll have more privacy, just the two of us . . .'

'It's fine, John,' Claire smiled through her tears, 'really it is. I'll be alright in a minute.'

'That's my girl; we won't let them get us down. Come on, chin up. I'll take you on a tour of inspection, and we can try to buy some equipment.'

'John, we've hardly any money —'

'I know, dear. We decide what are the most essential things we need, but I'd better warn you, the fighting here must have been quite heavy. The buildings are pock-marked with bullet holes, and there are small craters in the roads where grenades have exploded. There have been the most shocking atrocities carried out here by vengeful Japanese soldiers. They've invaded St Stephen's Casualty Hospital . . .' John's voice broke. He covered his face with his hands, and his whole body shook. 'They shot the medical officer who tried to block their entrance to the wards. They . . . they murdered three young British nurses, ra . . . ra . . . raped some of them, and even bayoneted patients in their beds.' John felt his pent-up wrath uncoil. 'Claire, oh Claire, it's horrendous what they've done. They're barbarians. . . savages.' He covered his face again, as if to erase the thoughts from his mind.

Claire hung her head, 'And I grumble because the room is so small. John, I'm sorry —'

'No, darling, it's not just the room. You've been through a lot, we all have . . . war is terrible . . . not to mention Alice, darling, you were so good with her, she just made me so mad —'

'Yes, poor Alice, poor Gordon . . . I wonder how they're going to cope . . .'

'At least we're in a healthy spot. The Japs probably decided on it because it's isolated from the rest of the Chinese in the Colony, and access by land can be easily controlled. It really is a good place to be interned, and quite beautiful with the two bays, and the mountains in the distance. At least we have space and fresh air . . . so different from that dreadful hotel. Claire, there are six dead Canadian and Indian soldiers in St Stephen's College – we'll have to start giving them a decent burial.'

'Yes, of course, John . . . their poor families, they'll be so distraught when they hear what has happened to them here.'

It had been a long, emotionally tiring day, but as Claire methodically sorted out the equipment she had hurriedly packed, she tried to throw off the feeling of despair which was threatening to engulf her.

She took a deep breath and tried to calm herself. Keep busy, that's the answer, keep busy, she told herself. Then set to with renewed strength.

There was nowhere to store anything, they would have to leave most of what they had brought with them in their cases. This task done, and having found her Bible, she sat down to read while she waited for John to return.

Two hours later John came back, his clothes, and face streaked with dust and dirt.

'You look exhausted,' Claire said, with a sharp intake of breath, as she gazed into his tired eyes.

'I'll be alright after a good night's rest, but what I really need is a lovely refreshing bath . . .'

'What a hope,' sighed Claire.

'Well, come on, let's go and have a look round. We seem to be free to move about at will. I think the Japs are going to leave us to run the camp ourselves.'

No one bothered with them as they set off on a tour of inspection. They stopped to speak to several friends and acquaintances whom they had not seen since the siege had begun. In the distance, they could hear the sounds of hammering, and as they made their way towards the noise, they saw Chinese labourers installing rolls of barbed wire about six feet high. The labourers appeared frightened and did not look up as John and Claire approached them.

They discovered that several buildings had been set aside for the Americans and Dutch. There were still people rushing around looking for accommodation. Unlike John and Claire, who had selected a small room, many families were trying to locate the largest rooms they could find.

'They're just being selfish,' declared Claire, hotly.

'After the experience of the hotels, you can hardly blame them,' John replied, with understanding.

The wide open expanses of Stanley led people to believe there was plenty of space for everyone. They were wrong, the accommodation was hopelessly inadequate for so many of them.

'We must get organized – it's essential,' said John.

'Yes, you're right, but where do we start? It's chaotic.'

'Well firstly, it looks as though we need a residence officer who will allocate rooms, rather than let the strongest take the most space. A democratically elected council . . . that's what's needed. It shouldn't be too difficult to set up – we've got plenty of people here who are used to organizing businesses, and all the government officials. Surely someone will take charge and get this confusion sorted out.'

'Yes, what a mess . . .' Claire looked around her.

'It's quite hilly and rocky . . . it doesn't look very fertile,' John remarked, then added, 'the two sandy bays on either side of the peninsula make it look like part of the Cornish coastline. That's Stanley Bay, on that side.' He pointed west. 'And that's Tytam Bay on the eastern side, by the three-storey building.'

They made their way towards St Stephen's College, hurrying to keep warm as the evening had turned chilly. On the threshold, they stopped dead; the colour drained from John's face.

Claire's hands flew to her throat, as if the strangled cry that escaped her was born of suffocation.

A buzz of voices met their ears, and immediately an odour of excreta and rotting bodies assaulted their nostrils. Over by the window there was the body of a soldier, slowly decomposing. On the walls Japanese characters had been written in blood.

Claire thought she was going to faint – even her war experiences had not prepared her for a sight like this. John reached for her hand and dragged her out into the fresh air.

'It's horrible, horrible . . .' Claire's words trailed away as she rushed outside. Her body shaking as she propped herself against the wall. John did his best to comfort her, but his own stomach was retching. He jerked round when a familiar voice hailed him.

'Dr Grayson,' he said with a sharp intake of breath. 'It's good to see a familiar face.'

'Dr Aldcott, yes, it's good to see you too. How are you?' Then, noticing Claire's ashen face, he turned to her. Taken aback, Claire tried a smile, but she was overcome again with a wave of dizziness.

'It's horrible . . .' was all she could manage to say. John and Dr Grayson supported her between them until the dizziness subsided.

'Thank you, I'll be alright now, it was just the stench.'

'Yes, it's a sorry business, all this killing . . .' muttered Grayson.

'We must see that the soldier has a decent burial,' John declared as soon as he had satisfied himself that Claire was recovering.

'It's going to take some contriving to get that mess sorted out,' said Grayson, with a sweep of his hand in the direction of the college.

'Have you found accommodation?' Claire asked him.

'Yes, yes, with only myself to think of I didn't feel it mattered too much, but I've managed to find a space in the college building. I'm in one of the upstairs rooms. The police have been allocated the classrooms. They've already begun to divide their block with thin wooden partitions. All the windows have been shattered during the fighting, and they've found some sacking which they propose putting up as a temporary measure. Some of their Chinese wives have come into the camp with them. They could have remained outside had they so wished – in my view they should have done so. I'm sure they would have been more help . . . But where are you?'

'We have a tiny room just big enough to hold bunk beds. It's in one of the bungalows, at the northern end of the camp, nearest to Stanley Village.' John explained. 'I believe they were formerly used for housing the European staff from the prison.'

'I see the Japs have reserved the best position,' Grayson indicated two very nice bungalows strategically placed on the highest rise.

'Oh, I guess that's for the Commandant and his staff.'

'Quite so. They can watch our every movement . . .'

'Then we had better watch our step,' said Claire, her colour restored.

'It's a relief to know that the Japs are allowing Dr Bonham Carter to remain outside, to supervise the town's health services,' said John.

'Yes, he's a very forceful character, with a reputation of being quite ruthless in matters of health,' Grayson smiled wryly. 'We've already been told to convene a meeting for all medically trained people to come along and pool ideas.'

John smiled back. 'So I understand. I've been scouting around. There's a pleasant three-storey building facing the sea, which I think would be ideal for a hospital.'

'You mean the building next to the prison?'

John nodded. 'Yes, that's the one.'

Grayson's eyebrows shot up. 'There'll be plenty of work to keep us occupied, that's for sure, and the sooner we get started, the better. Good day, Aldcott, Mrs Aldcott.'

Indeed there would, thought John, and a sense of desolation swept over him at the realization of the amount of human suffering around them.

CHAPTER XII

Stanley Camp

'Claire, you were very wise to advise me to get the smallest room,' said John. 'You know there are thirty people living in the bungalows which were only designed for one family.'

'Poor things, however will they manage?'

'They don't – all sorts of rows have broken out, it's awful. Some people are marking the floor with chalk to demarcate their territory.'

'I can understand that,' replied Claire.

'One fellow I bumped into told me he had been threatened that if he dared cross over the line, he would be killed.'

'Oh, I do hope the war won't last much longer,' sighed Claire.

'It's such a shock after the way we used to live; I wonder if we'll ever be able to adapt.'

'I think we've made a good start – once we get the hospital set up, and settle into a routine, things will begin to improve.'

An icy knot of anxiety formed in Claire's stomach – she could not share John's optimism. Life for the expatriates in Hong Kong had been extremely comfortable. She doubted they would find these conditions easy to cope with.

For the first few days, John and Claire had to queue for their food. The evening meal was served at five-thirty, but they quickly learned that if they did not get in the queue early, they would go hungry. Twice a day, the kitchen served dried boiled rice and a vegetable or meat stew. There was not much of it, and it often tasted musty.

'Claire, don't eat those little black bits,' John warned.'They could cause dysentery.'

'Why, what are they?'

'I hate to tell you this, but I think they're cockroach excreta!'

'Oh no . . .' Claire almost screamed.

'Steady, don't spill it, or you'll be hungry during the night.' John reached out a steadying hand and just managed to grab Claire's plate.

Some of her precious rice spilled on the ground, but John was quick enough to save most of it.

'You'll get used to it, in time . . .'

'Never,' she declared.

To John's amazement, there was quite a crowd already gathered in the leprosarium when he arrived for the first meeting of medical staff. He looked around and nodded to several acquaintances. Then, while he waited for the meeting to begin, he did a head count. The number totalled forty doctors, and about a hundred nurses. He looked around at the bare walls and hoped they had been disinfected.

A stocky man with iron-grey hair clapped his hands and asked for silence.

'My name is Grant, Dr Edgar Grant. I have been appointed senior medical officer here by Dr Bonham Carter, the Director of Medical Services.' He cleared his throat and welcomed everyone, then lost no time in outlining his proposals for the setting up of medical services in the camp.

John was impressed by the way he handled the meeting, his plan was well thought out and he was concise and businesslike. It was agreed that the hospital should be set up immediately, and should be known as Tweedy Bay Hospital. He also proposed they should have a medical association consisting of all the doctors, dentists and pharmacists. All meetings should be minuted and medical records should be kept of each person in the camp. A murmur of assent echoed around the room.

'There's just one more thing before we break up,' Dr Grant went on. 'It has occurred to me that this building could be used to house the medical staff and clergy. Our rations could be brought here from the hospital and so avoid us having to queue for food. It's too time-consuming, and our time can be better spent caring for our patients. Don't rush over moving, the most important job is to get the hospital set up. All agreed?' Hands shot up all round the room, and the meeting ended.

By the time the hospital was ready for occupation they had managed to acquire seventy beds, which they divided equally between the sexes. Most doctors had managed to bring some equipment with them. By pooling all resources, they were able to fit up the operating theatre, but they had very little else, and few drugs.

A week later people from the Peak began to arrive in lorries. They came laden with as many possessions as they could contrive to pack. John, who was present at the time, saw them drawing up and went to greet them.

The first person to alight was Prosser, closely followed by his wife. John went forward, hand outstretched.

'We seem to meet in the most unexpected places,' John remarked, struggling to feel some sympathy.

'Oh, it's you, Aldcott.' A disgusted smirk curled around his lips as he looked at John. 'So even the distinguished members of the medical profession haven't escaped internment then.'

John ignored the sarcasm. 'No, we've been here a week already. As you can see, it's pretty grim. The camp's already crowded. I don't know where they'll find room for all the people from the Peak, but come on, I'll show you where to go.'

'They'll have to give us decent accommodation, or there'll be trouble,' Prosser scowled. 'Here, Aldcott, make yourself useful and carry some of this stuff to the goddamn sty they've allocated us.'

John tried in vain to resist the temptation to gloat at Prosser's discomfort, and feeling guilty at his lack of charity, he offered assistance. He shot a smile at the elegantly dressed Virginia, who smiled back, again only with her mouth, her eyes still held a look of utter sadness.

John followed behind the billeting officer as he led them over to the Indian quarters.

'A pretty mess the Government's got us into,' Prosser moaned, staggering along with a heavy suitcase in each hand. 'I thought Hong Kong was supposed to hold out for six months, not three weeks. Now our home has been taken over by Jap officers, and we've to come to this dump. It's an absolute shambles, the civil servants should all be shot. The Army didn't put up much of a fight —'

'I'm sure they did their best,' said John. 'A lot of brave men died resisting the overwhelming Jap superiority.'

'Brave men my foot – a lot of wimps if you ask me.'

'Flesh and blood was all we had, which wasn't much good against their machines . . .'

Being the first of the Peakites to arrive, Prosser demanded the largest room.

'Good God almighty!' Prosser exploded, a look of incredulity distorting his face, as he looked around at the cramped conditions. Each flat had a washroom fitted, with a tap, stone benches ran along two sides, but there were no cooking facilities, and they had only a squat toilet. All the rooms were entirely bare.

'You can't seriously think we can live like this. Why, we can't swing a cat, let alone put our beds in here. I demand something better.' He turned angrily to the billeting officer.

'You can demand all you like,' the man replied, wearily. 'It'll get you nowhere, but I'd better point out that this room will have to be shared with another couple —'

'You must be joking! What on earth do you take us for? Don't you know we had one of the biggest houses on the Peak.'

'Well, now you'll learn how the rest of the world lives out here.' He made a quick exit before Prosser could gather his wits about him to protest further. 'Serves you right, you need taking down a peg or two. You're the type who give the British a bad name out here,' the officer slung back over his shoulder.

Fortunately, Prosser did not hear the billeting officer's parting shot – he was too busy cursing and swearing.

He was right, though, thought John, they were his own sentiments exactly.

'Really, I can't believe it, I can't possibly put up with this,' Prosser was fuming.

'Doesn't look as though you have a choice, so you'd better get used to the idea.' It was the first time Virginia had stood up to Prosser in John's hearing.

She'd have to pay for that remark, John rightly guessed, as he glanced first at Virginia, and then at Prosser. Two red outraged spots appeared on Prosser's cheeks, he raised his hand and before John could intervene, struck Virginia a resounding slap across her face, sending her reeling. There was a shocked silence in the room.

John felt his temper rise and he clenched his fists. 'You louse —' but he got no further. The billeting officer was back with another couple. They had been close neighbours, but were not on speaking terms with the Prossers.

'You'll have to share this room, there's no other accommodation,' the officer announced, with a glance of triumph at Prosser.

'You bloody sadist, there's no room as it is —'

'Don't blame me, blame the Japs, I'm just doing my job.'

Prosser went an ugly red. 'It's absolutely disgraceful. What do the Japs think we are . . . bloody animals or something? They've no respect for us at all. We, who created the British Empire. Bloody Nips. They'll soon realize they've bitten off more than they can chew. Let 'em just wait till this war's over —'

'They regard us as a defeated people, and therefore have no "face". They think of us as being completely subservient to them, and the sooner we realize this the better,' John interjected decisively and then hurriedly took his leave. 'The pig-headed swine,' he muttered to himself,' he's going to have a hard time here, there's no doubt about that.'

He blurted out the whole sorry episode to Claire later that day when he returned to their room.

'You know, dear, Prosser hasn't changed, and you were right, he does beat his wife. I wonder why she's stayed with him all this time.'

'Goodness alone knows, probably because she has no way of supporting herself.'

'No wonder she looks so withdrawn.'

'Poor Virginia —'

'And what about the couple whose bad luck it is to be picked to share with them —'

'It doesn't bear thinking about,' Claire agreed.

'The accommodation here is hopelessly inadequate. With our poor diet, there's bound to be a lot of illness and infections.'

Claire picked up their plates and smiled at John. 'If we've to look after others, we have also to look after ourselves, so come on, we'd better join the food queue, it's almost four o'clock.'

So the days and weeks went by, and the camp settled down to an uncomfortable routine. For most adults, their main occupations were queuing for food and fighting bed bugs. The children were being left to their own devices. Parents were glad to push them out of the overcrowded rooms where they were liable to irritate others.

'It's about time someone did something about all these kids.' Norman Watson was the first to voice his concerns at the mid-week Bible study group. 'They're becoming a nuisance, and getting completely out of hand. We need to come to some arrangement about their education.'

'There are plenty of teachers around. Surely they could be persuaded to help,' suggested Norman's wife, Enid, who was also Claire's friend.

Claire reflected that most of the adults were so pre-occupied with their own problems, they were content to leave everything to the experts to organize. She had come to know Norman well. He was a Civil Servant in the education department, a middle-aged man with a vast knowledge of the Chinese. He had met Enid when she was working in a hospital in Kowloon, and they had been married just six months.

'You're a good organizer – why don't you get things moving?' she ventured to suggest.

'Yes, you're just the right person,' agreed the others.

'That's settled then. I'll set about it tomorrow.'

Norman was as good as his word, and within two weeks schools had been organized for the children. The Japanese refused to provide books or equipment.

'Never mind, they can sit on straw mats,' Norman insisted. 'The primary and secondary schools will have to be run alternately in the morning and afternoon, in St Stephen's College. I've got enough qualified teachers to help, and also volunteers. I'll have a word with the Red Cross and see if they can get some desks, but more important, pens and books.'

The next morning, John and Claire were thrilled to receive a parcel from Storm.

'I wonder if the Japs are allowing local people to send in food parcels, or do you think Storm is putting herself in any kind of danger?' Claire looked at John with concern.

'I suppose if the Japs start being unpleasant, she'll stop. I'm sure she has enough common sense to do that.'

'She doesn't lack common sense, but her loyalty to us might overrule it . . .' Claire replied, tersely. 'If only we could get some news of the outside world, life here might be a little more bearable.'

'I'll get a newspaper,' promised John. 'It'll probably be full of propaganda, but at least we may be able to read between the lines, and get some idea of what is happening outside.'

Copies of the *Hong Kong News* were sent in to the camp daily with the rations, and were free of charge for anyone caring to collect one. John had not had the time nor the inclination to do so, but Claire's worried face prompted him to find one.

That night he returned to their room, his face grave, a newspaper tucked under his arm.

'Singapore has fallen, Claire,' he exclaimed.

'Oh no! I thought Singapore was supposed to be impregnable.'

'So did I,' replied John. 'It had lots of heavy guns, and a huge garrison. The outlook for the Allies looks very grave. I'm afraid this war is going to last a lot longer than we first thought. Britain is busy fighting Germany – the far eastern war is bound to take second place. The American Navy seems to be having a hard time as well. Those in the camp who think there's going to be a speedy release for us are going to be disappointed.'

Claire grabbed the paper and read for herself. 'Do you think we'll win in the end?' she asked, anxiously.

'According to this the Japs are making rapid advances and the Royal Navy has suffered total annihilation.'

'You mustn't believe all you read in the papers, dear. That's one of the reasons I haven't bothered to pick one up, they're full of enemy propaganda.'

'At least it'll be useful as a supplement for toilet paper, and give us something to read.'

'Is it worth it, if you end up feeling more depressed?'

'Yes, it's better than nothing,' said Claire, emphatically.

'I'm sure the combined strength of Britain and America can defeat the Germans, Italians and Japs, but it'll take time to mobilize all resources, and recapture the lost ground.' John reasoned.

'Canada will be doing its bit too,' Claire observed. 'I wonder if my brothers will be called into service? I sure wish I could get some news home to say we're alright; they must be very worried about us. I long to get news of the kids too. I still miss them unbearably . . . they're so far away . . . I can't help worrying about Storm too . . . I wonder if we'll ever see them again —' Claire's voice broke and she swallowed hard.

'Darling, don't say that . . . don't even think it. We must do all we can to stay as healthy as possible. This means getting our vitamin C. A good source is from the pine-needles around the camp.'

'Yes, the children are being organised to collect them,' replied Claire.

'I wish you'd eat the weevils you spit out in disgust. They're a good source of protein.' John remarked on a note of reproof.

'Ugh, John, they turn my stomach —'

'Never mind, don't think about what they are, just swallow them down. Make sure you don't eat any uncooked food, even lettuce. We don't have any medicines for dysentery, so prevention is better than cure.'

'I've been told that the Japs have said if we make any fuss, the men will be separated completely from the women and children,' breathed Claire, distress in her tired eyes.

John flicked a strained glance at her and replied, 'That would be a disaster, it would split families, and the civilizing effect of family life would be lost.'

'John, I'm really worried. I bumped into Alice today and during our conversation she let slip that Gordon had purchased some Cheddar cheese. When I asked where he got it from, she flew into a rage, and told me to mind my own business.'

'Oh dear, so internment hasn't changed her for the better . . .'

'No, but that's not what's worrying me,' Claire went on, 'if she can buy cheese, where's it coming from? And if the Japs find out, all hell will be let loose.'

'She probably received a food parcel from outside.'

'No, John, I don't think so, food is just as scarce outside, besides she would have said. No, there's some other explanation.'

'And if I know my wife, she'll try to find out,' teased John, on a lighter note.

'You bet I will —'

It was several days later when Claire's curiosity was rewarded. The food queue was the best source of information, and there Claire learned the answer to the mystery of the food supply.

'It's the Police stealing the food,' she blurted out to John when he returned from a hard day in the hospital.

Perplexed John asked, 'How do they do that?'

'Well, the Police have taken over the duties of collecting rations from the depot. They do the cooking and serving the food. In their wanderings around the camp, they discovered a warehouse where extra food is stored, enough to feed the camp for six months, or so the story goes. They've become quite organized in raiding the store, and no doubt making quite a profit for themselves.'

'Phew...' John drew a deep breath.

'There'll be trouble, they're bound to be found out,' said Claire.

'So why are we not getting the food legitimately?'

'It's strange, isn't it?'

John's brows drew together in a worried frown. 'Unless, of course, the Japs are deliberately trying to starve us —'

'That's wicked, if the food is there. I thought because of the war, we were unable to import it,' mused Claire, 'yet, there seems to be food available, people with money or valuables are smuggling it in over the wire, cigarettes as well. More people are smoking, including those who didn't previously. I guess it helps combat the pangs of hunger.'

'Claire, don't you think it's time we moved to the leprosarium? A room has been allocated to us,' John suggested.

'I guess you're right dear, but after a long day's work I seem to feel too tired to bother.'

'Is that really the reason, darling?'

'Oh, John, you know me so well,' Claire confessed, laughing. 'No, it's only part of the reason. I'll really miss the camaraderie of the queues.'

'You mean the gossip.'

'Well, what's wrong with that?' said Claire, grinning ruefully.

'Nothing ... but it'll save a lot of time and leave this space for others.'

'You win then, I'll see about it.' Claire surveyed the room and sighed. 'It certainly won't take much moving —'

John gave her a hug. 'I'll find out if I can borrow one of the wheelbarrows they use for distributing the food rations.'

'We certainly can't be accused of laying up for ourselves treasures on earth, that's for sure.' Claire stifled a sudden sob.

John drew her into his arms again and held her tight. 'Don't cry, darling, I know it's tough, but it can't last for ever.'

'It already feels like for ever,' she wept, the tears she had tried to hold back overwhelming her. 'I feel so hungry all the time'

'I know, it's hard to think of anything else but food.'

'You're just skin and bone already. If this goes on for long, we'll all die of starvation . . .' Claire broke off for a moment to compose herself, then went on, 'You know, John, I think something should be done about the distribution of food. The rumour is that some people are so hungry they're drawing more than one ration. This means there's not enough to go round. They say the cooks are getting perks as well.'

'It's probably true, but I can't see that we can do anything about it.'

'Surely you can. A ration book system should be introduced, then food would be shared more evenly.'

'That's a brilliant idea, I'll put it forward at the next meeting,' John promised, faithfully.

During the first two months, the internees were left to run the camp themselves. Gongs were sounded for them all to queue up for their food and water ration from the communal kitchen. They had little interference from the Japanese guards.

Then one day they were ordered to line up on the football field.

'Oh no,' cried Claire, when she received the order. 'It's raining sheets, we'll all be soaked.'

They stood motionless in the rain for two hours and were searched by Indian guards. When they were eventually allowed back to their rooms, cold and wet, they found that all their possessions had been turned over. Anything which was army issue, such as groundsheets, army water bottles, and the camps two typewriters, had been confiscated. The order was given that the food stores should be locked to prevent the internees from pilfering. Three keys were held by the most trusted people in the camp. As a result of the prolonged stand in the cold and wet, several of the older people went down with colds which developed into persistent coughs.

By the end of March, the weather began to turn warm. Fearing a possible outbreak of tropical diseases, the hospital staff began to clear a small ward in readiness for emergency use.

* * *

The Service in St Stephen's Hall was packed that Easter morning. As John and Claire rose from their seats to join in the triumphal hymn, 'Jesus Christ has risen today', they felt their spirits lift.

They had been stripped of all their earthly possessions, humiliated by the enemy, had their faces slapped if they had omitted to bow to the guards, and some had been beaten, for real or imagined misdemeanours. They were vulnerable and completely at the mercy of the Japanese, but no one could take away their faith and trust in God.

So, gradually values began to change, and many people came to realize that their wealth and position held no security. Their only security came from those things which are eternal.

CHAPTER XIII

Repatriation

When John and Claire no longer had to queue for food, news was slow in reaching them. It was a total surprise when they learned that the Americans and Canadians were to be exchanged for Japanese. Their initial response was to dismiss it as just rumour.

'No, I think it must be true,' Enid Watson commented. 'The Japs have begun to treat them better, they're being provided with more food, and they're being allowed to contact Chinese friends outside the camp, and what's more they've each been given ten US dollars.'

'Yes, that's right,' Norman confirmed, eagerly. *The Hong Kong News* reported this morning that the Swedish ship, *Gripsholm*, left New York with one thousand and ninety eight Japanese and Thais on board, bound for Lourenco Marques, Mozambique, where the exchange is to take place.'

'That's great,' breathed Claire, 'perhaps it won't be long before we're all released.' For a while, depression at the lack of food and the general feeling of deprivation in the camp became less pervasive, so sure were they that they would soon all be free again. Thoughts turned instead to what they would do with their new-found freedom. But their joy soon turned to bitter disappointment when they realized that the British were not to be released.

In late June when the Americans and Canadians were ordered to pack up, there was great excitement. Claire, however, was in a quandary – she loved her children and her husband equally, and she was caught up in the most agonizing dilemma. Should she accept this chance and go home? The thought of leaving the camp and all its appalling conditions behind was very tempting, but how could she bear to leave John? Even if she did decide to go, would she be able to get from Canada to England?

'John, what shall I do?' she asked, desperately confused.

Unhesitatingly John replied, 'Of course you must go.'

'It's not that easy. I long to see the children and make sure they're alright. I keep wondering if Luke has been called up. June is probably a difficult teenager and needs me. I know your mother and Amy will have done a good job caring for them, but I still feel anxious about them, as if part of my own body is missing.'

'Then what's stopping you?'

'Oh John, you know.' There was desolation in her voice. 'I . . . I . . . how, can it be right to leave you?'

'Look, darling, I understand. I'd feel the same way if I had to make the decision. But if Hong Kong is re-invaded, we may all be killed by the Japs, and if they don't invade we could starve to death. You have a chance of freedom and I think you should take it.'

Trying to suppress tears, Claire said, 'But I wouldn't have a moment's peace, knowing I'd walked out on you.'

'I'd miss you terribly, Claire,' there was a catch in John's throat. 'I love you so much, and the thought of losing you is almost unbearable. But the children need you too. I'll understand and support you, whatever you decide to do, but I'm afraid, dear, it has to be your decision . . .' Then on a more decisive note, he added. 'Why not talk it over with Mr Pickering – he'd make a good sounding board, and help you reach a judgement.'

'That's a good idea. I'll try to think up all the pros and cons before I go to see him. I'll get him to pray with me about it.'

Claire was quick to seek the loving counselling of Mr Pickering. A strange peace seemed to flood her heart as they prayed for specific guidance. Rising from her knees, her mind was made up. She smilingly thanked her Minister and went in search of John. They had planned to meet in the quiet of the cemetery, by the side of the camp.

Without preamble Claire blurted out, 'I've made my decision.'

John felt his heart twist over and he caught his breath. With an effort, he kept his voice low and calm. 'Good, Claire. That must be a load off your mind, uncertainty is so hard to live with —'

'John, I feel my place is with you, sharing in the hardships, as well as the good times. We made our marriage vows twenty years ago, and just because we're in a hole now doesn't seem to me to be any reason for altering them —'

A strangled sound escaped John and the tears began to roll down his cheeks. He gathered Claire into his arms and they clung together, their tears mingling. At that moment, John knew he had never loved her so much.

'Oh Claire,' was all he could manage. She was so gallant and loyal, it tore at his heartstrings.

Claire was the first to recover her composure. 'You know, John, I'm afraid I was beginning to lose faith in the goodness of God. Whilst Mr Pickering was praying, though, I felt a calmness sweep through me. I'm still scared at what the future holds, but I know I must trust in God, and He will give me the strength to carry on . . . There's so much to do here.'

'Darling, I don't know what to say. I'm so proud of you, you're so unselfish. All I could think of was how much I would miss you.'

With this weight off her mind, Claire was able to throw herself into work more wholeheartedly. For the next few days she was kept busy giving smallpox and cholera inoculations to the Americans and Canadians who were to be repatriated.

'Why aren't you going?' several people asked her, when they learned that she was Canadian. Some were amazed, others impressed at her reply. One couple, who lived in Toronto, promised to deliver a letter to her parents. All the internees were making the most of the opportunity given them by the Japanese. They were all being allowed to send a letter of 150 words.

Days went by, and still nothing happened about repatriation, then a great shout went up when a ship was sighted off the Stanley peninsula. Everyone who was free to rushed up to the high ground of the cemetery to get a proper view. The vessel had a black hull, with large white crosses painted on either side, and an illuminated cross on the superstructure. A huge Japanese flag was fluttering from the jack mast.

A great shout went up from the crowd. With a wave of excitement, the Americans and Canadians seemed to be experiencing a resurgence of energy as they sprinted down the hill. John and Claire, and a number of their British friends and colleagues, made their way more slowly – some were light-headed and faint through hunger. A Japanese soldier stared gloomily at the smiling throng, shrugged his shoulders and turned his back on them. The crowd suddenly stopped in its tracks and Claire was almost toppled by the force of bodies which bumped into her.

'What is it, John, what's happened?' she asked, anxiously.

Craning his neck, so that he could see over the heads of the people in front of him, he exclaimed, 'Someone has fallen . . . come on, Claire, we may be needed. I'm a doctor, please make way,' he pleaded, as they pushed through the multitude.

'It's Gordon,' Claire gasped, as she stared down at the haggard face and emaciated body. Beside him stood Alice, wringing her hands, a look of utter helplessness on her face. John sank to his knees beside the sweating, exhausted body. Gordon's breathing was shallow, the sweat was standing out in beads on his forehead, as John tried to examine him.

'What's wrong with him, is he going to die?' Alice's voice was jerky and unco-ordinated.

'I'm not sure, we must get him to the hospital as quickly as possible so that I can examine him more thoroughly,' said John.

By the time they reached the hospital, Gordon was again in a state of collapse. Two days later he died, the first victim of starvation, a distraught Alice by his side. She had refused to leave him.

'He gave me most of his food,' she wept. 'Oh, it's too awful to think about it. I shouldn't have taken it, but he insisted.'

Alice was inconsolable for days.

'Your husband must have loved you very much to sacrifice his life for yours,' Grayson told her bluntly. John, standing beside him, cringed at his tone. Alice looked up into his face, and whispered, 'I didn't deserve such love,' then turned sadly away.

John, repeating all that had taken place to Claire that evening, asked anxiously, 'Do you think you could go to her, she's going to need help to get over this?'

'Yes, of course,' was Claire's immediate response. 'Poor Alice . . .'

Although it was a hot humid day, nearly all the camp turned out to watch the departure of the Americans and Canadians.

'I can't help thinking of all the good food they're going to get soon,' was the constant cry from those left behind.

'Don't torture yourself by thinking about it, Claire,' John tried to caution her, but it was no good, the more Claire tried to put it out of her mind, the more it weighed on her. The procuring of food was an all-absorbing occupation for most people in the camp.

When it came to the Canadians' turn to be repatriated, Claire was surprised and delighted to be given her Canadian friend's worldly goods. In Stanley terms, it was a bonanza.

'Oh, thank you,' Claire faltered, almost overcome with emotion and gratitude, as she surveyed the contents of the gift box – spoons, knives, forks, crockery, food and clothing.

'Rather a motley assortment,' her friend grinned.

'It's like being given a fortune. I'll miss you both. God bless, don't forget to pray for us, and let my family know we're both well.'

They all hugged each other. Claire was rather quiet for several days after her friend's departure. John understood her grief, and tried to be as supportive as he could.

They were able to mix jam, or brown sugar, with their rice and boiled lettuce, to make it tastier. Claire had been wondering how she was going to replace her worn-out shoes and clothes. Apart from their hospital uniforms, which had to be washed daily by hand and placed under their mattresses to press out the worst of the creases, they had only the clothes they had worn on the day they entered the camp. When the weather had turned warmer, Claire had cut off the legs of John's trousers and had turned her skirt into shorts. She realized they would be totally inadequate for the winter, but they could only live one day at a time. The clothes her friend had given her were a size too big, but no one bothered about such trivialities. They were just glad to have something to exchange for their rags.

With the departure of the North Americans, the whole camp became inspired by the hope of repatriation. But as the weeks and months went by, hope was turning to bitter disappointment. Then in September, a petition was sent to London requesting that repatriation be arranged for women with children. Several women tried to become pregnant in order to qualify. Claire's friend, Enid, was one of them. When her pregnancy was confirmed, they celebrated with a few friends. The feast consisted of the luxury of a boiled egg each with their bowl of rice.

'Well, what was the verdict?' John was asked as he returned from a meeting with the Colonial Secretary, Mr Maynard, who handled the external relations of the camp with the Japanese. John looked round at the eager faces of the doctors and nurses, and shook his head.

'Not good news, I'm sorry to say. Mr Maynard accused us all of disloyalty.' Disgust was written large upon his face. 'He said he was powerless to help, and he thought it might be the intention of the British Government to keep British residents in Hong Kong, to maintain the morale of the Chinese, and their interest in the Allied cause. He said if the women and children left, it would be like rats leaving a sinking ship.'

'Why on earth should he think it disloyal to leave Hong Kong?' A flush had spread across the paediatrician, Dr Evans's pale face. 'It's not as if we're doing any good here. We're not contributing to the war effort or helping to defeat the Japs. We're just sitting here rotting away, slowly starving to death.'

'Maynard thinks loyalty in wartime calls for everyone to place their lives, and all they hold dear, at the disposal of the cause. He didn't think we should approach the enemy power to transmit the message to the beleaguered British Government.'

'That's going over the top a bit, as far as loyalty is concerned. Maynard must be an idiot if he thinks staying here is going to help the war effort one iota.' Dr Grayson, as usual, did not mince his words. 'Maynard's really going to make himself unpopular in the camp if he holds to that view.'

'And does he think we are being disloyal to want to improve our lot?' put in Dr James. 'The conditions here are dreadful, and I've heard that in Shamshuipo military camp in Kowloon they are even worse. Whatever happened to the Geneva Convention – haven't the Japs heard of this? Prisoners of war should receive the equivalent food of local troops. What did Maynard have to say about that?' The doctor sat down again a shadow of his former self.

'When this was discussed with the Japanese Governor,' said John, 'he argued that the food is similar to that which is given to their soldiers, but that their soldiers are taught to live off minute amounts. Mr Maynard said that the Japanese have no excuse for starving us. The British Government, through the Red Cross, remit £10,000 each month, for the relief of civilian internees and war prisoners. Also, in godowns throughout the Island, adequate food supplies have been stored against such emergencies. He believes that this food is being shipped to Japan.'

'Surely something can be done about the state of the food we receive,' an angry voice from the back of the hall demanded.

John thought of the dirty, low-grade rice they were expected to eat, sometimes with cockroach excreta, or cigarette ends, and even the occasional dead rat in it. He shook his head again. 'I'm afraid it's useless to complain, the food is inspected on arrival at the camp, but if the Colonial Veterinary Surgeon rejects anything as being inedible, we go without and nothing is sent to substitute it. So it seems the more we complain, the more likely we are to have our rations cut.'

'We're already getting signs of malnutrition, particularly in some of the older people,' another of the doctors observed. 'There's also the danger of an epidemic of cholera and dysentery spreading, because people are becoming careless over cooking food and boiling water.'

'True,' agreed Dr James, 'we must try to impress on everyone the need to be meticulous in this area. Any suggestions as to how we can improve things for ourselves?'

There was a stirring in the room, several hands shot up, and one after the other they stood up to offer suggestions. The secretary was kept busy taking notes as ideas came thick and fast.

'Yes, Dr Green?'

'How about setting up a soya bean milk factory. Soya beans are more plentiful than cows' milk, and the milk could be used to feed the children?'

'Bones from the inedible fish and meat could be ground up to produce calcium, this could be added to the children's food to help bone and tooth growth.'

'I've noticed that some people in the camp are beginning to grow their own food, so why don't we do the same? That way, we could provide extra vegetables to supplement our diet?'

'Salt and cooking oil are almost unobtainable, there's plenty of salt water around us, so how about organizing groups of people to bring it up from the harbour, to be used for cooking purposes.'

A pretty young nurse stood up. 'Bed bugs are driving me mad. I can't sleep. Has anyone any suggestions as to how this can be dealt with?'

Dr Grayson rose and looked around with tolerant amusement, until his gaze rested on the young nurse. He cleared his throat. 'There are three main methods of dealing with bugs. You can scrape them off with a knife, which is rather laborious, or you can paint them with kerosene, if you can get it, but the most effective method is to turn the bed frame on its side once a week, and give it a good hammering. You'll find the bugs will drop off in a shower on the floor. Combine that with standing the bed legs in tins of salt water, and you should be able to keep the problem to manageable proportions.'

'Thank you, Dr Grayson,' said John as the nurse sat down again, smiling. 'Now, on a more positive note, I'm glad to report that the children are doing very well with their lessons; they are certainly less of a nuisance now they are occupied. They're also getting some milk financed by the Red Cross; this too will be distributed to hospital patients.' He judged it time to draw the meeting to a close. 'Thank you all for attending, I've taken note of all your suggestions. We'll meet again in two weeks' time. This will give the working committee a chance to consider your proposals, and get some action. I believe we can only overcome our problems by working together as a community; everyone must play their part. I am confident that God will strengthen us as we face each new difficulty together. We have a great deal of talent in the camp – engineers, scientists, teachers, people with practical skills. These must be put to good use for the benefit of us all.'

As time went by, John began to understand why the poor often lived in such squalid conditions. Life became such a struggle with so much to contend with that he and Claire had little vigour left for the niceties of life. All their efforts seemed to go into bare survival. Even some of the pleasures of the camp began to wane, as energy levels dropped.

John and Claire still managed to get down to Tytam Bay for a swim at least once a week, but others found the steep climb back up was becoming too much for them in their weakened condition.

Claire and John, along with several friends, often gathered together at the end of the working day, for prayer and Bible study. They would watch the lights of the fishing boats from Stanley Village sparkling around the islands off the Stanley Peninsula. It was a beautiful sight, they feasted their eyes on it, and it gave some healing to their souls after the squalor and deprivation of the camp. They could see the Southern Cross among all the bright stars, and they would watch the moon glistening on the water, the waves breaking up its image at the water's edge.

'All that lovely fresh fish they are bringing in makes my mouth water at the very thought of it, Claire said wistfully one day.

'The Japs are being particularly cruel in not allowing us to buy it,' grumbled Alice who, since the death of her husband, had taken to visiting John and Claire regularly.

'Well it doesn't make much difference to us, we haven't the money anyway. I spend so much time thinking about food and the meals we had before the war, that I get quite depressed,' Claire remarked – gloomily for her.

'Well, we're going to do something about it. Since it was suggested at the hospital committee meeting that we start growing our own vegetables, I've got a few volunteers together. They've promised to make a start,' John's tired eyes lit up with enthusiasm.

'It's a good idea,' said Alice, 'but I've heard lots of complaints from those who have already started a garden. Before it's ready to harvest, others come along, and pinch it.'

'Then we'd better find somewhere where it will be safe.' Claire was thoughtful for a moment, then suggested, 'The flat roof, over the leprosarium perhaps.'

'Ideal.' John beamed at Claire. 'It'll be hard work, but all the residents will help, I feel sure.'

CHAPTER XIV

The Camp Develops

The idea to start a garden on the roof of the Leprosarium was taken up enthusiastically by the residents. The doctors and nurses, and anyone interested, pitched in to help. They began to scrape soil from the rocky hillside and made a human chain to carry buckets of it up to the roof and arrange it in beds. Seeds were obtained through the black market and a rota was drawn up for watering and attending the plants. Wood ash from the cooking fires was saved and garbage from the rubbish bins was collected by Doctor Jones, the youngest doctor in the camp. He caused great amusement at the next medical committee meeting when he proudly stood up to report on progress made.

'Time used to drag, I had so little to do, but now I have regular work, queueing for two hours each day to get sewage.' His eyes twinkled mischievously. 'I have plenty of time for reading while I'm waiting.'

Claire smiled as she thought of Doctor Jones deriving consolation from doing his studies, standing in the queue for the septic tank. But it's like that here, she thought. We have all, out of necessity, had to learn new skills. It's those who keep themselves occupied and mentally stimulated who will survive.

She thought of all the short courses put on by the academics in the camp, covering a very wide range of subjects. She had been particularly glad when the Americans had bequeathed their library to the camp when they were repatriated.

Claire had been so deep in her own thoughts that she missed some of what the other speakers were saying. She was finding concentration hard. She made a determined effort to keep her mind on the subject. They were all trying to do their bit to make life as bearable as possible.

Dr Grayson was now on his feet, talking about his attempts at cultivating yeast from sweet potatoes. Mr Pickering took the lead amongst the clergy to build ovens of red clay with wood as fuel to bake bread. The electricians in the camp were engaged in making electric ovens from concrete blocks, with the elements from wire fixed to flat sheets of roofing taken from the ceiling panels of St Stephen's school.

In time, as shoes wore out, a banker became an expert at making shoes out of bits of old rubber tyre and wooden clogs. A former horse dealer turned into a good baker. An eye specialist learned to be a good wood cutter. A stockbroker was transformed into a chicken farmer. A barrister became a hairdresser, cutting hair for a cigarette.

John never ceased to wonder at the change in Alice, since she had begun to join in the prayer and Bible study. Her face had taken on a strange serenity, and the most surprising feature of all was that she had stopped moaning.

'Penny for them.' John was so deep in thought that he was unaware Claire was talking to him. Alice gave him a gentle dig in the ribs.

'She's offering you a penny for your thoughts.'

'Oh, that's funny, I haven't heard that expression for years, and what's more, neither of us has even got a penny.'

'You were miles away though.'

'No, not really, I was just thinking how much we've all changed . . .'

'Well you can say that again.'

'You know, one of the best things to come out of the camp is that the old social distinctions of pre-war Hong Kong have gone,' said John.

'You mean the sort of white superiority practised by the British here in the twenties and thirties,' queried Alice.

'Yes,' replied John. 'It was totally wrong.'

'I think it was based on arrogance. Surely now people will realize that we are all human and vulnerable. When the war's over it will be time to build a new partnership with the Chinese. I think great things will come of it,' declared Claire heatedly.

'Well, there's no class distinction here. Even the Attorney-General has to queue for food, waiting in line for a couple of hours like everybody else,' put in Alice.

'I'm not sure everything's as equal as all that,' remarked Claire. 'I saw Prosser yesterday.' Her brows knotted in a frown. 'You know, John, he's been rather conspicuous by his absence. He looks remarkably fit, and very clean and tidy. I could swear his shirt and trousers are new.'

'Black market, I bet, whoever this Prosser chap is,' exclaimed Alice.

'Oh yes, sorry, I should have explained,' said Claire, 'he's a fellow John went to school with.'

'Yes, and if I know Prosser, he'll be the ringleader in any kind of double-cross and be making the most of exploiting a difficult situation. He speaks Cantonese, so he would be able to trade with the Chinese and Indian guards.'

'A good chap to keep in with then,' commented the unsuspecting Alice.

'He's a born rogue,' sighed John. 'I'm afraid he has few scruples.'

'Scruples or not, seems he knows how to survive,' observed Alice almost admiringly.

John recalled this conversation many months later, as the queues at the block clinics grew longer, and the hospital wards became congested. There was a desperate shortage of drugs and medical equipment.

John, who had been toying with his conscience for weeks, made up his mind. Gritting his teeth, he set a determined course towards the Indian quarters. He made straight for the room where he had last seen Prosser, but there was no sign of either him or Virginia. Retracing his steps, he stopped beside a child squatting on the ground outside, playing with two sticks.

'Can you tell me if a man named Prosser is anywhere around?' John enquired.

The child stared at him for a second, then snatched a glance over his shoulder, and in a conspiratorial whisper asked, 'The horrid rich man?'

John thought the description probably fitted Prosser well, so he nodded.

'Over there.' The child pointed to a two-storey block, with a balcony extending across the front. It stood out from the rest of the block by its freshly whitewashed appearance and colourful curtains.

John thanked the child and, eager to get his mission over and done with, hurried in the direction indicated.

The door opened at his knock to reveal an immaculately dressed Prosser, a large cigar held between his teeth.

'Well if it isn't my old friend Aldcott. I wondered when you would be beating a path to my door. Come in, old chap, and take a seat.'

Inside, John gasped as he looked around him.

'Like a cup of tea with real milk and sugar?'

John loathed Prosser's supercilious manner, but at the same time he could not for the life of him avoid salivating.

'That would be lovely, thank you.'

Prosser clapped his hands and in a second Virginia appeared.

'Tea, and some cakes,' Prosser ordered. 'Looks like you could do with feeding up a bit,' he added giving John an odd side-glance. He smirked to himself as he noticed John's scrutiny of the room.

'Not bad by Stanley standards, hey old chap?'

John stared at the sparkling dining-room furniture, matching tablecloth and curtains, and two bedsofas. 'How've you managed to acquire all this?' he asked, his gaze sweeping the room.

'Just shows you, old chap, what a bit of entrepreneurial skill will do.'

'It certainly does.'

John longed to ask how he had managed to get the room just for themselves, but fearing he would not like the answer, wisely refrained.

The tea was brought in, china cups and teapot on a tray. Virginia poured the tea, handed John and Prosser a cup each, then offered John a plate of delicious-looking oat cakes. He could not believe his eyes, and it took the utmost self-control not to scoop them all onto his plate and gulp them down.

'Oh, have another,' Prosser invited, in a nonchalant manner.

'How can I refuse? It was delicious,' said John. 'You appear to be well supplied.'

'Well I do what I've always done. A bit of trading here and there. Mind you, it's a risky business. Three Chinese coolies I traded cigarettes with were beheaded the other day by the Nips, and a whole lot of us traders were rounded up and put in Stanley prison for a week. It's a hell hole. The screams of the tortured coming from the prison at night make your blood curdle. So I have to watch my step. I no longer trade for cigarettes, too much competition from the cops' Chinky women. One of 'em grassed on me to a Nip. That's why I went to the clink. She'll pay for it, though, you mark my words, I'm just biding my time.'

His features set into a menacing scowl. 'I'm interested in trading for food now. I've got some good connections. Is there anything I can get you?'

John shook his head, 'Afraid I've little with which I can barter now, and it's not for myself I've called on you, but for the hospital. You see, we're running short of drugs and vitamins, and we badly need to get an outside supply. The medical superintendent is a great chap – he's not been interned and supervises the town's health services. He has contact with the camps, and is able to supply drugs and equipment, but not in sufficient quantities to meet the demand.'

Prosser measured John with a long, steady gaze, and began to shake his head decisively. 'Too risky, old chap, not really in my line.'

John turned away, his business done. He murmured a hasty goodbye and trudged back to the hospital. It had cost him a great deal to lower his pride and compromise his principles. He was in a way relieved not to be beholden to Prosser. Only real concern for his patients had given him the courage to approach him.

Several days later, John was attending a patient when he received a message that he was wanted in the office. He completed his examination and tried to reassure his patient that they would do their best for him. In his heart, he knew that the only real cure was a well-balanced diet of bread, meat and vegetables. It was another case of beri-beri.

It was strange how the sexes differed, he thought, as he made his way to the office. The men with beri-beri, like the patient he had just examined, tended to lose weight, but the women were more likely to become bloated. There were so many of them now, struggling to get around the camp on swollen legs, their lungs waterlogged.

Nutritional disorders were by far their greatest problem. Deep in thought, he entered the office, and stopped dead in his tracks. Prosser . . . the last person he had expected to see, was deep in conversation with Doctor Williamson, the deputy medical officer in charge of the camp.

Prosser and Williamson looked up as John entered.

'I believe you know each other,' Dr Williamson said, by way of introduction.

'Yes, yes, we attended the same school in England.' John stammered, wondering what was coming next.

'Mr Prosser thinks he can be of service to us,' observed Williamson.

John's eyebrows arched. 'Really . . .'

'Yes,' broke in Prosser, a look of crafty speculation spreading across his face. 'My contacts have located a source of drugs and are able to deliver, but the price will be high for the risk I'm taking.'

John felt a shiver run through him. He looked at Williamson – his shrewd eyes were scrutinizing Prosser.

'Quite so, I understand that, but you were saying people write cheques to you to obtain yen.'

'Yes, they do,' replied Prosser. 'I've got a great pile of cheques and IOUs from internees as payment for my services which'll give me a base to get started from once the war is over.'

'Well, we know of a few of our patients who have Hong Kong dollars.'

Prosser perked up at the thought of business, and was immediately on the alert. 'No problem, just give me their names.'

'I'm afraid I'm not at liberty to do that, confidentiality still has to be maintained here you know —'

'Oh, stuff and nonsense,' Prosser reflected for a moment, then continued, 'OK, I'll deal through you. I'll change their Hong Kong dollars for yen if you like, for a commission . . . I can help the hospital too, with drugs. If you don't have the money now, you can give me an IOU . . .'

'We have Hong Kong dollars to pay for more supplies, if you can acquire them.'

'Sure, what do you want?'

'Quinine, and nicotinic acid, pain killers, sulphur drugs . . .' Williamson reeled off their requirements.

'Sure, sure, good as done, you're dealing with a pro here you know, Dr Williamson'.

John looked at his watch as he had work to do. Prosser, noticing the gesture, bent forward to examine the watch more closely. 'I've traded jewellery and gold as well. That watch would fetch a lot of yen, buy you eggs and sugar.'

'No, no I'll never part with this watch, it was given me by my father.'

'Suit yourself,' snapped Prosser. 'But don't blame me if you get some of the disgusting diseases knocking about here. I wish you every pleasure in your daily rice and boiled lettuce.' Then turning to Williamson he declared, 'I need cash up front.'

'Very well, come back in an hour, and I'll have the money for you.'

Prosser stood up, gave John a withering look, and Williamson a wet-fish handshake.

John and Williamson both let out a loud 'Phew' as the door closed behind him.

John cast a strained look at his boss, 'He's trouble, I'm afraid, has been ever since I've known him. As he said, he's good at his business and extremely successful, but I must warn you, he's crooked in all his dealings.'

'Yes, that's blatantly obvious, but we don't have a lot of choice.'

John shook his head sadly. 'No, more's the pity. I would normally avoid him like the plague.'

Trying to distract himself from thoughts of Prosser, John returned to his work. Entering the womens' ward, he was immediately called to examine a patient who had been admitted unconscious the previous night. A young, grim-faced nurse explained that she had been brought in by her husband who had found her lying on the steps of their block. She had been beaten into unconsciousness, but had come round during the night. It was the Chinese wife of one of the policemen swathed in bandages. She was shaking badly, even though they had piled on as many blankets as they could spare.

John scrutinized the patient's chart. Then looking up exclaimed, 'My goodness, Mrs Everett, whatever happened to you?'

With downcast eyes, she whispered, 'I've been beaten up.'

'Beaten up, who on earth would do a thing like that?'

'Oh, there's lots of nasty people in the camp —'

'Yes, that may be so, but not to cause injuries like this for no reason . . .'

'Oh, he had a reason —'

'He? You know the man who did this?'

'Yes, he's been out to get me since I informed on him.'

Prosser, thought John, I bet it was Prosser.

'You informed on him?'

'Yes, I'm a good Catholic. It was my duty.'

'And you informed on the three Chinese workers too?'

John thought of the shock waves which had reverberated around the camp a few weeks ago, when three Chinese workers had been beheaded for trading cigarettes, and Prosser's words came back to him.

'Yes, yes, but I didn't think they would be killed.' The Chinese patient began to sob, 'If I've done wrong, I'll pray to be forgiven.'

John's sense of outrage at what the woman had done melted away as he witnessed her guilt and horror.

John was shocked by the extent of Mrs Everett's injuries – her face had needed six stitches. Her body was black and blue all over and it hurt her to breathe. 'With injuries like this I think we had better get you X-rayed. This will mean sending you out of the camp to the French hospital,' he explained. 'You're going to feel pretty rough for some time; we'll have to keep you in hospital for a while.' He gave her an encouraging smile and turned to the nurse. 'We've only enough painkillers to allow one a day.'

Prosser had revenged himself in the only way he knew how, thought John, but how strange life was, he may also be providing the drugs to relieve her.

Mrs Everett was one of the last to be allowed by the Japanese to go out for X-ray. Soon after her return, rumours of a more sinister nature began to circulate around the camp. When a returning ambulance was stopped and searched, the patient was found to be hiding a wad of notes under his bandages. Everyone waited with a sense of foreboding.

Alice was, as usual, one of the first to hear the news, and rushed off to find John and Claire.

'The money was confiscated by the Japs and he's been put under arrest,' she blurted out, breathlessly.

For once even John knew what she was referring too. It had been the talk of the hospital for the last twenty-four hours.

'We'll all have to pay for this, you mark my words.'

Sadly Alice was right. Not many days later, the wife of the director of medical services, along with her daughter, were brought into the camp. The Medical Superintendent and the Chief Manager of the Hong Kong and Shanghai Bank had both been arrested. Later, other senior officers of the Hong Kong Bank, and health officers, were rounded up. The camp was stunned.

Prosser had managed to acquire all the drugs Williamson had asked for, as well as eggs and flour. To Williamson's delight he had also managed to come by some shark liver oil. Having deposited the drugs, he went in search of John.

'You're glad you agreed to use my services now, old chap, aren't you?'

John looked into the mocking eyes of his old enemy, and his heart seemed to drop to his boots. He longed to lean over and wipe the superior smile from Prosser's face, the smile which said, 'I've got you now, just where I want you.'

Insomnia, so prevalent in the camp, which had not as yet been a problem to John, began to plague him.

As time went on, the hospital staff noticed people complaining of what they called 'barbed-wire sickness'. Many of them showed signs of increased irritability and exaggerated ill-temper.

'I know of one young lady who bit her best friend so hard on the thigh in a fit of temper that she drew blood. She would never have done that in normal life,' Enid Watson told the little circle of friends gathered together outside the leprosarium.

'It's being cooped up that does this to people,' John replied. 'I've noticed concentration becoming more difficult for myself. My memory isn't so good these days.'

'Yes, and you're not sleeping so well, John,' Claire remarked, anxiously. 'Is it because of uncertainty about the future, do you think?'

'In most people's case it probably may be so, but my problem is an old one – Prosser.' He had not intended to worry Claire with this but he was so burdened by it that he felt the need to talk it through with the group. He asked for them to make it an urgent matter for prayer. That night he slept well for the first time in a week.

The next day was John's turn for duty in the clinic. He was in a better frame of mind, having shared his troubled thoughts and prayed for guidance. Even so, he was surprised when his first patient of the morning was Virginia Prosser. Strictly speaking she should not attend this clinic as she did not live in the district. John was puzzled by the visit.

'Well hello, what can I do for you?' he asked with a smile. He was shocked at her appearance. She was not as thin as most people in the camp but her skin was pasty and colourless, the eyes dull and vacant. She seemed broken and without hope. John listened attentively as she told him her symptoms.

He nodded sympathetically. 'It's the diet. Changing from your usual meat and two vegetables, and three good meals a day, to small amounts of rice and lettuce is an enormous change. A lot of people in the camp are getting these symptoms. They are caused by the absence of normal quantities of protein and fat. They should go away as you become more accustomed to the diet. I'm sure your husband can get supplementary rations for you,' he could not resist adding.

She laughed in a brittle way. 'You're the only one I can turn to. Thank you for not turning me away. You see I . . . I . . . think I'm pregnant,' she stammered.

'Apart from the difficulties of the camp, would that be a real problem?' John queried tentatively.

'Graham hates children, he'll be furious.' Virginia who had been trying desperately to hang on to her self-control, could contain herself no longer – she just broke down completely. Hard, hurting sobs that seemed to have been buried in her for years came from her. 'I'm sor . . . sorry, Dr Aldcott, but I can't seem to stop myself,' she wept, her shoulders shaking.

John let her cry, realizing the pent-up emotion needed an outlet. Presently she looked up and wiped the tears from her eyes.

'Would it help to talk about it?'

Virginia was almost overcome again by John's soft sympathetic voice and calm manner. With an effort she controlled herself, and nodded. 'I've found camp life unbearable. My husband gives me no support, and spends all his time on black market business. His greed and pomposity have isolated us from everyone else. Graham's only companions are his business associates. He keeps me a virtual prisoner in our rooms – I can't go out, as he has me watched. Besides, I have no friends, no one to talk to, nothing to do. It's driving me crazy. It may surprise you to know that I do have a brain – before we were married I trained as a nurse. But I'm rambling on, probably not making any sense of myself.'

'You're doing just fine,' John encouraged her.

'I can't understand how I'm pregnant as we seldom have intercourse. Graham accuses me of being cold and frigid and, as he puts it, takes his comfort elsewhere. He's having an affair with another woman in the camp, someone who was a high-class prostitute before the war. He bribes her with black market food and cigarettes. He's off with her now. That's how I've been able to slip out this morning.' Virginia stopped for breath.

'Why do you put up with him? Haven't you thought of leaving him?'

'Yes, many times, but it's not that easy. Where would I go? I never finished my training so I've no means of earning a living. Besides,

Graham supported my mother, too, for many years, I had to think of her, not just myself. Life wasn't all bad. I did have friends in Hong Kong. Graham used to go away on business for weeks on end and he didn't leave me short of money. He has his good points and is quite generous. I went sailing and played tennis. One could have a good time here, and I really lived it up whilst he was away. We gave spectacular parties, admittedly mostly for people Graham wanted to impress, but some were very nice.'

'And how long has he been beating you?'

'It started about six months after we were married. I longed to have a baby, but Graham was against the idea. When I got pregnant he was furious and accused me of having an affair. It was totally untrue. That's when he began knocking me about. I lost the baby . . .' The tears, still very near the surface, began to fall again, but she quickly wiped them away. 'If I'm pregnant, I dread to think what he'll do.'

'So you're worried because your periods have stopped . . .'

'Yes they've always been so regular, and I feel so peculiar. I'm tired and lethargic all the time, and some morning's lately I've been sick.'

'Well, without examining you, I can't be sure, but from what you've told me, I think it's highly unlikely you're pregnant. You're more likely to be suffering from anaemia, caused by lack of iron. It's quite common amongst the women here. If only you could get some fresh vegetables, that would give you all the iron you need. The Red Cross have sent us a parcel of multi-vitamin tablets. I'll give you some of those. I can do tests, if that would reassure you, but in your case I don't think it's really necessary.'

'No, no, I'm sure you're right,' said Virginia, evidently torn between relief and regret.

'My main concern is your general state of health. You cannot continue to be kept a prisoner and besides, you have talents which could be used in the camp. I don't want to cause more trouble for you, but if you did decide to leave your husband, I'm sure we could find work for you in the hospital – that would then entitle you to live in the leprosarium. None of us knows what the future holds, but please God this war will not continue for much longer. You know, there's no reason why you couldn't complete your studies, and earn a living for yourself. It'll be tough, but then nothing in my opinion could be worse than what you're experiencing at present.'

'Somehow you make it sound so easy. I should have stood up to Graham years ago, but . . . but . . . I . . . I just couldn't. Even now I'm terrified of what he'll do. If he knew I'd come here this morning he'd be furious, probably throw me out —'

'Well, would that be so bad?'

'No, not really, now I've talked it over with you. I've the feeling he could be doing me a favour.'

For the first time, John saw a look of defiance in Virginia's face. She got up and began to pace, as she tried to collect her thoughts.

'Dr Aldcott,' she said, at last 'I've taken up a lot of your time, but thank you, I knew the night you visited us at the Peak that you and your wife were different from any of Graham's other associates.'

'Well, if either my wife or I can be of help, you know where to find us.'

'Thank you again.' The face she turned back to John was full of quiet resolution, and there was a spring in her step as she left and quietly closed the door behind her.

Virginia had time to reflect on her conversation with John, for it was several hours before Prosser returned. She had not felt so good for years. It was true what her mother used to say, she told herself, that a trouble shared is a trouble halved. Why, oh why, had she let Graham dominate her all these years? I'll do it, she vowed, I'll stand up to him, even if he does beat me, it will be for the last time. I'm still young enough and fit enough to earn a living. With so many influential people around it would be an ideal opportunity to break away from him. She didn't need Graham any more and he had made it patently obvious that he had no love for her, she reasoned. Then she made herself a cup of tea and sat down to await Graham's return. The minutes seemed to drag by – she just wanted to get it over and done with before she lost her courage.

When at last she heard him approaching, the old sinking feeling began to return. He seemed to be in a good mood, for he was whistling and she had not heard him whistle for months. She jumped to her feet, not wanting him to have the advantage of looking down on her.

'Hello, had a good time with your girlfriend?' she greeted him as he sauntered nonchalantly into the room.

'What if I have?' he retorted, not attempting to hide his contempt for her.

Virginia took a deep breath – now or never, she told herself. 'I'm sure, as you have someone else in your life, you no longer need me. Ever since we came into the camp you've treated me like a slave, just to cook and clean for you, while you've been out on your black market business, and off with other women.'

'What if I have,' repeated Prosser, not getting the drift of Virginia's unaccustomed forcefulness.

'I've decided I'm not going to put up with it. You've kept me a virtual prisoner with nothing to do but household jobs, no social contacts. It's bad enough putting up with the privations of the camp, without the indignities which you place on me —'

'Oh, hoity toity, who do you think you are, and just who do you think will take you in?' said Prosser, with a mocking laugh. 'You know how crowded the accommodation in the camp is. I've got the best rooms for you —'

Suddenly brave, she rejoined, 'Yes and the less you say about the way you did that the better. I was so ashamed —'

'You ashamed! You were mighty glad to live here, and not in some of the other hovels. You go right ahead,' Prosser went on, sardonically. 'Just see how far you get. You won't survive five minutes in this camp without me. You need me more than I need you, you always have.' He gave a modulated snort, a sneer made deep lines around his nose and mouth, and then, before Virginia could duck, he hit her hard across her face.

'I'll show you,' Virginia threw at him, colour rising in each cheek as her anger mounted. 'Our marriage has never been much, but I put up with you because I thought, in spite of all your sarcasm and cynicism, deep down you loved me still. I was impressed by your wealth and power, and the pleasure that gave me. Strip that away, and you're just a greedy, self-centred black marketeer, and that's all you are.'

Prosser exploded, 'Shut up, you little bitch.' He slammed her hard against the wall. 'You can't do even the basic things, like looking after me, properly. You're useless, do you hear me, useless.' He hit her again, blood trickled down her face; there was a ringing in her head. 'You snivelling little guttersnipe. You might as well just curl up and die for all the good you do me,' he shouted towering over her as she cowered on the floor. This is it, she cried within herself, no more. I've had enough. As soon as he had gone, she would collect her things and move up to the leprosarium. She knew the pattern, it had happened so often. He would light up a cigarette, drink himself silly, and go off for the rest of the day. Then she would make her move.

She bathed her battered face and body. This done, she curled up on her bed and feigned sleep. Prosser began to drink. As soon as Virginia heard the door slam, she knew he had slunk off. Then, as fast as her bruised and throbbing body would allow, she set to work gathering her things together.

It was a very dejected, sorry sight that presented itself at the hospital. I've done it, she thought, and slid into a heap on the floor.

Virginia awoke in a strange room, her mind refusing to focus. She tried to sit up, but a pain in her arm and head made her flop back again.

Then a quiet, warm voice spoke to her. 'Take it easy, you're very weak, but you'll be alright in a few days.'

Virginia opened her eyes again and a spasm of panic shot through her.

'Would you like something to drink?' the pretty girl with red hair bending over her asked.

'Yes, please,' Virginia's voice, little more than a whisper, answered her.

'I'll tell doctor you're awake,' the pretty nurse turned away, and returned in a few moments with a warm, sweet drink.

Virginia thanked her and drank thirstily. Then the room swam out of focus again for a few moments, and she sank back on her pillows exhausted. The next time she woke, she felt stronger. She was able to sit up unaided, and to take stock of her surroundings. She smiled as a familiar figure came striding down the ward towards her.

'Well, hello, sleeping beauty,' John greeted her, 'how are you feeling?'

'Much better thanks, Doctor. How . . . how long have I been here?'

'A couple of days, you collapsed on the floor, and we've kept you under observation. Looks like you've been in the wars again, but there's nothing broken.' John smiled knowingly. 'Have you come to stay, we could sure do with another pair of hands?'

'Yes, yes please, I've come to stay.'

'Good, then Claire will find a space for you to live, and work for you to do when you're feeling up to it. In the meantime, you need a good rest, and building up a bit. I'll get Claire to come to see you, perhaps tomorrow.'

'Thank you again, my talk with you gave me the courage to walk out on Graham. I hope I never give you cause to regret helping me,' she said, blinking back the tears.

It was two weeks before Virginia was well enough to leave the safety of the hospital. Claire had come to see her several times and she looked forward to her friendly visits. 'There's always work needing to be done in the hospital. John was telling me you started training —'

'Yes, but I never qualified.'

'That doesn't matter, you could work as a nursing auxiliary. It would be good experience, and I'm sure would be a benefit when completing your studies after the war. You'll get all your food from the hospital kitchen and you'll find all the staff very friendly.'

'Thank you, you and your husband have been very kind. I'll work hard, I know it'll be difficult at first, but it'll give a purpose and direction to my life that I've been lacking for years.'

Virginia was eager to learn – what she lacked in skill she readily made up for by sheer hard work and a willingness to please. She proved particularly good in the children's ward.

The single nurses, when they heard of her husband's brutality unhesitatingly made space for her to share their crowded room and she quickly settled into her new environment.

To Claire's astonishment and delight, one evening Virginia asked if she could attend the Bible study.

'You'll sure be welcome,' was Claire's immediate response.

The Bible studies seemed strange to Virginia at first, as the women there talked of things she had never thought about. The Bible was an unknown book to her and she could only recollect strange stories from her schooldays.

Corinthians, the book they were studying, was a complete mystery. The fruit of the spirit seemed a very odd concept – she had never experienced much joy or peace in her life. It had been difficult to feel joyful when she was always looking over her shoulder in fear of her husband making a scene.

But she liked the fellowship and support of the other women who were always around her, available to discuss anything which was on her mind. It was a tremendous encouragement after her years of isolation.

It was almost a month since she had left her husband, and to the relief of everyone in the know in the hospital, Prosser had made no attempt to contact her. John was therefore taken by surprise when one morning, as he was walking to the clinic, he met Prosser. He tried to avoid him, but Prosser changed direction at the same time as John, and they came face to face.

'I see you've kidnapped my wife,' said Prosser angrily.

'Kidnapped your wife? What are you talking about? Your wife is working in the hospital, and living in the leprosarium, but she came of her own free will —'

'This is hardly what I would have expected of an old King's man,' Prosser flung at John. 'It's the sort of treacherous action I'd have anticipated from the Chinks. Don't ever come and ask for my help again to get drugs or anything else for you. As far as I'm concerned, you and the rest of the people up there,' he swept an imperious hand towards the leprosarium, 'are *persona non grata* for the rest of my life.'

'So be it,' replied John grimly, and walked off, controlling his anger with difficulty. He frequently contemplated the causative factor for Prosser's aggressive and acquisitive behaviour. Had he at an early age been a victim of some crippling deprivation? There must be some explanation for his behaviour, he reflected.

CHAPTER XV

A Friend Amongst The Enemies

At the end of John's clinic, he returned to the hospital to complete another hour on duty. There was quite a crowd gathered in the office. Doctor Fraser, was the first to speak. 'We've just heard that there's been a number of arrests. It would seem that the Japanese authorities suspected there were radios in the camp. They've been taken to Stanley prison.'

'Oh dear me, no . . . do we know who they are?' John asked with growing concern.

'We understand one was the former Defence Secretary, one of the senior policemen, and three former radio engineers who were in the Broadcasting Company,' replied Doctor Fraser. He went on after a brief pause, 'One of the engineers was seen digging in the blazing sun this morning, under the supervision of a guard. He had to dig for hours, and eventually uncovered a wireless set. It had apparently been buried for some time.'

'That's terrible . . . we must do something —'

'Yes, exactly, we've decided to protest,' broke in Doctor Pomfret, one of the civilian doctors in the camp, who had recently been transferred from Shamshuipo military camp in Kowloon. 'We can't just let them get away with this.'

They talked shop for some time and then dispersed to the wards.

The next day John was doing a ward round and stopped beside the bed of an elderly patient.

'Hello, how you feeling?'

'Dreadful. The screams coming from the prison were so horrendous I've hardly had a wink of sleep . . .' John felt his pulse, and the man continued. 'They must be torturing the arrested internees to make them confess,' he shuddered. 'What a wicked lot these Japs are.'

'They're certainly the most cruel race I've ever come across. I think it must be the military regime they have, and the militaristic training they receive, which accounts for it,' replied John.

'They say Japanese boys are spoilt until they're about eight, and then toughened up after that . . .' chipped in the patient in the next bed. 'This soft, hard approach must have a detrimental effect on them, but the women, wow, now they are —' John moved on down the ward, so he was not to hear any more about the exploits of his patient with the Japanese women, but he was left with the impression of a pair of twinkling green eyes, in what once must have been a comparatively handsome face.

'Quite a one with the ladies in his time, no doubt,' John smiled to himself.

The military trials were held, but the protest made by the representative of the internees was ignored. A few weeks later, the five men were taken to a hillside by the prison and shot in the back of the head. Morale in the camp plummeted.

It was at this stage that one or two of the seriously sick patients, who had put up a brave fight, drifted into listless apathy and gave up the struggle.

The entertainment committee did their best to liven up the atmosphere, putting on monthly shows. Some were exceptionally funny and helped to lighten the gloom. Food supplies worsened as month after month they heard the American aeroplanes, or the muffled rumble of bombs being dropped on the city.

John and Claire were particularly concerned about Storm and Lily Kwok.

'They must be having a terrible time,' Claire confided her anxieties to her friends, Enid and Alice. 'Food is dreadfully scarce in the city.'

'Yes, but it's great to know we haven't been abandoned. The Americans have kept their promise, surely help isn't far away,' said Enid, hopefully. She had been forced to sell her wedding and engagement rings to buy extra milk for her baby son Brooke after he failed to thrive.

'That's all very well,' chimed in Alice, 'but we're obviously being badly affected by the blockade.'

John, returning from a hard day's work, dropped a kiss on his wife's head, and sank down wearily on the ground beside her.

'Well, what've you been doing, apart from putting the world to rights?' he enquired, as cheerfully as he could.

Claire smiled. 'We were talking about the raids – anything of interest happened at the hospital today, dear?'

'Well, yes, as a matter of fact there has. I met a Japanese pastor today, the Reverend Sigara Nanataki. He told me that before the war he used to be a minister at a Lutheran Church in Hiroshima. He spent two years training at a seminary in America, so his English is good. His church was closed by the government at the beginning of the war, and he was called up to be an interpreter.'

'How wonderful, I've never met a Japanese Christian.' Claire's eyes shone with pleasure.

'Well, you soon will – he told me he would be worshipping with us. He couldn't stop long this morning for fear of being accused of fraternizing, but he said he would come back tomorrow afternoon to look around the hospital.'

'Are you sure he's genuine?'

John noticed the alarm in Alice's voice. 'Well, I'm in two minds myself,' he admitted. 'On the one hand, he may be a Christian, or on the other hand he could be a Japanese spy, trying to entrap us. After the horrors of those executions, I can't be sure. There must be spies in the camp —'

'We'll have to be very careful,' cautioned Claire.

'I guess I could sound out two of my colleagues who worked at Shamshuipo. They must have come in contact with him. He told me he had been transferred from there.'

Over the mid-morning meal of rice and boiled lettuce, John briskly related his concerns to Dr Pomfret.

'I remember him well in Shamshuipo camp. He was the only Jap who never did anything cruel to the POWs,' Dr Pomfret observed. 'In fact, to let you into a secret which I don't want you to pass on, he brought in some medical instruments for us to use. As a Jap, he was never searched when he came into the camp. As far as I can tell he did nothing to hinder their war effort, but he's certainly helped to save lives. Yes, I would stake my life on it he's to be trusted.'

Reassured, John was delighted that afternoon to personally give his new friend a conducted tour of the hospital.

Reverend Nanataki was amazed at the cleanliness and layout of the hospital. 'You've done a marvellous job here,' he enthused.

'We've done our best in the circumstances. We're short of drugs and equipment, but by sheer hard work we've managed so far to prevent an epidemic of any kind,' John replied.

'Yes, things are very bad for all of us,' John saw a spasm of pain cross Nanataki's face as he spoke and realized, at that moment, that the Japanese could be as cruel to their own people whom they considered traitors, as they could to the enemy. He quickly changed the subject.

'Do you have any family back home in Japan?' he enquired.

Rev. Nanataki's face softened. 'Yes, my wife, a teenage son, and daughter of seven. My first wife died of typhoid, and my two older sons from my first marriage are in the army, one in Java and one in China.'

'You must miss them very much,' John sympathized. 'I too have a son and a daughter. We sent them back to England to complete their education, before the war started. Claire and I went through agonies at parting with them. At the time we thought it was the right course of action, now we are not so sure. It is so hard sometimes to know what to do for the best for them.'

'Yes,' agreed Rev. Nanataki, 'I guess all missionaries suffer this dilemma.'

'I've an adopted Chinese daughter, too,' continued John, 'but she is still in Hong Kong. We received one parcel from her early in our internment and have heard nothing since. That's one of the hardest things to bear, not knowing what is happening to our families.'

'Your daughter's in Hong Kong, and you say you've not heard from her?'

'No, it's very worrying.'

'Perhaps I could help. Would you kindly give me her name and address, and I will try to visit her.'

'That would be so very kind.' John knew he could trust this man, and wondered how he could have doubted him, he radiated such warmth and love. He smiled and then grew serious. 'But would it be safe for you?'

Rev. Nanataki regarded him with a straight, level gaze. 'I will not take unreasonable risks, Dr Aldcott. You give me her name and address. Maybe I can bring you some information as to her welfare.'

'We named her Storm; she may have returned to our address in Bowen Road, or she may have gone to live with our amah, Lily Kwok.'

Rev. Nanataki produced a small notebook from his right-hand pocket. 'Here, just write down the two addresses.'

John nodded his thanks, wrote quickly and handed it back.

'Storm speaks good English. She's a fine Christian, she trained in needlework and tailoring, so if you need anything in that line, I'm sure she could help.'

'Good, that can be my reason for visiting, just in case I am followed. I'll ask her to make a shirt for me for special occasions.' Rev. Nanataki laughed at his little deception. 'Now you do something for me, please?'

John nodded affirmatively.

'I would like to pass on messages from the prisoners in Shamshuipo camp to their relatives here, but I need assistance. Perhaps you would be good enough to aid me by using your knowledge of people in the camp.'

John's face lit up. 'Yes of course, delighted to help you if I can. They do so long for news of their loved ones.'

Rev. Nanataki continued to visit the hospital. Whenever he saw John, he would smile and give a stiff little bow, then shake his head sadly. 'No news, my friend, of Storm.'

Several months passed and then one evening, John happened to be alone in the stillness of the office writing up his reports, when a shadow crossed his paper. He looked up into the now familiar face of his Japanese friend. John smiled in greeting, but there was no answering smile on Rev. Nanataki's features – he wore a sombre expression, and his eyes were downcast.

John's heart gave a great thump – something was amiss. Something awful had happened to Storm was the first thought which penetrated his mind.

When he spoke, the words were gritty with apprehension. 'You've news of my daughter. . . ?'

His eyes still downcast Nanataki replied, 'Yes, I've seen your daughter, she is living with your old amah, Lily Kwok, in your flat in Bowen Road. They are both in good health. Storm has set up a little business in the flat, and makes uniforms for the Japanese officers, and clothes for some of the Chinese people living in the area. She is earning enough to keep them from going without food.'

'That's wonderful news —' A great tide of relief swept through John. Then he saw the great sadness in Nanataki's face. 'You have bad news. Please, what is it?'

'Yes bad, very bad, I'm so ashamed of my countrymen.' He hung his head and the words seemed to be almost wrung from him. Then he looked at John, his face contorted with pain. 'I have to tell you this. Your lovely daughter was raped by drunken Japanese soldiers after the capture of Hong Kong. She has a son, a beautiful little boy of two years . . .'

'Oh no, no.' John was aghast, stunned. Storm, the beautiful little girl they had loved and protected – raped and assaulted. He turned away, and buried his face in his hands, as he felt a flame of red hot anger forming in his stomach, burning him up, almost consuming him.

'The brutes, the drunken brutes. Poor little Storm,' he wept within himself. He wanted to rush to her and shield her. Nanataki, struggling with his own emotions, remained silent. At last John looked up, fists clenched at his side, controlling the tide of blazing emotion. He said, 'Thank you for telling me.'

'I'm so terribly sorry that this should have happened to your daughter.

I'm afraid it was battle fatigue and drunkenness which caused them to do this terrible thing.'

John's face, a study in agony, his voice a strangled sob, got out the words, 'At least she's still alive.' Then noticing the anguish on Nanataki's eyes, he added, 'It took courage for you to tell me.'

'So much sadness, such difficult times, food is scarce in the city. The people suffer there too.'

'But Storm is well —'

'Yes, and the little one. Your Lily Kwok is a good Christian. She minds the baby well. Your daughter has weathered the ordeal, she is very brave. She told me you rescued her and took care of her. She is sad she cannot send you food, but they have so little. She loves you very much, and your wife —'

'Oh, however am I going to break the news to Claire, she'll be so distressed, but we're indebted to you for bringing us word of her. We now know she's alive. We've been very anxious about her.'

'I'm sure your daughter will survive this terrible war with the help and support of Lily Kwok, a remarkable lady. If there is anything I can do to help you through this situation, then please don't hesitate to ask me.'

'I know war brings out the worst in people, and can turn them from decent people into monsters,' said John, painfully. 'It is the struggle for survival at its most basic. None of us come out of war with clean hands.'

'I'm sure you're right,' acknowledged Nanataki, 'but sad to say there are humans who will always run out of control. I sometimes think God gives men too much free will – they are prone to doing evil with it,' he said sadly. 'Just remember, my friend, God knows and understands how we feel. After all He died on the Cross for us. That is proof of His love indeed. But I must leave you now, my friend. God be with you.' Nanataki bowed and took his leave.

Watching him walk away, John was again struck by the selfless courage of this man who risked his life daily. If he was discovered by the Japanese guards to be helping the enemy, he could be killed. He might be small in stature, thought John, but he had a huge heart. He lingered another hour, trying to sort out his jumbled emotions. Then, determined not to put off the harrowing task of telling Claire any longer, he filed away his records, closed the hospital door quietly behind him, and crossed the cinder tracks to the living quarters.

Claire sobbed, as she thought of the rough hurting hands, that must have bruised her precious Storm's young tender body. For the fact she had not been there when Storm needed her most, and for the innocent little life which had been born out of Storm's terror. 'Why, why, why has this to happened to her?' she cried in her misery. John shook his head – he had no answer. He could only hold her close and endeavour to comfort her, whilst knowing there was no comfort to give. Eventually the tears ceased, then John tenderly wiped her face.

'You know, Claire, for years I've tried to find a reason for evil. Some wickedness is beyond rational thought.'

Claire shook her head sadly. 'Yes, sin has certainly blighted the world, and brought with it much suffering.'

'But we have the assurance that Jesus broke the power of sin on the Cross, when he took its curse on Himself, setting us free from its penalties and power,' declared John.

'We must pray, then, that the evil done to Storm will not destroy her goodness,' Claire announced emphatically, forcing a smile.

'Yes, I believe Storm's faith was strong, and she will know that God was in the trouble with her.' John was quiet for a few moments then added, 'At times like these, Claire, I don't know how people manage without God.'

'No, neither do I,' replied Claire.

'I just hope that Storm will be able to hold on to Jesus's promise that He knows and understands, and that that knowledge will sustain her.' Claire remained silent, and John went on, 'At least she's alive, and I just know we'll see her again.'

'I wish I could be so sure,' whispered Claire, as the tears began to fall again.

John saw a good deal of the Reverend Nanataki over the next few weeks. He was talked of with love and respect among many of John's friends in the hospital.

'He seems a good bloke,' Dr Grayson said to John one evening when they were alone together in the office.' The Japs are kind to the children, but he's the only one who is kind to everyone.'

'Yes, and if he's discovered he could be in grave danger, but he seems unconcerned about his own safety. He's been invited to the children's nativity play on Christmas Eve —'

'Christmas, oh good gracious, yes, it's only about two weeks away, our third Christmas here.'

There was hardly a dry eye amongst the 500 ragged internees, as the Christmas story was retold once again. The sewing group had gone to great lengths to have all the costumes just right for the three wise men, Mary and Joseph, and the shepherds.

The children sang 'Away in a manger', their sweet voices trained to blend harmoniously. All the congregation joined in the Carol 'Silent

Night', then the Reverend Nanataki was asked to give a rendering of a well-known Japanese carol.

'Certainly,' he replied, with a broad smile. 'How about "Once in Royal David's City"?' The pianist struck up and the audience listened attentively to the familiar tune, and the unfamiliar Japanese words. A spontaneous round of applause broke out as he took his seat, and for a brief moment there was a feeling of peace and reconciliation between the two peoples.

'I've enjoyed the nativity play very much,' he twinkled at John. Then dropped his voice to a conspiratorial whisper. 'I have a little gift for you, my friend. I will bring it to you later.'

A surprised little smile spread across John's face. 'That's most kind of you —'

Nanataki waved his thanks aside. 'I just wish I could have bought a little gift for all the children for Christmas,' he sighed, then continued, 'I would like to help you all more . . .' he shrugged his shoulders sadly.

'There is something which would be an enormous help to the whole camp,' John responded. 'Most of the people here are suffering from pellegra and beri-beri, as you can see by their swollen legs. We so badly need vitamin tablets and nicotinic acid to make up for the deficiency in our diet.'

'I'll see what I can do.' Rev. Nanataki left with a very determined expression on his face.

'Please be careful,' cautioned John.

Nanataki clasped John's hand and smiled broadly. 'Do not fear, my friend, I am never searched.'

Edith, Alice and Claire had been saving some of their meagre rations so that they could have a little treat on Christmas Day. Norman had insisted on paying over an IOU to Lane Crawford to add to the party fare, and between them they had been able to assemble what was, for them, a feast. Alice had nothing to contribute except her share of the day's rations and so had volunteered to cook the meal.

It turned out to be a kind of corn beef hash, with fresh vegetables from their garden. The gardeners had watched over their little plot as if it contained the crown jewels, so resolute were they that everyone in the leprosarium should have some fresh vegetables for Christmas.

John and Claire stayed chatting for a while after the Christmas Day service, knowing that their meal was in the capable hands of Alice who, since the death of her husband, had shown herself to be very resourceful.

With the cheerie words of 'Merry Christmas' from all their friends ringing in their ears, the two couples, along with little Brooke, made their way back to their block.

Alice, flushed from her exertions, greeted them warmly. 'Merry Christmas,' she beamed, and handed them each a mug of hot watery tea. 'I managed to find a few pine needles to give it a bit of flavour.'

'And what else?' enquired John, sniffing his brew.

'Ah,' laughed Alice, 'just a bit of spice and sugar I've been saving up.'

The weather was warm and sunny enough for them to be able to sit out on the veranda. Alice had arranged the two remaining chairs, an upturned bucket, and two small boxes around a larger box which they could use as a table, and had set out their odd assortment of cutlery. In the centre of the table she had placed a tiny posy of silk flowers.

'From one of my old hats,' she explained when this small gesture of love and thoughtfulness was acknowledged.

Then with a flourish, Norman produced from a bag he had been carrying very carefully, a large red cracker, made out of material, and beautifully decorated with sequins in the shape of stars.

'It's lovely,' they all gasped.

'Well, little one,' said Norman to his wife, 'stand up and take a bow. It's taken her hours to make.'

Enid blushed and smiled shyly.

They were just enjoying the meal, when John spotted Rev. Nanataki crossing the track. Leaning over the balustrade, he waved and sang out 'Merry Christmas, come and join us.'

Nanataki gave an answering wave, and shouted back, 'I was coming up to see you.'

They all welcomed him like an old friend, for that was how most of the internees thought of him now. He had become one of them.

'Happy Christmas,' he greeted each one with a little bow. 'I've a little something for you.' From his pocket he produced a small Christmas pudding. 'Not quite what you asked for,' he smiled at John, 'but it will make your meal a bit more festive.'

'Oh wonderful,' was the general chorus. 'Thank you so much,' said Claire. 'What a treat. Can you stop and enjoy a meal with us?'

'That is most kind, but no, my friend, I must not stop. I'll join you all for Carols at three this afternoon. I look forward to that. It will remind us of happier times.'

John wanted to say something to ease the pain Nanataki tried to hide, but knew that no words could really express the deep hurt of being separated from loved ones, not knowing if they would ever meet again.

It was several days before John was to meet up with Nanataki again.

'I've managed to obtain the medicines you require,' he whispered to John. 'Can we go somewhere quiet where we will not be observed.'

'Yes, of course.' John whispered back. 'Please follow me.'

He led the way to the dispensary where they were unlikely to be seen by anyone. Unbuttoning his coat, Nanataki extracted some flattened parcels, attached with string around his neck.

'My heart begins to go boom boom,' he smiled, 'when I smuggle something into the camp. I fear I may be searched, but I never am.'

'Thank goodness for that, from what I've heard of the Kempetai that could be most unpleasant.'

'I'm in the hands of the Lord, I will trust Him. I do not take unnecessary risks, I try not to arouse suspicion. That is why I do not spend too much time at the hospital.'

'I can understand that. We all have to be careful. I fear there are spies in the camp. Some people will do anything to get extra food. Thank you so much for all you do for us.'

'It is my pleasure, my friend.'

John was sad to notice that as time went by, Rev. Nanataki was seen less and less. Then suddenly his smiling, encouraging face was there no more, and the supply of medicines he had been smuggling in ceased. Weeks later, they learned that he had been sent back to Japan.

'Bang goes another supply of vitamins,' said Dr Grayson.

'I suppose he was being too friendly for the liking of the Japanese Commander.'

'Most likely moved to another job where he has less contact with prisoners.'

'I fear we've lost a good friend,' said John sadly.

'And the latest rumours don't sound too good . . .'

'What do you mean, Dr Grayson?'

'Haven't you heard we're being taken over by the military? Our new commander is to be Colonel Hattori, from the Shamshuipo camp.'

'Oh no,' cried John, 'I've heard he's a real nasty character.'

CHAPTER XVI

Stanley Military Camp

Life for the internees had been difficult for the past two years, but under military rule it became far worse. Rations were cut, and no reason was given. Now, they had to assemble for roll call twice a day in all weathers. Electricity was cut, and water was supplied every other day. News was slow in reaching them, but the truth that the war was going against the Japanese was beginning to filter through.

Air raids were more frequent, and they realized ships with food were unable to get through. As every available Japanese soldier was needed, forty Formosan guards were recruited to patrol the camp.

'Did you notice them doing cartwheels, and poking fun at the Japs behind their backs?' said Enid, as they were returning to their rooms after roll call.

'They've no respect for them. A real corrupt and uneducated lot of ruffians,' Norman warned.

'They've got into the black market quicker than anyone. I saw one guard near the Indian quarters with Prosser. He was shaking out cigarettes from his trousers and battledress. I couldn't count how many packets there were,' observed John.

'The Formosans speak a language that can be understood by the Cantonese, but I'm blowed if I can understand them,' said Norman, who was quite fluent in Cantonese. 'They seem to hate the Nips as much as we do. They're after jewels, gold and clothing, so there must be a ready market in the city. They must know the Japs are going to lose the war, and they're trying to make as much money as possible.'

'If the Formosans had their way they would strip us of all we have,' remarked Claire. 'John vowed he would never sell his watch, but that's all we have left.'

'Prosser tried to persuade me to part with it months ago —'

'Well he's a wily fellow, and knows everything there is to know about the black market, so it must be worth quite a lot. I have a few contacts in the camp. Would you trust me to get a good price for you?' Norman asked.

'That's very good of you – bartering's not really in my line.' John removed the watch from his arm almost reverently, thinking of his father.

Two days later Norman called in, a mischievous grin on his face. 'You were right. I've been able to sell it for sixty thousand yen. I have contact with a Formosan who, after a bit of haggling, agreed to buy it for that.'

Norman handed over the money. 'Wow, I didn't realize you were such a whizz . . .' John was relieved to have the worry taken off his mind. 'Thanks a lot.' Then turning to Claire he said, 'Now we can buy food on the black market.'

'With prices as they are, it's not going to last long,' cautioned Norman. 'It's amazing how values have become distorted in the camp. There are so many cheques and IOUs floating around. A few people are going to be very rich after the war.'

Claire was doubtful, 'Do you really think so?'

'Yes, dentists and traders will make a lot of money —'

'Not if we all starve to death, or die of malnutrition. My legs ache so much now, it's as much as I can do just to walk to the hospital. Life is becoming more trying by the hour. It's a pain having to preserve every drop of water for flushing the toilet or watering the gardens. It's just so ridiculous only getting water once every five days —' Claire's words were drowned by the shrill of the siren.

'I'd better get back to Enid, she hates to be alone during the raids,' shouted Norman, and dashed off.

When the siren went, all the internees had to remain in their rooms. Their routine was completely disrupted until the all clear sounded.

'It's OK now, darling, I'll be off to the women's fellowship meeting.' Claire dropped a kiss on John's cheek and hobbled off across the campus to the the communal meeting room. John watched her go, his face sad. Claire's legs were full of sores like so many in the camp. They had to keep them bandaged to keep the dust out. They were getting like human machines, mechanical, apathetic, resigned, he thought, and the lack of mental stimulation too was so depressing.

John continued to watch Claire making her slow laborious way. She had to stop several times to rest, but at last she was out of sight and he turned again to his book. His power of concentration was poor, and it was not long before his head began to nod and his book slipped from his hands.

He was having such a lovely dream. A table was spread before him, laden with mouth-watering dishes of food. He had just reached out to help himself to a delicious looking hunk of fruit cake, when Claire exploded into the room, gasping for breath.

'John, John, come quickly,' she cried.

For a stunned second John stared at his wife's distraught face, then managed to find his voice.

'What . . . whatever's the matter?'

'It's a drunk soldier, in the womens' quarters, he's . . . he's threatening one of the women. Come on, oh come on, quickly.' Panic was written all over her ashen face.

She grabbed John by the hand. He leaped up in an instant, and tried to calm Claire, all the while struggling to clear his mind and make sense of what she was saying to him.

'OK, I'll run over there and see what I can do,' he said, at last. 'You'd better go straight to the Japanese headquarters, and get an officer to come to the scene immediately.'

They dashed off in opposite directions as fast as their aching legs would carry them. Breathlessly John pushed the door open. The terrified women were huddled together. The soldier, obviously very drunk, was trying to drag one of the women across the room, while the others were desperately clutching on to her.

'Leave her alone,' shouted John. The soldier dropped the woman's hand, and in a voice slurred with liquor answered something in Japanese which John did not understand. Then he staggered towards John and in English rapped out, 'You kneel.'

John immediately went down on his knees, knowing that not to do so would be courting disaster. One of the women screamed as the sergeant fumbled with his cigarette and reached for his revolver.

He held it to John's forehead. John felt a sour bitterness in his mouth. This was fear, cold and solid and strong, shaking him, catching at his breath and at his blood. What a way to die.

He closed his eyes. Thoughts from the past flashed through his mind, of Claire, his mother, his children. 'I'll never see them again.' The sergeant's laugh was evil. 'I'm in your hands Lord —'

But he got no further with his prayer. Claire came bursting through the door closely followed by a Japanese officer. For a stunned second, her eyes took in the scene, then without thinking she lunged herself at the sergeant knocking him sideways. Sinking to her knees beside John, her screams echoed though the building.

The officer barked an order at the sergeant, who straightened himself, saluted sloppily, and slunk out of the door, closely followed by the officer.

John, clasping Claire to him, shuffled awkwardly to his feet, his face gaunt and haggard.

'It's all over now, darling,' he whispered to Claire, still holding her tight. The women crowded round, and it was only then that he felt himself trembling all over – he had to hang on Claire to support himself. He brushed off the women's thanks and, not trusting himself to speak, indicated to Claire that they should get back to their quarters. Leaning heavily on each other, they left. Quite a crowd had gathered outside.

'That was a courageous thing to do,' someone shouted out. 'You deserve a medal.'

'You weren't afraid of the bastard, that's the way to treat them,' called out another voice.

Little do you know, thought John, as he mopped the sweat from his brow and smiled wanly.

'I was terrified,' he confessed to Claire, as they at last reached their quarters, 'you were the courageous one, darling. I just did what I thought was best in the circumstances. I knew I couldn't stop him as he was armed.'

'You were brilliant, dear,' Claire insisted.' I'm so proud of you.'

'No, Claire, it was nothing, you were the real hero, it was a very risky thing to do.'

'John, it wasn't. As usual, I didn't stop to think. I just reacted to the situation. Thank God you're safe —'

'He could have killed you too,' he shuddered.

Within an hour, the news had spread through the camp. Alice, as usual heard it in the food queue, and hurriedly ate her bowl of rice, anxious to find out for herself how her friends had coped with their ordeal.

'We're fine now,' John reassured her, 'but I don't mind admitting we were both petrified at the time. I have cold sweats every time I think about it —'

'How about coming along to the concert tonight? It will take your mind off it.'

John and Claire looked at one another, and then smiled their thanks at Alice. 'It was good of you to come over. Yes, of course we'll come along with you. What time does it start?'

'In ten minutes, so we'd better get going or all the best seats will be taken.'

They crossed the parade ground, remembering to bow as they passed the guards. When Claire stumbled, Alice and John held her arm. She was still feeling rather weak and light-headed. The entertainments committee organized a monthly show, a programme of lectures on an endless variety of topics, and the occasional concert. Alice went to most of them, but John and Claire were usually too tired.

There was a steady stream of emaciated prisoners stumbling along the paths, all making their arduous way towards St Stephen's Hall. The shoes they had worn into the camp had long since disintegrated. Many preferred to walk barefoot, and others struggled along in wooden sandals. These were just two pieces of wood, kept on with string or canvas strips held by nails. The better-off favoured using cut-up rubber tyres, which seemed to last the longest. John smiled to himself – what a motley lot they were, he thought.

'I'm sure you'll enjoy it tonight,' Alice was saying. 'There are some very talented people performing. Tonight's show was written by Charles Granger, one of the teachers.'

They sat six rows from the front and waited for the hall to fill up. Five minutes later the show began; it was a musical comedy, 'Mimi'. John and Claire had not laughed so much in years. In the middle of the performance, just when the audience were really enjoying themselves, there was a disturbance behind. John looked round.

'There's some Japanese photographers come to take pictures of us,' he whispered to Claire sitting beside him. As the cameras flashed everyone looked round. Then a young child in the front row raised his fingers in a victory sign. Soon everyone was doing it, even the people on the stage. The audience chuckled as the Japanese turned on their heels and left the building in disgust. The following day, all concerts and gatherings were barred for several weeks.

Norman had not been present at the concert. Their little son was suffering from earache and they were having disturbed nights. He had called to ask John if there was anything he could suggest to relieve the pain.

Sadly John shook his head. 'We have nothing to give you, I'm so sorry,' he responded.

'Just thought I'd ask, I guess I knew the answer, things can't get much worse . . .' then Norman chuckled, 'I hear you were at the concert the other night.'

'Yes, yes I was,' replied John, laughingly. 'It's a shame all the entertainment has been stopped, but somehow it seems worth it to prevent the Japs using pictures of us enjoying ourselves.'

'For propaganda, you mean? They wanted to pretend that they are treating us well —'

'Yes,' John grinned. 'It was a bright little lad in the front who started the victory signs.'

'Then everyone followed his lead, and the photographers were taking pictures of a sea of victory signs,' added Claire.

They all laughed together, then on a more serious note Norman observed drily, 'The world needs to know just what a cruel lot these Japs are. The only decent thing they've done, as far as I can judge, is to institute the communal gardens. The sweet potatoes have helped improve our diet.'

'I heard that they've given extra rations to the men who work the gardens,' said Claire.

'Yes,' declared Norman, cynically, 'and that's the reason some of the idle so and so's volunteered to work in them.'

John turned to Norman. 'Did you know it's been decided to give over some of the rooms here for a sanatorium for tuberculosis cases?'

Norman raised his eyes. 'You mean tuberculosis has broken out —'

'No, not exactly. Because of the poor conditions, people who caught it when they were young are now having a recurrence of it,' explained John.

'Have you drugs to help?' asked Norman.

'No,' replied John. 'All we can do is give them rest.'

Silence fell on the room. It was Norman who broke it again. 'It can't last much longer —'

'That's what we keep saying —' muttered Claire.

Norman continued, 'Italy has surrendered. France has been recaptured, it's only a matter of time before Germany falls. You can tell the war is going badly for the Japs from the way the American bombers have free access all over the sky —'

As if on cue, the shrill of the siren blasted out. 'See what I mean?' he shouted.

CHAPTER XVII

The End of the Road

With the rapid fall in temperature at the approach of the Chinese New Year, morale slumped to its lowest ebb for most of the internees. It was boosted only by the sight of the American planes.

On Monday, 15 January, the air-raid alarm was sounded, and the noise of explosions lasted for most of the day. The walking patients in the hospital sat huddled by the windows in their blankets trying to keep warm as they watched the planes passing overhead.

John and Claire remained at the hospital overnight, and with morning came the sound of another alarm. Everyone rushed towards the window and watched with horrified fascination as someone nearest shouted out, 'He's missed —'

'What's happening? Missed what?' Went up the general cry.

'One of the single-engine bombers dived onto a half-sunken ship in Stanley Bay. He released his bomb, but it was too late and he missed his target'.

Several small bombs were dropped in the bay in close proximity, shaking all the buildings in the camp. The noise was deafening. Guns from the prison barked incessantly and guards fired rifles at the attacking planes. Terrified patients were screaming, then in the midst of all the din and commotion a tremendous explosion rocked the whole camp.

'Something's been hit,' bellowed a voice in John's ear. 'Look! Look at all that smoke.' John peered in the direction he was pointing. A great cloud was rising from one of the buildings near the cemetery.

'Come on, we'd better see if anyone's been hurt,' John shouted back. Several doctors grabbed what equipment was available and ran off in the direction of the dense smoke. As they approached the bungalows, over the sounds of the droning aircraft, John could hear cries of 'Help'.

'Looks like it's had a direct hit,' he shouted to his colleague, Dr Pomfret. Several people from the adjacent buildings had already arrived and were pulling at the rubble from where the groans and screams were coming.

John and Dr Pomfret were the first doctors to arrive on the scene. They quickly turned their attention to the bodies lying on the grass, while the other rescuers continued to drag people from the wrecked bungalow.

The first four were women. John examined them, but found they were beyond help. 'Must have died instantly,' he said as he looked for signs of life. Another woman was badly injured. 'We must get her to the hospital straight away.' Several more people were brought out, and willing hands came forward to carry them.

'That's the lot, I think.' someone shouted.

'Are you sure?' came back another voice. 'I think I can hear something. Quiet everyone.'

They all listened intently. Sure enough, a faint cry of 'Help, help' was coming from under the ruins.

'Keep calling,' said Dr Pomfret, 'We're trying to get to you.'

They continued to tear away at the bricks and concrete. It was hard work for the near-starving rescuers, but still they persevered.

'There he is. Hold on, we'll get you out.'

John and Dr Pomfret watched and waited as the last remaining bricks which were pinning the victim's legs were carefully removed. Then a great cry went up from the waiting crowd as the last casualty was pulled clear of the wreckage. John bent to examine the body. He was covered in blood and dust.

'He's alive, but unconscious. Stretchers here quickly, we may be able to do something for him.' The patient moaned. John took a closer look, and froze. Aloud he said, 'It's Prosser, oh my goodness, it's Prosser.'

Prosser was lifted gently onto the stretcher and John walked beside him as he was carried to the hospital.

Days of uncertainty followed, as Prosser hovered between life and death. Virginia sat motionless beside him, waiting. Graham needed her now, as never before, but her mind was in torment. She knew she ought to be thankful that he was alive, and to be praying for his recovery, but she could not. Guilt lay heavily on her, and the anger at his treatment of her and the evil life he had led seemed to dominate her emotions.

John, too, was suffering his own inner conflicts. As a doctor, he mourned the fact that full medical treatment could not be given, but so grave were Prosser's injuries, it was doubtful he would have survived even under normal medical conditions. When John's duties ended for the day, he would sit for a while with Virginia. Each seemed to find some comfort in the other's presence.

Prosser never regained consciousness and four days later he died.

The Anglican clergyman led the funeral service. Prosser was buried in the cemetery, transported in a coffin by Catholic pall bearers, as he had no friends to carry it to the grave. Even the coffin was a communal one, with a removable bottom, for out of necessity it had to be used again and again. John, Claire and Virginia were the only mourners. Prosser's black market associates had no interest in him now.

A headstone was put on his grave, taken from a pile of granite stones in the camp. Two Russian prisoners carved his name on the stone. There were no tears shed as he was laid to rest alongside the others in that quiet cemetery. Yet, John was moved to sadness and regret for harbouring such bitter feelings toward him. He acknowledged he had made no effort to discover the real hurt and anguish which possibly lay at the root of Prosser's behaviour.

CHAPTER XVIII

Liberation

As the shortages increased the hunt for firewood became more and more difficult. Everything combustible was burned. Furniture, floorboards and even the doors to the internees' apartments were sacrificed. The food problem worsened. Even the *Hong Kong News* was banned, and the Japanese captors, being unable to accept defeat, became more arrogant. Only the black market flourished.

'The Formosan guards must be making an enormous killing. One of my out-patients, who lives near the road, told me he can hear guards dragging sacks of food along the roadway at night to exchange for valuables,' John told Claire, as they sat outside again now the weather had become so much warmer.

'You're right,' said Claire. 'The food the Formosans are trading is keeping us all alive. I'm afraid the effect of internment on most people has been to degrade them. The thin veneer of culture and civilization has dropped away. I had my hair cut today by a leading barrister for two cigarettes.'

'It's a good job neither of us smoke. Our cigarette ration has proved invaluable,' observed John, ruefully. 'I guess, though, what you are really saying is that the effect of hunger is to destroy our finer instincts, and feelings —'

'Yes, that's exactly what I mean. It's difficult for people to be moral under conditions of poverty. I've come to see, too, that if we hope as missionaries to win people for Christ, we need first to ensure they have sufficient for their basic needs.'

'I believe Jesus knew that, for the gospels tell us before He began to preach to the people He gave them food,' John pointed out reflectively.

'Yes, I never really thought of it like that before.'

Changing the subject Claire asked, 'Have you met the two guards who hang around the hospital?'

'No, dear, I don't think so,' replied John, with a puzzled look.

'One is called Saigo and the other Tageoka. The children love them as they give them food. There is always a group trying to hold their hands.

They call them "Sago and Tapioca".' Claire smiled, and then became serious again. 'Even while I was there on duty, I noticed five people come up to Tageoka with rings, brooches, and one had a camera.'

'The trouble is they are so ill-disciplined, with the result internees are punished by the Japs. The reason we haven't had any sugar for the last month is because the Formosans raided the Japs' stores,' mused John.

Several days later, 'Sago' entered the hospital. He stood staring at Claire for several moments before approaching her. Claire had not seen him enter. Startled, she looked up, and she was surprised to see huge tears running down his cheeks.

'Whatever's the matter?' she asked, her voice warm and gentle.

'You've been watching, you know what we've been doing,' he cried. 'When it's all over, you won't chop my head off will you? I've not done you any harm —'

'No, of course not. We're a Christian country and don't chop people's heads off the way the Japanese do,' declared Claire.

'The Americans are going to invade soon. Then we'll all be killed by their flame-thrower tanks. I'd rather be invaded by the British, they're less ruthless.'

'You just keep bringing the food in, and I'm sure you'll be alright,' Claire reassured him. 'Keep us informed of all the latest news about Allied advances as well. If you do that, a lot of us will put in a good word for you when the Americans arrive —'

'I certainly will,' said Sago, his tears turning to smiles. 'I don't like the Japs any more than you do. They've colonized my country and been very brutal.' He turned to leave, then as an afterthought turned back to Claire, and continued, 'I heard that your Mr Churchill has been defeated in the general election.'

Claire was amused at his words but, hiding her smile she replied, 'So Britain has a Labour Government now. Let's hope that the full force of the British and American armies that defeated Germany will be turned on the Japanese.'

Sago lowered his voice to a confidential whisper, 'They're blasting trenches in the hills and building up defence areas all around the camp.'

'They obviously have no intention of giving up Hong Kong without a struggle then,' replied Claire.

Sago looked around him anxiously, 'I must go, I'll keep you informed,' he promised as he slouched off.

Two weeks later, news came that all the technicians were to be taken to

Canton. When John heard it, he sought out Duncan Roberts, one of the hospital technicians.

'We're probably to be held as hostages,' Duncan observed. His face creased with anxiety. Then he added quietly, 'We know so much about running Hong Kong, my guess is they'll take us out of the city in case of an invasion, so that we can't get Hong Kong going again.'

'The Japs must be pretty desperate to resort to a trick like that. God be with you, my friend.' They parted at the steps of the hospital, their faces grave.

The rest of the camp speculated wildly as they watched over 170 technicians being packed into a junk. Despair gripped many of them as the junk disappeared into the distance. That afternoon as they met under the trees for the weekly Bible study John asked the group to pray specifically for Duncan and the rest of the exiles. As the meeting was about to break up Claire related what she had learned from Sago.

'There'll be more fighting and killing,' wailed Alice, then in a jerky, somewhat unco-ordinated voice she added,' what do you make of the latest rumour?' When she was sure she had everyone's attention, she continued, 'In the food queue, this evening, I heard everyone talking about a terrible bomb. They said its flash was brighter than a thousand suns, and it's devastated Japan —'

'Someone's imagination working overtime, no doubt.' Norman summed up the feelings of most of the group, who were too polite to voice them aloud to the incorrigible Alice.

When, the next day, the wonderful aroma of cooked meat permeated the camp, Alice rushed off to find Claire.

'It's true, it's true, real meat after all this time. It will only be a tiny portion each, but they say there's more to come . . . toilet paper and soap, too. Oh, it's all too much to take in. Whatever does it mean?'

After Alice left, Claire continued to sip her black market tea, yet she felt a sudden heaviness descend on her. She could not throw off the feeling. The rumours of the bomb devastating Japan continued to circulate. It sounded horrible, sinister. Claire did not know what to think or believe. It must be the inertia, she told herself – patience was never her strong point. John was not due in for another hour as he had been summoned to a committee meeting. So Claire decided to go over to the Indian quarters and have a chat with Norman and Enid. She scribbled a note on a used packet of cigarettes, their way for the last two years of communicating to each other, as they had little other means. 'Gone to see Enid and Norman' she wrote. She'd be in time to see little Brooke before he was settled for the night, which would cheer her up, she decided.

It was a beautiful warm evening. Claire stopped to chat to several people as she passed. As she neared her friends' block she saw they too were enjoying the last of the sunshine. She waved and called out. Brooke looked up from playing in the dirt, saw her, and with a whoop of joy came running up to her. 'Auntie Claire, Auntie Claire,' he cried. Claire waited with arms outstretched as he ran to her. She scooped him up and gave him a big hug.

'What a big boy you're getting,' she said, putting him down, and rumpling his fair curly hair. Brooke smiled up at her, 'Car car,' he chanted, holding his hand out for Claire to admire his new toy.

'My, that's a lovely car.'

'Mine,' said Brooke, clutching it tightly to him.

Norman strolled over to welcome Claire and laughed indulgently at his small son. 'His first toy – I bought it from Lane Crawford with an IOU.' He grinned. 'He won't part with it.' Then turning to Brooke he said, decisively, 'Now young man, time for bed, Mummy's waiting for you. Say goodnight to Auntie Claire.'

Brooke held his angelic little face up for a kiss. 'Night, night, Auntie Claire,' he said sweetly.

'Night, night, darling,' Claire bent to kiss the upturned face, and waved as he toddled off.

'Come and take a seat. Enid will join us as soon as she's settled Brooke.'

'I can't get the news of the bomb out of my mind,' Claire confided to Norman. 'I can hardly believe we may soon be free. Do you think it's true?'

'Oh, I think it's true all right. I managed to get a paper from the guards. They've started smuggling them into the camp. I wanted to find out what's going on. All this speculation is getting too much —'

'And did you read of anything significant,' Claire demanded, impatient now for news.

'Oh yes, it was headline news. It said, in view of the continued loss of life and because of his great love for his people, his Imperial Highness has decided to end hostilities.'

Claire was stunned. 'So the war is over. I can't believe it, I was expecting more raids, more killing . . . but . . . There's been no excitement, nothing.'

'No, the news hasn't been formally released.'

'What an anti-climax, after all these years of sorrow and suffering. So what do we do now?'

'We must just wait, something's bound to happen before long.'

Claire and Norman chatted companionably until Enid joined them and Norman then regaled them with stories from his past experiences.

'It's good you haven't lost your sense of humour,' laughed Claire. They were still laughing at Norman's droll telling of how, soon after arriving in Hong Kong, he had been sitting next to a very well-dressed British lady at a hotel dinner. The lady, who was obviously on the lookout for a husband for her only daughter, had regarded him as a suitable candidate, only to recoil in horror when he told her he was head of the sanitation department. They were still chuckling when John strolled over.

'What's so funny,' he asked, his eyes twinkling. The tale was not spoiled by the retelling.

Norman, who always came straight to the point, then enquired, 'What was the meeting about?'

John took a deep breath and smiled round at everyone. 'It's over. It's all over.' His voice rose to a gleeful shout, 'We're free.'

'We know that,' interrupted Claire, in prosaic tones. 'Norman read it in the paper.'

'Oh, really, well now it's official, Japan has accepted the terms of the Potsdam Declaration, which involved absolute surrender.

'A notice is to be posted up informing everyone of the fact, and to recommend everyone remains in the camp. There are to be no demonstrations, no cheering, no celebrations, for fear of reprisals. It was odd – one of the Formosan guards came in to turn on the water. He was in civilian clothes. He suddenly looked round at everyone, rolled his eyes, and gave a thumbs up sign. He looked so incongruous, I had a job to keep from laughing out loud.'

'Can we leave the camp then?' asked a bewildered Claire.

'No, we must wait, the administration of the camp is to continue to function as normal for the time being.'

'You mean our years of fear and tension are over – we are no longer at war, but we carry on just the same?'

'Yes, darling, for the time being.'

Claire found it hard to believe that it really was all over. As she and John returned to their quarters, they noticed people gathering in little groups all over the camp. The air was alive with bubbling exuberance. Several people had risked hanging out flags. Only the guards' faces revealed their stunned disbelief.

'They accepted all the propaganda that's been put about, so they are totally unprepared for the surrender,' John exclaimed.

'John, look over there, whatever's going on?' said Claire.

John stopped in his tracks and turned to look in the direction Claire was pointing. 'Smoke. It's coming from the Japanese Headquarters. I bet they're burning all the records.'

Sleep was impossible for John and Claire that night. At last, after three and a half years of internment, they were free – they could relax after all the fear and tension. Yet nothing seemed to have changed, except now they had more food than their constricted stomachs could take.

Stories of the devastation of Hong Kong soon reached them. They were safer in the camp than outside, until law and order was restored.

For two days they hung around, waiting for something to happen. The Japanese guards, to console themselves, got drunk. The internees, who were flying Union Jacks, were asked to take them down for fear of what might happen.

That evening a thanksgiving service was held at St Stephen's Hall. Over a thousand people of every denomination crowded there together and worshipped, giving heartfelt thanks to God for their deliverance. At the close of the service, they were told that their first visitors would shortly be arriving from the city, and from the military camp. There was a ripple of excited voices and many eyes filled with tears of happiness.

'I wonder if Storm will come,' Claire whispered to John.

'Of course she will,' was his confident reply as he looked at her in anticipation, and his fingers tightened on hers.

For two hours John and Claire stood craning their necks, watching for the bus which would herald their visitors. They longed for a sight of Storm. A million times Claire had rehearsed over in her mind their first meeting. Their Little Storm, herself a mother now, but under the most tragic circumstances. How was she? How had she survived? Why had this terrible thing happened to her? Would they have the right words, the healing words to say to her? Round and round went the questioning in her mind.

At last a cry went up as the first sign of dust clouds could be faintly seen on the horizon.

'They're coming,' was the shout, as the shape of a bus could now be distinctly seen, winding its slow laborious way along the dusty road.

At last the bus came to a standstill. The British police officers, now in charge of the camp, clothed in what was left of their uniforms, moved forward to the barricade as the first visitors alighted from the bus, laden with food and clothes. John spotted her at once.

'What did I tell you, Claire? She's here, she's here,' he screamed, above the noise of the waiting crowd. He grabbed Claire's hand and they pushed their way to the front.

John ran forward, his arms outstretched, a joyous welcome on his face. He saw Storm hesitate, then she gave a radiant smile. With a cry of joy, she ran towards him. Tears streaming down her face, she threw herself into her father's outstretched arms, they clung together, laughing and crying. Then it was Claire's turn to gather her daughter to her, their tears mingling. Exhausted by their emotions, they held Storm from them. After so much time apart, it was difficult to think of anything to say as they stood in silence, gazing at each other.

'Oh, my darling, it's so good just to see you, to hold you,' breathed John. He clasped her close again. 'We've been so worried about you. You've suffered so much —'

'We've lived and prayed for this day, for so long —' murmured Claire, huskily.

'You heard —' Storm hung her head, trying to hide the hurt in her eyes, her voice barely audible.

'Yes, darling, we heard, and we've had you in our hearts . . .'

Claire looked into Storm's strained and anxious face and ached for her. 'We were just so sorry we were not there for you —'

'I was so ashamed —' Her eyes filled with tears again.

'You have nothing to be ashamed of —' said John fervently.

'I couldn't understand why God allowed this to happen to me. At first I was so angry with Him, and full of bitterness towards the Japanese soldier. I hated him and everybody. I was so frightened I just wanted to die. I would have done something dreadful, if Lily Kwok had not been there. She stayed with me all the time, and would not let me out of her sight. Before the baby was born, I thought I would hate him too. I wanted to give him away and to shut out all the hurt and pain. But when he was born, Lily Kwok made me hold him and really look at him. I didn't want to, but she made me. When I held him, he looked so tiny and helpless, I knew I could learn to love him.' Storm looked up for the first time, and there was an expression of profound love and joy on her face. John and Claire held their breath, almost afraid to intrude. The look of joy faded and a spasm of pain took its place. Storm hesitated, John and Claire waited. Then the words burst from her. 'I did right to love him, to keep him, didn't I —'

'Yes, darling, you did right, absolutely right.' They both held her tight.

'We're your family and we love you very very much, and we'll love your little one too,' said John, caringly.

A dazzling smile spread across Storm's face, the sadness slipping away.

'And now we have a beautiful little grandson,' John went on. 'When can we see him? You didn't bring him?'

'I wanted to be sure you would love him too,' Storm smiled shyly. 'He's in the bus with Lily Kwok, I made her wait —'

'Oh, you dreadful child,' John teased, trying to relieve the tension, 'fancy keeping us in suspense. Go and get them immediately. We've waited far too long already.'

Just a signal was all that was needed for a beaming Lily Kwok to come tottering forward, a beautiful dark-haired, dark-eyed toddler clinging to her hand. She looked older. The years have taken their toll, thought Claire as she hurried to embrace her.

Storm drew her child forward then, turning to the man who had rescued her all those years ago, she blurted out, 'I've named him John, after you, because you rescued me, and have shown me so much love, and tenderness —'

All manner of mixed emotions crowded in on John as the tears fell unchecked again. He remembered the little girl who had won his heart so long ago and he wanted to hold her, protect her again from all the hurts and evils of the world. Wiping his cheeks, he looked from Storm to her son. He smiled. 'John, come and give Grandpa a big kiss.'

He stooped down to the solemn-faced child, and his heart missed a beat as he remembered the same look on Storm's face – the look of bewilderment when he had to leave her at the orphanage.

'My first grandchild, what a lovely feeling it gives me,' he murmured. The child obediently lifted his face to be kissed, first by John then Claire. They all laughed as he immediately turned and ran to his mother and buried his face in her skirt.

They sat out in the sunshine, sheltered by the trees, and talked as if somehow they could fill in the years in which they had been apart. Storm and Lily Kwok marvelled that so many people could have survived in such cramped quarters for so long.

'What're things like in the city?' John asked.

'Very bad,' Storm said, sighing deeply. 'The Japanese arrested people on the streets at random, and tortured them to see if they had any information. Most people were so scared they stayed in their homes, only going out to buy food. Food has been very scarce and very expensive. We survived as I found work making uniforms for Japanese officers.'

'It was good of you to send us the food parcel, when you obviously needed it as much as we did,' said Claire gratefully.

'I just wish I could have sent more, but I was taken in for questioning after delivering the parcel. I was so frightened, I was accused of being a collaborator. I explained to the Kempeitai that my adopted parents were in the camp. Then I offered to make new uniforms for the officers, and they let me go. Lily Kwok wouldn't let me risk sending another one.'

'You were right to do that.' John turned to Lily Kwok. 'The Kempeitai were extremely unpleasant. We saw what they did to the Director of Medical Services. When they released him into the camp, after keeping him in prison for some time, his hair had turned white, his face was haggard and he was almost bent double.'

'The church is in ruins,' Storm remarked sadly. 'When the electricity was cut off, the roof was stripped for wood, and the stones were used for building a new tower on Government House, which of course the Japanese took over. There are few cars or buses in the city – we believe they've all been shipped to Japan for scrap metal. They've wrecked homes and neglected public services, and lots of Chinese people have just disappeared.' Her voice broke, 'It's just horrible . . .' she shuddered.

'And the hospital?' queried John.

Storm shook her head, 'It's been bad for them, working under Japanese rule.'

'We must try to make something beautiful out of the ruins,' John declared when the time came for the visitors to leave.

'It's going to be alright,' breathed Storm. A dazzling smile spread across her face and the sadness slipped away.

With promises of further visits, they reluctantly said their goodbyes, and waved non-stop until the bus was lost to sight.

On 29 August the Royal Navy arrived, quickly followed by a visit from the newly appointed Governor of Hong Kong. At last they could laugh and cry, hug each other and dance for joy openly, all fear of reprisals gone.

Everyone dropped what they were doing and stood to attention as the Union Jack was raised. 'God save the King' was followed by a representative of each national group raising its flag.

Then as they watched, a gentle breeze blew up and the flags were lowered to half mast. The last post was sounded. 'Oh God our Help in Ages Past' was sung as aeroplanes flew overhead.

The Admiral spoke of those who had given their lives. As bugle notes wafted to the far corners of the camp, and the Japanese flag was torn down, a mighty cheer went up at the sight of the Union Jack fluttering in the breeze over Headquarters.

'We're free, we're free.' The triumphal cry rang out.

Epilogue

As John and Claire, along with the many friends they had made during their internment, boarded the bus to take them back to the city, most heads turned to take a last look at the camp which had been their home for the last three and a half years. A strange stillness seemed to have gripped everyone, as they mulled over their memories.

The years had been filled with hardship and sorrow. John thought of all those who had endured the suffering with grace and dignity. He realized that they had found a certain comradeship in shared troubles. Many new friendships had been formed. God had not forsaken them, many times during their captivity they had been conscious of His strength upholding them. They must learn to put bitterness and hatred aside. All had suffered, and it was only in true love and forgiveness that they could hope to rebuild their lives, and become whole again.

Perhaps he reflected that it was the combination of a military government and warfare which had led the Japanese to be so cruel. Then he acknowledged that not all their captors had been evil – there were those who had shown compassion. He remembered his friend, the Rev. Nanataki, how he had risked his life so many times to help them. After all, he thought the ground is level at the foot of the cross.

The bus lurched, jolting John out of his reverie. They had climbed the hill and joined the main road. Now he could look down into the city he remembered so well, and the harbour, always teeming with ships. 'Good grief,' he exclaimed, 'the harbour is completely empty, there's not a thing moving on the water. Not even the ferries are crossing to Kowloon.'

'No,' said the driver, 'the American bombers have done a good job, most of the ships have been sunk or damaged.'

They drove on through once familiar streets, now deserted and dirty. An odd shop was open, but shoppers looked drab and furtive.

'What a shocking state it's in,' mused John. 'We've almost got to start to rebuild from scratch. It's going to take years to restore order out of the chaos.'

At Central the bus stopped. Norman turned in his seat, 'I'm getting off here, I can't wait any longer to find out what's been going on,' he stated, flatly.

John turned to Claire. 'Do you mind if I go with him, dear? You can go on to the hotel, I'll join you later.'

Barely waiting for Claire to reply, John and Norman alighted from the bus. They walked in silence through the deserted streets. Pale, sad faces peered from behind upstairs windows. They made their way to the Peak tram. 'Would you believe it? Look, John, the cable's broken,' exclaimed Norman. 'The trams out of use, shall we walk?' John nodded determinedly. It was swelteringly hot and the steep climb up the Peak tramway to Kennedy Road was exhausting in their weakened state. They had to stop several times to catch their breath. At last, panting and dripping with perspiration, they arrived. They stopped and stared, horror registering on both their faces. Union Church was just a pile of rubble. The memorial to the founder of the church, the Rev. Dr James Legge, was the only large stone left.

A growl, low and distant, like the roll of a train on a faraway bridge, began to stir in Norman's throat. 'The barbarians,' he hissed. 'God's house reduced to rubble.'

'Christians have worshipped here for years, and we must make sure they continue to do so,' said John.

There, in the dust and rubble they knelt in prayer. Then rising from their knees, John vowed, 'We'll rebuild it. A new Church with a fresh vision will arise here, and God will bless it.'

'Yes,' echoed Norman. 'We'll rebuild it.' They parted there, and John made his weary way along Bonham Road towards the hospital. He stopped outside the doors and gazed around him. At least the hospital remained intact, he mused. He pushed open the doors and stepped inside, walking the familiar corridors. He hesitated before pushing open the door of the office. There, at the same old desk, looking older and sadder, was David Schom. 'My old friend,' John cried.

David Schom's face broke into a radiant smile. He jumped to his feet and they clasped each other warmly.

'How have things been for you, my friend,' John asked.

'Pretty bad,' came back the grim reply. 'We've been short of drugs and equipment. The Japanese have been in charge, and very arrogant. They made it clear they didn't trust us and interfered constantly. They tried to humiliate us. It's been a very difficult time, but you, my friend, have had it much much worse. You are a shadow of your former self.'

'Well they tried to starve us, and we, too, were often humiliated by them. When people forgot or refused to bow, they had their faces slapped, and some were beaten.'

'Yes, they've committed the most horrendous atrocities.' Then a smile crossed his face, and he added, 'Yet it has not been all bad. Twelve of the new nursing staff have become Christians, and the spiritual side of our work has continued, albeit more surreptitiously.'

'That's wonderful,' breathed John. 'Our faith too has sustained us and given us courage to keep going in the face of so much hardship.' Then John added earnestly, 'Valuable lessons too were learned in the camp, which I trust will be built on in the future. The dreadful attitude of British superiority fell away, and I trust it will never return. We must all work to build up a new partnership on spiritual, social and economic levels.'

'That is good, my friend, and Claire?'

'She has been wonderful. She could have left the camp earlier when the Canadians were repatriated, but she chose to remain with me. We've had ups and downs throughout our lives, but our marriage has helped sustain us both in all the difficult times. I've so much to be thankful for.'

'And now, my friend . . . ?'

'We'll go back to England, to see our families.'

'And what of the future?' David Schom looked anxiously at John. 'You'll come back?'

'Why yes, of course, there's so much to be done to rebuild our city, and our church.' Then his eyes twinkled mischievously, 'After all, you must remember I'm a Hong Kong boy.'